THE GUESTHOUSE BY WATERSMEET BRIDGE

THE WATERSMEET BRIDGE SERIES
BOOK 2

JULIE STOCK

CLUED UP PUBLISHING

Cover Design: Fully Booked Design
Editing and Proofreading: Bryony Leah Editorial

For my mum who was my greatest fan.

CHAPTER ONE

What was she doing here? It wasn't the first time this thought had gone through Cara Rafaelli's head. In fact, it was all she could think about since returning from Watersmeet Bridge. She'd got back late last night after a glorious weekend with her grandma to find no sign of Phil – or any of their flatmates, for that matter. So much for him 'missing her like crazy' and being 'desperate to see her as soon as she got back'. He'd have spent the whole day down the pub with his mates and rolled in drunk before crashing out until this morning, she told herself, and sure enough, that was exactly what had happened. Same as every weekend.

Now it was Monday morning, and she was sitting at her desk staring out the window, daydreaming about being back home in Watersmeet Bridge. She'd taken this job at a solicitor's office in Exeter six months after leaving university, when she'd finally had to acknowledge jobs for arts graduates were few and far between and companies weren't exactly crying out for someone with no experience. But now she'd been here for two years, and she was fed up. There were no chances of promotion even if she wanted them – she wasn't a trained solicitor and didn't want to be – and despite the experience she'd gained, Cara had no real sense of achievement.

But she'd decided to stay here after university so she could continue to experience life in a city, and then, once she'd met Phil, living with him in Exeter seemed like the right choice. She'd had enough of the quiet life back at Watersmeet Bridge only just a few years ago, so wouldn't she end up feeling the same if she went home again now? She just didn't know for sure. What she did know was that she hated her job, and it was only a matter of time before she started looking for something else.

And then there was Phil. She didn't feel like their relationship was going anywhere important either. He still behaved like a student and didn't seem bothered about getting a regular job so he could pay his way. He was quite happy to let Cara pay for everything, and all of a sudden, the sense of being trapped was overwhelming her.

Her computer pinged with another email, and she reluctantly tore her gaze away from the park across the road, back to her screen. She kept herself busy for the rest of the day, but as soon as she was making her way home, her mind returned once more to the idea of leaving her job. But she still had the room she shared with Phil to pay for. Cara made up her mind to talk to him about it that evening. At least if he got a job, she might have some flexibility to start looking for something else.

'Hello. Anybody home?' she called out after closing the front door. There was no response.

Cara took off her coat and hung it up in the hallway before going through to the lounge. She glanced across at the open-plan kitchen on her way through and couldn't believe the sight before her. The table and all the surfaces were covered with dirty dishes. She'd left the kitchen spotless when she'd gone to work, and as she was always the first to leave, this mess had to be down to one or all of the others. Of her three flatmates, only Tim had a job and he was pretty good at clearing up after himself too, which left Phil and his partner in crime, Chris, as prime suspects. She wouldn't even be able to make herself a drink given the state of the kitchen. She sank down onto the sofa and put her head in her hands. She'd cleaned up after them so many times that they probably expected her to do it by now, but she'd really had enough.

Irritated, she stood up and went through to the bedroom she shared with Phil, thinking she might feel better in their private space, but when she opened the door, she found her boyfriend sprawled across the bed.

'Phil! Get up now,' she cried, her fury with him finally getting the better of her. When he didn't stir, she picked up a nearby cushion and thumped him with it.

He groaned and turned over, squinting at her through half-closed eyes. 'Whassa matter?' he grumbled incoherently.

'I've been at work all day, and you've done nothing. That's what's the matter,' she shouted at him, ending on a half-sob.

He rubbed his eyes and attempted to sit up but failed and fell back down on the bed again. Cara stared at him in despair, wondering just what she had to do to make him see how upset she was. Abruptly, she turned and left the room, slamming the door behind her. She grabbed her bag from the living room and went back to get her coat before leaving the flat and returning to the High Street.

She had no idea where to go, but she was determined to find somewhere with some peace and quiet to be on her own for a while. She spotted the coffee shop further down the road with its lights still on and decided to drop in there while she calmed down. She hated feeling so incapable of sorting her life out. She'd given Phil so many chances, and yet he continued to let her down, but she still couldn't quite bring herself to break up with him.

When they'd first met, he'd paid her so much attention, taking her on fun-filled dates and buying her flowers, making it easy for her to fall head over heels in love with him. It wasn't long before he asked her to move in, and she'd jumped at the chance, excited by the prospect of their future together. Looking back now, she could see that was when things had started to go wrong. He'd started taking her for granted, and criticising her for the slightest thing. Now, she wondered if they'd ever really been compatible at all.

She still loved him despite his many faults, and desperately wanted things to work out between them. But this time, she wasn't sure how much more she could take.

By the time Cara returned to the flat, Phil was nowhere to be seen, but he had at least tidied the place up. She had no idea where he'd gone but could make a good guess he'd sloped off to the pub as usual, so she went to bed early to avoid any further conflict with him.

Cara spent most of her lunch break the next day pondering whether she could afford a place of her own, and with those thoughts came the realisation she was no longer committed to her relationship. She couldn't even be bothered to have it out with Phil, for goodness' sake. There really didn't seem to be any point to carrying on if that was how she felt.

At the same time, she couldn't afford to rent on her own, so she'd have to look for another flat share but with people she didn't know. That thought made her feel marginally worse than staying where she was. She took a sip of her coffee and stared out the window of the café she'd taken refuge in. No wonder she felt so trapped. She just had no idea what to do for the best.

She made her way home slowly at the end of the day, dreading a repeat of the day before. This time, though, she found Phil waiting for her in the living room. Everywhere was spotlessly tidy – suspiciously so.

'Hey,' she said as she put down her bag. 'Good day?'

'I think we should talk,' Phil replied, sidestepping her question.

She raised her eyebrows, thinking surely that was her line, but she hadn't had the courage to say it. 'I agree,' she said instead, feeling slightly optimistic about this apparent overnight change in her boyfriend. She took a seat in the armchair opposite Phil and dared to hope.

'I know you've been paying all the bills, and that hasn't been very fair on you. I am sorry about that, but I don't think things are working out between us any more, so I think you should move out. You can take some time looking for somewhere else, of course, but I've spoken to the others, and we're all agreed.'

Cara was so flabbergasted that she was speechless for a moment. 'Well, it was kind of you to discuss our situation with them before me, but despite that, I've come to the same conclusion. Things aren't working between us, and I'd prefer to move out and live on my own. You're going to have to move out of our room, though, while I look for somewhere. So you can go and get your things now.' She stood up to emphasise her point and made her way to the room, trying to disguise how much she was shaking from having stood up for herself for once.

Fifteen minutes later, Phil had disappeared again without further discussion, and after Cara closed the door, she fell onto the bed and succumbed to her tears. Even though she'd expected to end up alone eventually, she would never have expected Phil to make the first move. She hated to admit that it hurt to be so easily dismissed after all this time together.

So now she had no choice but to find a new place to live and try to afford it on her own. She had no idea what sort of accommodation she could expect on her meagre salary, nor the sort of people she might have to share with. Her heart sank even further at the thought of it all. Still, there was no better time like the present, she thought, and that spurred her on to wipe her tears away and pull out her phone to have a look at what was available to rent online.

An hour later and she was feeling even more despondent, if that were possible. There was very little to rent in the city, and what was available was so far out of her price range it was impossible for her to consider. Her stomach rumbled suddenly, and she remembered that she'd had nothing to eat since lunchtime. The prospect of going out to the kitchen to see if there was anything for dinner filled her with dread. She didn't want to bump into any of her so-called flatmates.

Then she heard the door buzzer go and guessed they'd ordered something in. Despite her difficulties with Phil, they'd all spent many great evenings together, bonding over pizza and wine, and she felt deep sadness at the thought that those good times were now definitely over. Cara sighed and decided to change into her pyjamas. She'd just finished pulling on her top when there was a knock at the door.

Opening the door a crack, she found Tim, the tidy flatmate, standing there shuffling awkwardly from side to side.

'Hi, Cara. Look, we've not long ordered pizza, and I wondered if you'd like some. I'm sorry everything's so awkward, but I don't want you to hide away in your room.'

She was touched by his kindness and wondered fleetingly if Phil had lied about them all having agreed that she should move out.

'Thanks. That would be great.'

She followed him out to the kitchen and saw he was on his own.

'The others have gone out already and won't be back till later, so you're fine to sit here without interruption.'

Cara fetched a plate from the cupboard and took a seat next to Tim at the table.

'Thanks, Tim. I really appreciate this.' She took a bite of her pizza and closed her eyes at the taste of the melted cheese and pepperoni.

'I'm sorry you're going to be moving out. How do you feel about it all?'

'Honestly? I have no idea what I'm going to do next. I can't find anywhere I could afford to rent in a decent part of the city, and I don't want to take the risk of living anywhere else on my own. I just have to hope something will turn up, and soon.'

The sound of her phone ringing woke Cara early the next morning, and she groaned as she picked it up.

'Cara? Is that you? It's Penny here.'

The familiar sound of her grandma's voice overwhelmed her emotions, and tears sprang to her eyes. 'Hello, Grandma. Yes, it's me. Is everything all right?'

'Never mind me,' Penny replied in her usual no-nonsense voice. 'I'm worried about you. You didn't seem yourself at the weekend, and I wanted to check in on you before time runs away with us as usual.'

'I'm sorry for worrying you, Grandma. I...'

'You've nothing to be sorry for,' Penny interrupted. She hated being called Grandma, and despite everything, Cara had to smile. 'But will you tell me what's wrong?'

And so Cara told her about Phil and his ultimatum.

Penny cleared her throat, and Cara waited, wondering what she was going to say next. 'Well, good riddance to him, that's all I can say. And it's good timing that I'm calling now, because I have a proposition for you that may just solve all our problems.'

'All our problems?' Cara echoed. 'What do you mean?'

'Look, I'm too old to run Watersmeet View on my own any more, so I want you to come home and help me like you used to in the old days.'

Cara gasped, but her first thought was concern for Penny's health. 'What do you mean you're too old? Are you ill?'

'No, don't fuss. I'm fine. I'd just appreciate some help, and as you worked here with me at the guesthouse for years, I know you know what to do. And it sounds like you need a fresh start too.'

'Oh, Grandma, I would love to come home and help you run Watersmeet View.' Cara could hardly believe her good luck.

'Your room is still here just as you left it, and you know this is your home. Let me know when you're ready to travel, and I'll transfer you some money for the journey if you need it. I can't wait to have you back home again.'

Cara said goodbye and closed her eyes briefly. Now she'd be able to go home to Watersmeet Bridge with a job and somewhere to stay all sorted. Things were beginning to look up at last.

She glanced around the bedroom she'd shared with Phil for the past couple of years and heaved a sigh of relief. She'd be glad to see the back of it.

She got ready for work with an extra spring in her step and then spent a few minutes preparing her resignation letter. She'd decided to ask if she could leave as soon as possible, using up her holiday days and taking unpaid leave if necessary. She didn't want to work a day longer than she had to.

Fortunately, her boss was more pleased at her announcement than she'd expected, so maybe she'd jumped before she was pushed, but she didn't care. She only had to work till the end of the week, and then she'd never have to listen to complaining customers again. Well, the ones who were buying and selling houses, at any rate.

Back at the flat, she started sorting out her things and getting rid of anything she didn't need to take home with her. She still ended up with a large suitcase full of clothes and assorted other bits and pieces, as well as a huge rucksack, and she hadn't packed all the last-minute items yet either. She sank onto the bed with a groan, wondering how she'd transport it all to and from the stations. She'd get a taxi this end, she decided, and then she'd ring her friend, Zoe, to ask for her help at the other end. And there was no better time for that conversation than right now.

'Hello, you. To what do I owe this pleasure?'

She could sense Zoe's smile in her voice, and the thought filled her with joy. 'Well, you'll never guess what's happened, so I'll just tell you.'

Cara filled Zoe in on the conversation with her grandma.

'Oh my goodness!' Zoe cried when she'd finished her tale. 'It will be just like old times, being able to see each other as much as we want, and to catch up all the time.'

'I know. I can't wait to get back home and see Grandma every day and to see you more often as well.'

'So are you coming back for good, or will it just be for the summer?'

'Oh no, it's time to come back for good now. My love affair with the city is well and truly over. I knew the minute I got back here after my last visit.'

'And what about Phil?' Zoe asked.

'That love affair is also over, but it has been for a while, if I'm being honest.'

'Crikey, this really is going to be a completely new start then.'

'Yes, and I'm looking forward to it. So you'll be able to pick me up when I get there then. Are you sure you don't mind?'

'Of course not. Just send me a text with your train arrival time, and I'll see you there on Saturday.'

Cara said goodbye to Zoe feeling much better and then cast her eye round the room to see if there was anything she'd forgotten. She was pretty much sorted, and so she got ready for an early night before her last day at the office tomorrow.

As she climbed into bed, she was sure she wouldn't be able to sleep since she was such a mass of combined nerves and excitement, but she drifted off easily thinking about the Devon village she'd grown up in and the countryside she'd missed. Now she'd be able to have that fresh start Zoe had mentioned, and to take some time to get her life in order.

For the second time in recent weeks, Cara was making the train journey from Exeter to Barnstaple, but this time, it would be for good. She was going back to the only place she'd ever called home, and she was looking forward to seeing her friends and Penny again, and to getting back to life in Watersmeet Bridge in time for spring. After five years away in Exeter, first at uni and then blinded by what she'd thought was the love of her life, it was definitely time for a change.

She stared at the beauty of the river valleys the train passed through on its way towards the North Devon coast. The trees on either side of the train line were still heavy with overnight rain, but there were patches of blue sky above, and weak beams of sunlight were trying to make their way through the trees.

As the train wended its way home, Cara's longing to get back to the community she loved only grew, along with her need to try to repay them for all they'd done for her family, first when her dad left them unexpectedly to go back to Italy, and then when her mum died. She heaved a sigh as thoughts of her mum threatened to flood her mind. It didn't seem to matter how many years had passed – the grief was always there, waiting to catch her out at the most unexpected times.

She gave her head a slight shake, trying to stop the sadness building up on her. Instead, she focused on what would be waiting for her when she got home. Her grandma had always been as strong as an ox and had run the family guesthouse for years, so Cara understood that things must be bad for her to have asked for help. Especially since Cara had only worked in the guesthouse a handful of times when she was young – despite what her grandma believed – and so she had absolutely no idea what was involved on a day-to-day basis.

She bit her lip as once again she considered all the skills needed to make breakfasts, do all the cleaning, and keep guests happy, unsure she had any of the necessary experience to help run the guesthouse at all. Still, Penny had asked for her help, and she would learn quickly, she hoped. After working at the solicitor's office, she was pretty good at filing, answering the phone, and making cups of tea – but she didn't have a lot of other experience, as Phil had been only too keen to remind her. She rolled her eyes as she thought of how often he'd sought to undermine her already fragile self-confidence.

The difference now, though, was that Penny loved her and had always been there for her, and as a result, Cara would do anything for her grandma. She knew the guesthouse had always meant so much to Penny – and to her own mum, Angela – so it was important to keep it in the family now. Although Cara had never known her granddad, the guesthouse was his legacy, and as such, she'd do everything in her power to keep it going.

There was no denying things must have become very difficult for Penny in recent years. It had never occurred to Cara that her grandma might be too old to be running the place at seventy-five, but looking back now, she could see that perhaps the time for her grandma to ease up a little and rest a bit more had long since passed. Cara only wished she'd understood that sooner.

As the train rounded a bend, she looked across to the other side of the carriage for a better view of the valley. Instead, her attention was caught by a man seated at the table opposite hers, hunched over his laptop. His suit jacket was draped across the seat next to him, and his shirtsleeves were rolled up, drawing her eyes to his tanned forearms. As he typed, his muscles flexed, and she found herself wondering what he did for a living. She was mesmerised for a moment, until she heard a cough and looked up, straight into his face. His lips tilted up in a half-smile, and she blushed furiously at having been caught staring. Then, mercifully, his phone rang, and they both looked away.

It wasn't far to Barnstaple now, and the excitement she was feeling at seeing Zoe built inside her. Zoe had been working at a bistro in the village when Cara was last living at home, and she wondered if she was still at the same place. She owed her a massive apology for not keeping in more regular contact, but she was sure Zoe would forgive her, because that was the sort of friend she was.

The train pulled into Barnstaple shortly afterwards, and as Cara made her way outside to look for her ride to Watersmeet Bridge, she felt a bit better, instantly forgetting the man on the train. As soon as she left the old stone station, she smelt the familiar sea air which always buoyed her mood. She looked to her left and right quickly, dragging her suitcase behind her, and then her face lit up when she saw Zoe waiting for her.

'Hi there, stranger,' Zoe said a moment later as they hugged each other furiously. 'It's so good to see you back home.'

'And you,' Cara replied. 'I'm sorry it's been so long and that I missed you when I came home last time.'

'Damn right, it has. But I'll forgive you this once. It was my fault for not seeing you last time because I was working.' Zoe laughed, and Cara immediately felt better. They reluctantly let go of each other and turned to climb into the car.

Cara stashed her bags on the back seat before joining Zoe in the front. 'We'll definitely see more of each other now, won't we?'

'I'd like that,' Zoe said with a quick glance her way. 'Although I'm sure you'll be pretty busy at the guesthouse.'

Cara nodded but didn't say anything more. She had a massive challenge ahead of her, but for now, she was just glad to be back home again, where she belonged.

CHAPTER TWO

'So, what happened with you and Phil?' Zoe asked as they made their way towards Exmoor National Park.

Cara didn't quite know how to tell her what a colossal disaster her whole life had become.

'We just had nothing in common in the end, and I finally realised I'd been fooling myself for far too long about that. And just when I was working myself up to tell him I was leaving, he jumped in first and told me to leave.'

'What a bastard!'

'Yes, that just about sums him up. And so here I am, back at Watersmeet Bridge. But I'm looking forward to it. I've got my itchy feet out of my system, along with men, for the foreseeable future.'

'I'm sorry about what happened with Phil,' Zoe told her. 'But it sounds like you're well rid of him.'

'I'm sorry too for being so rubbish at staying in touch with both you and Grandma, but I'm so glad to see you now. I want to know everything that's been happening with you too.'

Zoe glanced across again before returning her attention to the road. 'Well, I'm still working at The Bistro, which is great, and I love it. And I've finally got together with Ed.'

This time, it was Cara's turn to be surprised. 'I can't believe you didn't tell me about that development! Although if I'd have been in touch more often, I would have known. Things are obviously going well between you, and I'm glad about that.'

'They are, yes. I can't believe my good luck.' She almost whispered that last bit, and Cara smiled before falling silent and turning to look out the window as they made their way across the moor towards the coast.

In no time at all, they were almost at Lynford, where the lush green countryside gave way to the neat rows of houses and various businesses of a seaside town.

'I'm pleased to see so many of the larger hotels are still here and doing business,' Cara commented as they passed through the outskirts of the village.

'They're all competition for the guesthouse, though, aren't they?'

'To some extent, I guess, but the village has always been able to support lots of different hospitality businesses. At least, it has in the past,' she added as an afterthought, mindful of all that had gone on in the world in recent times. She wondered how much of an impact all that had had on the guesthouse's fortunes.

They continued alongside the river, down towards the village centre, and Cara sat up straighter in her seat, looking out for one of her favourite spots. But then Zoe turned right to go the back way round the village to the guesthouse.

'Why aren't you going across the bridge?' Cara asked with real disappointment.

'We can't drive across the old bridge any more,' Zoe told her.

'Since when?' Cara was shocked to hear about that change.

'It's been a couple of months now. It was always a bit dodgy, allowing traffic to use it. You must remember that.'

'I used to love standing on Watersmeet Bridge, though, and watching where the waters of the two rivers eventually meet.' Cara hadn't been into the village itself on her last visit, there hadn't been time.

'Pedestrians are still allowed to use it, don't worry,' Zoe told her.

She drove the car expertly up the hill, away from the harbour, and circled the village before turning along the road leading down to the High Street. She pulled up in front of the guesthouse a few minutes later.

Cara climbed out and stared at her childhood home, taking in every detail this time now she was going to be home for good. The guesthouse had been built in Victorian times but had only been oper-ating since the end of the war. Cara loved the colourful bricks on the front of the house and the white sash windows. And then there was Penny's beautiful garden. How she'd missed it all.

'My shift starts at The Bistro soon, so I must go, but give my love to Penny, won't you?' Zoe said, putting Cara's bags down in front of her.

Cara turned to give her friend another hug. 'Thanks so much for everything, Zoe. I'll see you soon.'

'You'd better,' Zoe warned with a laugh before climbing back into her car. 'And good luck with everything. I hope you know I'll do anything I can to help you. You only have to ask.'

Cara watched Zoe go before turning away from the guesthouse to take in the view in the other direction. She was rewarded with the magnificent sight of the river and the bay down below. She took in a deep breath and released it again, marvelling at how good it felt to breathe in the sea air. It really had been too long. She gathered her bags and made her way through the garden to the front door, which she found open, as always.

'Cara! Oh, sweetheart, you are a sight for sore eyes.' Penny came round the desk and put her arms out for a hug.

As Cara put her arms round Penny, she was able to hide her reac-tion from the woman who'd become so dear to her since her mother had died. When Penny had said she needed her help, she'd thought it would just be due to her age. She was her grandmother after all. But this was different. Penny looked ill even though she'd said she was fine. And Cara could feel how slight her body had become since she'd last seen her.

They stepped apart to look at each other properly, and Cara couldn't hide her thoughts any more.

'Now, don't look at me like that,' Penny said. 'I'm just getting old, that's all. The morning rush is over, so let's make some tea and sit down for a chat.'

Cara put her bags down behind the desk in reception, noting that it had hardly changed in the time she'd been away. It could certainly do with a lick of paint and some more modern furniture. She followed Penny through to the kitchen, full of regret for having left it so long before coming home. Penny went to fill up the kettle but winced at the weight of it.

'Here, let me do that.' Cara stepped in and took over, and for once, Penny didn't argue.

'My hands aren't as strong as they used to be. I think it's just arthritis, but that's to be expected at my age.' Penny pulled a face, and Cara remembered just how proud she was.

She made two cups of tea and set them down on the table before taking a seat opposite Penny.

'It is so good to see you, but I have to admit, you seem a lot more fragile than when I was last here,' Cara ventured, knowing that she might offend Penny but needing to tell her of her concerns anyway.

'Well, I'm in my seventies now, aren't I? I've worked hard all my life, and it's taking its toll on my health, which is why I need your help.'

'You know I'll help out in whatever way you need. You've given me a lifeline just when I needed it.'

'To be honest, Cara, I just can't do it any more. It's too much for me to run the guesthouse at my age, which is why I want to hand everything over to you.' Penny paused to let what she'd said sink in. 'But look, we're really busy at the moment, so I can't talk about it now. Let me remind you how everything works, and then we can talk again later.' She stood up and finished her tea before disappearing back towards reception, leaving Cara speechless behind her.

After Cara unpacked her stuff back into her old bedroom, she joined her grandma in the kitchen for dinner, and that was when all the bombshells started falling.

'The doctor has signed me off and suggested I get away from here so that I'm not tempted to do any work,' she began. 'So I'm finally going to take my friend, Hamish, up on his offer to go and live with him at his cottage in the village.'

Cara's fork clattered back onto her plate in shock. 'Hang on a minute. You didn't say you were going to be moving out. I thought I was coming back for us to spend some more time together.' She sounded pathetic, but she didn't care.

'I'll still be in the village, so I won't be that far away,' Penny reassured her. 'But the doctor says I'm seriously ill, Cara. If I don't give up work at once, I'll probably be dead within a few months.'

Cara's hands flew to her face. She took a minute to absorb what Penny had said. 'What's wrong though? Is it just exhaustion?'

'I am old, there's no doubt about that, and I work too hard. Have done for years. I need to take things easy, because my heart isn't what it once was, and he says I'm at great risk of a fatal heart attack.'

'Oh, Grandma. I'm so sorry. I wish I'd come home sooner.' She hated herself for losing touch with this woman she loved so dearly, and who had welcomed her back with open arms and no judgement.

'Don't you dare feel guilty,' Penny admonished her. 'You're young, and you have your own life to live. You don't owe me anything.'

'Yes, I do, and you know it. I owe you everything, and even though I do have my own life to live, you're the only family I have, and I should have made more of an effort to keep in touch with you.'

'Well, look, you're here now, and I can't tell you how glad I am about that. You mean more to me than anything, and if you can help me out now, then so much the better.'

'I do want to help, but I'm very worried about running the guesthouse when I don't have the first idea about how to run a business on my own. I want you to get better so we can run the place together.'

Penny pursed her lips. 'I don't think that's going to happen, sweetheart. It's time for you to take over from me, and for me to retire and take it easy. My will's all written, and I know what I want to do with Watersmeet View when I die. I always meant to pass it over to you, and you needn't worry about managing the business. You've got it in you, and with the help of Zoe and the rest of the community, you'll be fine.'

Cara frowned. 'Hang on. First of all, you're not going to die for a long time yet, Grandma.'

'Well, not if I retire and hand the reins over to you, sweetheart, no. And I have every confidence in you, even if you don't have any yourself.' Penny rolled her eyes, and Cara laughed, but she was a bag of nerves.

'But I can come and ask you for help when I need it?' she checked, avoiding the awkward discussion they were on the brink of having.

'Yes, of course, but woe betide you if you fall foul of Hamish by coming to talk to me about the business all the time. He's my fierce protector,' she said, and Cara could see just how much she loved him as she said those words. Penny took a deep breath, and Cara held hers, wondering what she was going to say next. 'So if everything works out, I want to transfer the guesthouse into your name straight away. I want to enjoy the rest of what's left of my life with Hamish without having to worry about this place, and you're the only person I can trust it with.'

Cara was speechless this time as the full weight of her grandmother's plans finally hit her.

Hamish came to collect Penny after dinner, once she'd packed a small bag of essentials to last her until she could come back for the rest of her important things.

'I'm very glad to meet you, Cara,' he said with a soft Scottish accent and a twinkle in his eye.

'Likewise,' she said, trying not to reveal just how abandoned she felt once again, with the only family member she still had leaving her on her own to fend for herself. Her reaction was a little unfair, she knew, but her family did have a habit of disappearing or dying when she least expected it, and Penny was all she had left.

Once they'd gone, she checked everything was in order before making her way past Penny's sitting room and bedroom, and finally, on to her old bedroom, right at the end of the corridor. She opened the door, noticing this time how it still creaked, and marvelled at the ever-present reminders on the wall of the pop-star favourites of her youth, as well as the tattered old bedspread that was still spread across the old single bed. Being back in this room always made her feel like a teenager again. She would definitely have to do something about that now she was back home for good.

She got herself ready for bed, dreading the early start she'd have the next morning. Lying in the small single bed, she struggled to come to terms with everything that had happened to her in the past twenty-four hours. She'd wanted a fresh start, though, and this was definitely it, and she couldn't begrudge her grandma the rest she needed nor the new life after all the years she'd spent working. It was going to be a challenge, but Cara was up for it, and maybe it would be the making of her. She hoped so, because she didn't want to fail. She wanted to make a success of the guesthouse, to make her grandma proud of her, and to have something all of her own at last. She fell asleep full of positive thoughts about turning the guesthouse around and making a go of things in the future.

The sun was just coming up as Cara stumbled along the corridor the next morning to the guesthouse's kitchen, ready to throw herself into the task of producing a hearty breakfast for the five guests staying with them.

As she put on an apron, she cast her eye round the tiny space and wondered how on earth her grandma had managed to produce food in this cramped area for all these years. Despite having helped out at Watersmeet View a few times when she was growing up, this was the first time Cara would be completely in charge, and the mere thought of it threatened to overwhelm her. But she simply had to do it for Penny. Her grandma's poor health had come as a shock, so she'd had no time to think about whether she was up to such an enormous challenge. She'd just had to say yes.

Taking a deep breath, she went through to the dining room to make sure everything was set up there first, before the guests started arriving from seven o'clock. All the tables were clean at least, so all she had to do was to put out the cereals and the fresh bread for toast, together with the pastries, which had been stored in the pantry overnight. After collecting the milks and juices from the fridge, she made her way back into the kitchen to assemble her ingredients for the cooked breakfasts.

Cara swiped her hand through her long hair, pushing her fringe out of her eyes, before using one of her many hair ties to pull it out of the way. She really would have to see about getting it cut when she had a moment, but with things as they were, she had no idea when that would be. Having only just returned home without a penny to her name, it was going to be a while before she had any money to spend, let alone any free time to spend it in.

As she registered the tidiness of the kitchen as well, she wondered briefly when she'd have the time to clear up after cooking breakfast so everything looked this pristine tomorrow morning. Just as a hint of panic started to tighten her chest, the door to the dining area creaked open, signalling the arrival of the first guests, and everything else went out of her mind.

She made her way back out to the dining room and smiled at two of their regular customers easing themselves down onto the wooden seats at their usual table in the window. Emily and her sister, Cecily, had been coming to the guesthouse every March for years, and it was good to see them again, even though they were now considerably older than the last time she saw them.

'Good morning, ladies. It's lovely to see you both.'

Emily glanced up and then squinted through an ancient-looking pair of glasses. 'Goodness, Cara, is that you? We haven't seen you in ages. But it's good to see you back.'

'It is me, back from Exeter at last.' She took out her pad and pen from her pocket, subtly trying to move them on to placing their order rather than allowing them to take a wander down memory lane, which she didn't have time for right now. 'What can I get you both on this bright spring day?'

She was just on her way back to the sisters when the door opened again to admit the family of three who were staying at the guesthouse for the first time. Cara took the ladies' hot food orders before making her way over to the family.

'Morning,' she said with a smile. 'Have you settled in okay?'

The dad glared at her. 'We've had hardly any sleep, so it's not been the best of starts. When did you last change the mattress on that double bed in our room? It was like sleeping on one of those water beds.'

Cara was speechless for a moment, unsure of the right thing to say. 'I'm very sorry you found the bed uncomfortable,' she said in the end, knowing that an apology and the acknowledgement of a complaint usually went a long way to taking the heat out of a situation. 'Perhaps I can talk to you more about it after breakfast to see what we can do to improve the situation?'

The man nodded before turning his attention to the menu, effectively dismissing her.

'If you'd like to help yourselves to juices, pastries, and cereals, I'll be back shortly to take your hot food and drink order.'

She dashed off to the kitchen to make a start on the cooked breakfast for the two elderly ladies, worrying all the while about how she'd deal with the complaint from the other guest. She had no idea how old the mattresses were but could well imagine how uncomfortable they might be. She'd have to sort something out for them later, but for now, cooking and serving breakfast had to be the priority. Once the sausages were underway, she popped out again with the hot drinks for Emily and Cecily before taking the other table's order.

The next fifteen minutes flew by in a blur of sausages, bacon rashers, fried eggs, and fried bread. She piled the plates high, adding beans, tomatoes, and mushrooms, before delivering the first two plates and then returning with the other three. She discreetly cleared both tables of used items before making her way back to the kitchen to start clearing up.

Cara stacked the used crockery in the dishwasher and made a start on the washing-up. Once again she marvelled at how Penny managed it all at the grand old age of seventy-five. She was considerably younger than her grandmother, but after just cooking breakfast for five people, she was exhausted. The guesthouse needed to get much busier if her brief check of the accounts was anything to go by, but if it did, how would she manage on her own? Maybe it was just as well things were quiet for now. She had plenty to worry about for the time being without encouraging more guests to come.

She went back out to the dining area to clean up once all the guests were gone and was struck by how much food had been left on all the plates. Was she that bad a cook, or was there something else at fault here? Yet another worry to add to her mental list of concerns. She cleared the plates to the kitchen, wiped the tables down, put everything away, and then went back to the washing-up. At least she knew how to do that.

***

'Zoe, hi, it's me,' Cara said when her friend answered.

'Hey. How's everything going? Bet it feels like you've never been away,' Zoe said.

'Well, it turns out my grandma's too ill to keep running the guest-house on her own, so she's asked me to take over for a while so she can rest.' Cara blew out a long breath.

'Crikey, that must have come as a surprise.'

'Yep, you're not wrong there. It's been a bit of a baptism of fire, to tell the truth, but I've survived so far, and it's all coming back to me now. Still, there's no doubt it's a lot of work for one person. I honestly don't know how my grandma's been managing on her own for so long. And I've only got five guests in just now, but even so, there's such a lot to do.'

'And how's the business going?'

Cara released another long sigh. 'Not good, by the looks of things, although I haven't had a proper look at the finances yet. There are very few bookings in the diary, but even if it does get busier, I just don't know how I'd cope. But I need to if I'm to turn this business round.'

'Hmm. It sounds like you need to come up with a marketing plan, and quickly. Finn and Olivia have done wonders with The Bistro. Olivia knows all about marketing stuff. I'm sure she'd have some good advice if you need it.'

'I'd love to meet her,' Cara said. 'I know Finn, but only vaguely. Now I'm back in the village, I really want to get involved in the community properly, and to get to know everyone again.'

'I'll have a word with them and see if they might have any suggestions for you, shall I?'

'That would be great, thank you. Although I can't afford to spend any money on marketing, so free ideas would be best if possible.' Cara groaned. She hated the very idea of marketing and promotion, and yet she'd agreed to take over a business that would need both to get it back up and running.

'Look, try not to worry,' Zoe said. 'You can do this, and I'll help you too. Let's get together soon and catch up properly. I really have missed you.'

Zoe rang off, and Cara put her phone back in her pocket before checking her to-do list for the rest of the day. As she'd mentioned to Zoe, there were only a couple of bookings in the diary, and none of those were coming up, so she had only the current guests to deal with, including the man with the uncomfortable mattress. But her main priority was to have a look at the accounts in more detail to see just how bad things really were.

She made her way to the kitchen along the corridor behind the reception desk, filled the kettle, and switched it on to boil for a fortifying cup of tea, gazing out the window at the gardens to the side of the guesthouse while she waited. The gardens were Penny's pride and joy, and by the looks of it, whoever had been doing the gardening was doing a great job of things. Cara wondered absently how much that was costing and then winced at the negative turn her thoughts were taking. The guesthouse needed to look good to attract people to come and stay, of course, but everything else was going to cost money too, and there didn't seem to be much of that around.

Once she'd made her tea, she walked back towards her grandma's office and took a seat at the ancient desk where the accounts book was kept. She was afraid to open the old-fashioned ledger, not knowing what she'd find inside when she did – and even worse, that she might not be able to understand it. She wished her grandma had used a computer and an online bank account.

Cara took a deep breath and opened the book, preparing herself for the worst, and after a few minutes, she breathed a sigh of relief. It was very organised and easy to follow, with income shown across one set of double pages and expenses across another, all written in her grandma's neat hand. However, having worked her way down both sets of pages, it was clear the guesthouse's finances weren't good at all. Quite simply, there were a lot more expenses than there was income.

The back of the book contained a plastic wallet full of invoices, and several of these looked to be overdue. She let her head fall into her hands. What was she going to do? She'd hoped there'd at least be some money to spare to do the place up a bit and buy replacement items like mattresses, for goodness' sake, but there really wasn't anything. And while she could get more customers in with some marketing effort, no one was going to want to stay in a dilapidated room with a lumpy old mattress to sleep on.

She heaved a sigh and stood up to cast her eye over the folders neatly stacked side by side on the bookshelf at the side of the desk, trying to see which one held the bank statements. Maybe there was a savings account with some money in. Her heart told her this was unlikely, but she still had to try.

After several minutes of pulling files out and checking them, though, there was no sign of any bank statements, which was odd given how organised her grandma was. She would have to ask Penny about that when she next saw her.

A quick glance at her watch told Cara she needed to abandon the search for now and get back outside to the guesthouse. She still had some rooms to clean, and while she was at it, she could check the mattresses in the empty rooms to see if there was a newer one the grumpy man and his family could have. But as she walked upstairs to the first floor, she pondered how she'd even begin to move a double mattress on her own, eventually concluding it would be impossible. Perhaps it might make more sense for the family to move to another room instead.

After checking the unoccupied rooms on the first floor, it was obvious only one of the mattresses was relatively new. All the others were decidedly old and needed replacing sooner rather than later, and they weren't cheap. Tears sprang to Cara's eyes as the weight of all she'd taken on settled on her shoulders. She wanted to make a go of this – she really did – but right now, it seemed like everything was against her.

CHAPTER THREE

Cara mopped her brow for what felt like the tenth time in half an hour. The kitchen was stifling even with the door open, and with all the rushing to and from the dining room, she wouldn't get a chance to cool down until service was over. After barely a week, she was getting better at cooking and delivering the breakfasts every morning, but it was all so relentless, especially when she was the only person working there.

They'd picked up another couple of guests who'd just walked in off the street yesterday, so Cara was even busier than before. Still, they needed every guest they could get if they were going to be able to keep the guesthouse running. There was a small amount of debt – although no mortgage, thankfully – but with no savings, they needed more guests and more staff as soon as possible. Still, she was trying to keep an open mind about the way forward, and to stay positive, as she'd promised Penny.

After speaking to Finn and Olivia, who owned The Bistro in the village, Zoe had let Cara know about a networking meeting for businesses taking place in Barnstaple later that morning, so she was hopeful something might come out of that when she went along. She was going to leave the front desk unattended, but with a message saying she'd be back later, and Zoe would drive her there. Cara had never learnt to drive as she didn't really see the need to, but it did make her dependent on others when she needed to travel away from Watersmeet Bridge, especially as the bus service no longer ran from their end of the village, only from Lynford itself.

She finished serving the breakfasts and cracked on with tidying up the kitchen and the dining room so she could get away quickly. There was always so much to deal with first thing in the morning, and she was on the back foot the whole time. After completing the morning dash along the corridor to her bedroom, she was back five minutes later dressed in the only smart pair of black trousers she had and a fitted multicoloured top. She'd given her hair a quick brush, but her fringe was already getting in her eyes, and she swiped at it self-consciously, wishing that she'd thought to pin it back before getting in the car.

Cara shrugged into her jacket and ran down the garden path and out onto the road, where Zoe was parked up waiting for her. She slipped inside the car, and Zoe started driving away as soon as Cara had done up her seat belt.

'Thanks so much for this, Zoe. I really appreciate it.'

'No worries, you know that. I have to go and get the fish for the restaurant anyway, so it's not like it's out of my way.' She wrinkled her nose, and Cara laughed.

'I must admit, I'm glad not to be in your shoes, even if I am worried sick about how this meeting's going to go. I've never been to anything like this before, and I'm sure to put my foot in it with at least one person while I'm there.'

'Ah, don't be so daft. You'll be fine. You're just the same as them, I'm sure of it. You all run small businesses, and you'll all have the same problems to talk about and share solutions for.'

'I hope you're right. It sounds like the right place to go for advice at least. I had a look at the accounts yesterday, and things are even worse than I realised, so we need to do something pretty quickly.'

'Have you got a website and social media and all that? That's probably a must these days, with everyone being online and booking things direct.'

'I have no idea. I should have looked, I know, but I just haven't had the time. I can't see my grandma doing all that, though, can you?'

They both chuckled at the thought of it. Penny was old-school and didn't believe in websites and the like, even though she was savvy in many other ways.

Cara turned to look at the lush green landscape passing by. She wished she had more time to get out and about in the village to appreciate the area rather than having to spend most of her time indoors. She sighed. If she could improve things at Watersmeet View enough that they could take on someone else to support her, maybe she'd be able to explore a bit more in time.

They soon reached the edge of Barnstaple, and Zoe followed the signs towards the town centre, where the hotel holding the meeting was located. When they pulled into the car park five minutes later, there were already a lot of cars and people milling around, and Cara's nerves increased further.

Zoe parked in a space and left the engine idling while Cara gathered her things and pulled herself together.

'I hope it goes well,' Zoe said. 'Text me when you're done, and I'll come and get you.'

'Thanks. I'll see you later.'

Cara stepped out of the car, waved goodbye to Zoe, and turned to follow everyone else towards the large, modern-looking hotel. As she made her way to the entrance, she found herself a bit daunted by so many small business owners in one place. She wouldn't have thought this many people would be free to come to an event like this in the middle of the week. It was certainly playing on her mind having to be away from the business for so long.

Once inside, she joined a queue of people for the registration desk, and as she waited, she learned there were a number of meetings going on that day, not just hers. She took a breath and willed herself to be calm. She could do this, and maybe she might get some useful tips out of it too.

Cara made her way towards the conference room, following slowly along behind the other attendees. When she next looked up, she was taken aback to see the man from the train standing at the door, greeting people as they arrived for the networking session. She was so surprised she stopped right in the middle of the corridor. He was wearing his smart business suit – probably one he wore to the office every day – and she frowned as she worried whether she should have dressed up a bit more. Or perhaps he was overdressed. She didn't know the etiquette for these things, and it made her anxious. Someone nudged her as they came past, which set her moving again. There was no way of avoiding him now.

'Morning, everyone. Thanks for coming,' he said as the group in front of her passed by on their way in. She liked the deep sound of his voice, and her stomach fluttered at the thought of meeting him any minute now.

'Good morning,' she said softly as she drew level with him at last.

'I'm Joe Harris,' he said, with a flicker of recognition in his eyes. 'Good to meet you properly.' He smiled and put out his hand to shake hers.

Cara was surprised at the tingle she experienced as their skin met. There was no hint of a smirk from him, thank goodness, and she was grateful for that considering how she'd been ogling him on the train.

'Likewise,' she replied at last. 'I'm Cara. Are you running the training session today?'

'That's right, so if you'd like to take a seat, I'll see you in there.'

She disappeared inside the conference room and found herself a seat in the middle of the room. Glancing around, she saw that most of the attendees were less formally dressed, just like she was, and she breathed a sigh of relief. At least she didn't stand out on that front.

A few minutes later, Joe appeared at the front of the room and coughed lightly to get everyone's attention.

'Good morning again, everyone, and thanks for joining me for this networking session today. It's really heartening to see so many of you from small businesses in the local area, and I hope you'll all get a lot from the session I'll be running today. What I'd like to start with is by asking you all for your questions, so I can get an idea of where to pitch things for you. So please feel free to tell me what you want to know.'

Before she knew what she was doing, Cara put her hand up and Joe's eyes settled on her at once as if he'd been hoping she might ask something.

'Yes, Cara. Can you tell me what your business is, please, and then ask your question?' He gave her a broad smile of encouragement, and her heart warmed.

'Hi, yes. I run a guesthouse in Watersmeet Bridge, in Lynford. Well, I only recently took it over, and I need to bring things right up to date, so my question is, should I have a website and be on social media to promote the business?' She sounded more confident by the end, but her heart was pounding after speaking in front of all these people.

'Thanks, Cara. That's a really good question. Out of interest, can I ask for a show of hands as to whether anyone else wonders about this?'

Half the room put their hands up, and Cara breathed a sigh of relief as she realised so many people felt the same.

'Great, thank you. I can definitely talk about that issue at some length. Any other questions?'

By the time Joe had gathered half a dozen questions, it was time for the first break. Cara stood up to go and get herself a drink and found herself mingling easily with the other attendees at the drinks table. As she moved away to one side, Joe appeared next to her.

'So, what made you want to take on the running of a guesthouse, Cara?' he asked.

'My gran has run it all her life, but she's in her seventies now, and not in the best of health either, so she's asked me to take over. I thought I was coming home to help, but now I'm in charge and I have no experience at all of running a business. And I'm not that great with things like websites and social media either. I could probably do with a course just on digital marketing.' She laughed to cover her nerves.

'I run courses for small businesses all over the country, and social media is the number one course people ask for. Everyone's nervous about it and needs help to get started, but it's not so bad once you learn the basics.'

'Where are you based then?' she asked.

'I'm in London now, so I'm just here to run a few of these sessions before going back again. My mum lives in Watersmeet Bridge, though, so I know the area. Well, I must get back,' he said, finishing his coffee, and with another quick smile, he was gone again.

Cara went back to her seat thinking about what Joe had told her and wondering how they'd never met before. Joe launched straight into a session about setting up a website and getting started with social media after that, and she was so busy taking notes she couldn't think about anything else. By lunchtime, he'd covered half the questions raised, and her brain was frazzled with all the new information.

She chatted to the other attendees over lunch and didn't get to speak to Joe again before the afternoon session. He was busy networking with the other attendees, so she didn't begrudge him not talking to her, but she found herself wishing he'd been able to come back, even if only for a minute.

At the end of the session, Joe received a huge round of applause. She'd overheard lots of good comments about him from the other attendees.

'Thanks so much for coming today, everyone. I hope you've found this useful. We do offer courses about specific subjects, so if you'd be interested in attending one here again in the future, please do let me know.'

Cara stood up to put on her coat and then sent a quick message to Zoe to let her know she was ready to leave.

'It was good to meet you, Cara,' Joe said, suddenly appearing again at her side.

'And you, Joe. I found this session so helpful. Thank you.'

'Would you be interested in attending a course here in the future?'

'I'd definitely appreciate the help, but I couldn't spare the time away from the guesthouse with things as they are. I'm sorry.'

'I understand. Of course.'

'Maybe I'll see you in Watersmeet Bridge sometime when you come home to visit,' she offered hopefully.

'Maybe, yes.'

She watched him walk away knowing she shouldn't even be thinking of getting to know someone so soon after splitting up with Phil, and certainly not someone who lived in London. Joe was out of her reach, and perhaps that was for the best.

After another busy morning making breakfasts and clearing up the kitchen, Cara was determined to get outside again for a little while. She finished up and then stepped out the back door into the garden behind the guesthouse. She took a few steps away from the building and then turned to look back up at her childhood home. She had fond memories of growing up here with her mum before she became ill, and of the time afterwards when the community had rallied round to look after her and Penny as they came to terms with her mum's death.

At the same time, there was no doubt of Watersmeet View's importance to the community. The guesthouse had survived many difficult times over the past one hundred years or so, and become like a reassuring beacon to the village. Its prime position at the end of the village overlooking the bay below, where tourists and villagers alike often paused to take in the view, also meant it must have featured in thousands of photos over the years.

She walked past the large storage barn to the front garden and along the path to the gate, keeping her eyes on the view as she got closer to the front wall that marked the edge of the property. She slipped outside and across the road to the railing overlooking the bay below, the magnificent river, and the sea in the distance. Cara took in a deep breath and released it again, marvelling at how good it felt to breathe in the sea air.

Leaning forward slightly, she looked to her left, where she could just about make out the point where the waters met, shimmering in the distance, just before the old bridge. Although she'd been shocked when Zoe told her about the bridge's weakened structure, she now thought it might be a good thing it had become pedestrianised. She looked forward to wandering through the village and across the bridge again sometime soon.

She crossed back over to the guesthouse's garden and made her way to the front door, which had been left open, as always. There was still a pile of paperwork to deal with, but there were also beds to change and rooms to clean. The family were leaving today, as were the other couple who'd come in off the street. Thankfully, the family had chosen to move to the other room for the rest of their stay, and as it had a sofa bed, the sleeping arrangements had all worked out fine. She only hoped it was enough for them to leave a positive review on the site they'd made their booking through.

Preferring to clean rather than tackle her to-do list, she grabbed the cleaning supplies and made her way to the top floor to start on the family room first. She made a mental note to ask Zoe to help her swap a newer mattress to that room as soon as she could.

As she began to change the beds, Cara thought about ways of saving money. She pulled out a fresh sheet in its wrapper from the linen pile she'd collected and then stopped and stared at it. There was no point in putting fresh linen on the old mattress if they were going to swap it, and there was even less point in changing the beds in a room she planned to decorate as soon as possible. In fact, if she was only going to let out a few rooms while the decorating took place, there was no point in paying for so much new linen at all. She put the new sheet to one side and concentrated on stripping the old sheets off.

It made sense for her to change the arrangement with their linen supplier – at least temporarily – while she got the decorating done. Pleased with that decision, Cara set about cleaning the bathroom, which led her to think about the cost of the toiletries they put in the rooms and all the tea- and coffee-making items. They could definitely afford to reduce their orders with their suppliers for the time being to save costs.

By the time she'd finished cleaning the family suite, the checkout deadline had passed, and she was able to move on to cleaning the other two rooms. Both sets of guests had taken the early checkout option, so she didn't have to worry about being at the desk to see them off. She would have liked to be, but she just had too much to do. Still, she worried about the image that presented to those guests and whether it would put them off coming again.

Cara couldn't help but fret about everything as she pushed the hoover round. The guesthouse meant so much to Penny and had been in their family for years, and the responsibility for keeping it going was a heavy burden. It was all much more than she'd originally signed up for, and she was full of doubts and fears about how she'd manage on her own. But more than anything, she wanted her grand-mother to get better, because she couldn't take it if something happened to her. Then she'd be completely alone in the world, with the additional weight of a run-down, unprofitable guesthouse on her young shoulders.

Once she'd returned to reception, Cara pulled out the paperwork that had begun to pile up and started going through it all. She checked the linen invoice first and was shocked by the cost of the twice-weekly cleans the local company provided. She pulled out her notebook and added a note to speak to them about it. She wanted to change their order as soon as possible.

Then she remembered about the wasted food from breakfast. She concluded she was serving up too much food, and wondered about creating a questionnaire for guests to complete on arrival, specifying what they'd like for their breakfasts, so she could just buy what was needed, rather than buying to excess.

By the time she'd gone through all the paperwork, she looked set to save enough money to get all three rooms on the top floor redecorated, and maybe the shared bathroom as well. Now she needed to speak to Zoe about helping her get a good deal on that decorating work. If her memory was correct, Zoe would know just the person to help.

After a quick lunch, Cara returned to her to-do list, which was already as long as her arm. There was a pile of invoices waiting to be paid, but Penny still hadn't given her access to the business bank account. She made a note to ask her about that when she next spoke to her. There was a delivery of clean bed linen due, although it would be much reduced now she'd given the linen company a call, and she also needed to get out to buy food for breakfast the following morning. The stress was already starting to get to her.

On top of that, Cara found herself spending quite a lot of her time thinking about Joe, and that was making it hard for her to focus. She'd felt a real connection with him at the networking session and if he didn't live in London, she would have liked to explore that further. But maybe it wasn't meant to be, or maybe she should keep to the promise she'd made herself after splitting up with Phil to forget about men for a while.

Grabbing one of the restaurant menus, she made a list of what they needed for breakfast the next day based on what she'd seen in the kitchen fridge and the cupboards earlier on, determined to start cutting down the food waste immediately. She'd get out for some fresh air and do the shopping. Everything would seem better after that. Penny had at least left her some money for food, so she picked up her purse and made her way outside.

'Morning, Cara,' a deep voice with a hint of a Scottish accent said as she stopped for a moment on the doorstep.

She turned to look and found Hamish kneeling in the flower bed doing some weeding. 'Hello, Hamish. I didn't realise you did the garden here,' she said.

'Yes. I've been taking care of it for a good few years, although my daughter Sheila's here more often than I am now she's moved to the village, so you'll probably see her next time,' he said, standing up slowly and stretching out his back on the way. He gave her a broad smile, his white teeth standing out in his tanned face.

'And how's Penny doing? Is she resting?'

Hamish's weathered face crinkled up into a smile. 'Reluctantly, yes. I'll be spending most of my time with her, so I can be there if she needs anything. How are you getting on with everything? I'm sorry you've been thrown in at the deep end, but we both really appreciate your help.'

'It has been a bit, yes, and it's taking me a while to get back into the swing of things after not having worked here for so long. But I'll get there. I just want to help Penny after all she's done for me. Anyway, I'm off to get some shopping, so I'll see you later, Hamish. Give Penny my love.'

She gave him a small wave and set off for the High Street. She was glad Hamish would be there to give Penny a hand should she need it. She had no idea if Penny had told him about her plan to give her the guesthouse. That was up to Penny to deal with.

Cara was almost at the butcher's when she saw Zoe coming the other way. She smiled at the sight of her friend, and her heart warmed to know this would become the norm for her now she was back home again.

'Morning! How's it going up at Watersmeet View? Are you starting to settle back in?'

'I haven't even had a moment to think about settling back in, to be honest. Penny's thrown me straight back into it and left me to my own devices. And she delivered another bombshell to me yesterday as well.'

'Ooh, do tell. I love a good bombshell.' Zoe's eyes lit up, and Cara laughed despite herself.

'She's saying she's moving in with Hamish and that she wants to give me the guesthouse – you know, to put it in my name.'

'Well, that's great news, isn't it? That means you can definitely stay here for good.'

'It is good news, sort of.'

'What do you mean, sort of?' Zoe narrowed her eyes.

'It's just such a lot of responsibility. I don't know how I'm going to manage it all.'

'Oh my God! Just say yes to all of it. I would. You've got nothing to lose by giving it a go.'

Cara started to protest but then realised Zoe was right.

Zoe took Cara's hands in hers. 'You need to start believing in yourself. You can do this – I know you can – and I'll do anything I can to help you. We must meet regularly so you can keep me up to date. Where are you off to now? I'm on my way to the fish market yet again, for my sins.' She wrinkled her nose.

'Ew. I'm off to the butcher's myself. But listen, before you go, could you have a word with Ed about doing some decorating work for me? It would have to be a bit at a time while I save up the money, unless he wants to learn creative writing in exchange.'

Zoe laughed. 'I'm not sure writing's his thing. He'll bite your hand off for some regular work, though, don't you worry.'

'Great! Thanks. Tell him I'll be in touch. Thanks for the pep talk. Have a good time with the fish then, and I'll see you soon.'

Zoe went on her way, and Cara continued along the High Street. Was Zoe right? Could she do this? Other people seemed to think so, but taking the whole business over was another level of commitment entirely, and quite different from just working there with Penny by her side. She definitely didn't have either the confidence or the experience to run the guesthouse on her own., but Penny had left her to it, and she didn't want to let her down. At least she had Zoe for moral support. And maybe this could be a new beginning.

She arrived at the butcher's and joined the queue of people waiting outside. It was good to see the village thriving, and she was so glad to be back in the community that had embraced her as one of their own. This was where she belonged, and if she could repay Penny and the community for all they'd done for her, she would be delighted. It was time to put the last couple of years behind her and move forward. She had a job to do and a roof over her head, and for now, that was all that mattered. Plenty of time to worry about everything else later.

CHAPTER FOUR

Cara had spent most of the morning researching how to build her own website, but she'd found the whole thing so confusing that in the end she'd given up. She'd tried to set up some social media pages next and found them just as difficult. It was all so frustrating. At least her email worked properly, which was vital as the only means of communication for bookings at the moment.

She took a break mid-morning to make herself a cup of coffee, and as it was a bright spring day, she took the opportunity to get some fresh air. Standing just outside the front doorstep, she took in the magnificent view of the bay. She counted herself very lucky to be able to see it again every day.

Cara hoped she'd have more time soon to get out and about and appreciate the area rather than having to spend most of her time indoors. She sighed. If she could just improve things a little at the guesthouse, she could take on someone else to support her and try to claim back some time for herself.

Or maybe she was mad to even think that was possible. Her thoughts drifted to Phil and how easily taken in by him she'd been, even when he'd started to criticise her for everything she did. She cringed inwardly at how happy she'd been to let him dominate her whole life, to the exclusion of her friends and her grandma. He'd put such a dent in her confidence that it was hard for her not to think negative thoughts about her new situation. One thing she did know for sure was that she wouldn't let a man do that to her again. Now she had this fresh start, she'd take full advantage of it and do all she could to turn things round, even if it was the hardest thing she'd ever done.

She hadn't realised just how much she'd missed Watersmeet View in the time she'd been away. But so much had gone downhill in her absence, and she couldn't stop berating herself for not coming home more regularly, or at least checking in on her grandma more often.

She turned around to look up at the front of the building, taking in the noticeable signs of deterioration once again, and she was saddened that the guesthouse was in such a state of disrepair. Despite the obvious work that needed doing, she hadn't even thought about the outside of the property. They really needed to get more bookings in to bring in more money first, so her priority had to be the inside of the guesthouse. But just how was she going to do it?

With a bit more motivation after some fresh air in her lungs, she returned to her desk and picked up the list she'd created of items to deal with. Their lack of guests was high on her list of concerns, but she had no spare money to market the guesthouse with either. She definitely needed to sort out a website and some social media, but she was beginning to accept she might have to pay someone to help her with that. She should talk to Olivia at The Bistro, as Zoe had suggested, to see if she might have some ideas for free marketing. And then there was the matter of the need to redecorate, but at least she'd made a start on that. She closed the list and took a deep breath. She needed to take it one step at a time and remember that she wouldn't be able to do everything at once.

As she was studying her to-do list, her email pinged to say she'd received a message, and when she went to look at it, she was surprised – and a bit delighted – to see it was from Joe.

Hi Cara,

I hope you don't mind me getting in touch with you this way, but I don't have any other contact details for you.

I've been thinking about you and your situation ever since we met the other week, and what I might be able to do to help. So I've managed to persuade my boss here to let me come down to Watersmeet Bridge for two weeks, with a view to offering some low-cost digital training to local businesses while I'm there.

I wondered if you would be interested in this, and if you could spread the word locally for me, please?

It would be good to see you again.

With best wishes,

Joe

Cara couldn't quite believe it. She read the email through quickly again, pondering the meaning of some of his words more than was healthy, if she was being honest. He'd been thinking of her and said it would be good to see her again. She had to admit to feeling exactly the same, and now he'd reached out to help her. She didn't even have to think twice about whether she'd be interested.

Hi Joe,

It's really good to hear from you. Thank you so much for offering to help – I would definitely be interested in some training. I can think of a few other local businesses straight away that would also appreciate your help, so I'll speak to them and let you know.

When do you think you will come? It will be great to see you again too.

Best wishes,
Cara

Cara presumed Joe would stay with his mum, since he'd said she still lived in the village, and then she found herself wondering if she knew her. But she'd been away for so long that she wasn't as familiar with all the people currently living here. She hadn't gone to school with Joe – that much she did know – so maybe he and his mum had moved to the village after she'd left.

Joe's reply came back quickly to say he'd be arriving in the next few days, and that once he'd settled back in at his mum's, he'd be in touch. They swapped numbers to make things easier, and now all she had to do was wait for his arrival.

After speaking to her grandma the next morning, Cara finally got hold of the business bank details, and following a long wait on the phone to the branch in Barnstaple, she managed to get them to send the necessary paperwork for adding herself to the bank account. Once Penny signed everything, she'd set up an online account to make their lives easier.

She went out mid-morning to run some errands and then took her time on the way back to the guesthouse, trying to soak up all the things she loved about the village: the cobblestones along the High Street, the glimpses of the harbour and the sea between the shops and the houses, the people who nodded hello to her as she passed by.

She stopped at the gate and glanced out at her favourite view briefly before turning into the garden and making her way towards the front door. This time, there was a woman tending the flower beds, and she remembered Hamish telling her about his daughter.

'Hello,' she said as she got nearer, waiting for the woman to look up. 'I'm Cara. You must be Hamish's daughter.' She smiled.

The woman looked up then and returned her smile before getting to her feet, pulling off her gardening glove and extending her hand. 'Nice to meet you, Cara. I'm Sheila. I'm here most days now that Penny's moved in with my dad. Are you happy for me to carry on with what I've been doing in the garden?'

'You do an amazing job, but I have to be honest and say I'm a bit worried about how I'm going to keep on paying you if things don't pick up.' She blushed with embarrassment.

Sheila patted her on the arm. 'Don't worry, honestly. I can come as often or as little as you like or can afford. I've got our latest invoice here, so you can see what we charge, and then we can take it from there. Please don't be embarrassed. We're all trying to make ends meet.'

She turned to her rucksack and pulled out an envelope, which she gave to Cara.

'Thanks, Sheila. I really appreciate your understanding. It's a lot for me to get to grips with just now.'

'I'm sure it is, but you seem like the right sort of person for the job. Just take your time, and you'll get there.'

'Thank you. That's kind of you to say. I'm just about to pop the kettle on for a cup of tea. Would you like one?'

'I would love that. Thank you,' she said with a chuckle.

Cara went indoors, and her heart already felt lighter after talking to Sheila and getting that confidence boost. She checked in quickly at the desk, and then, satisfied there were no issues, she carried on through to the kitchen. After putting the kettle on, she quickly unpacked the shopping before making two cups of tea and delivering one back to Sheila.

It was such a lovely day that Cara stood on the step to drink her tea rather than going back inside.

'I don't remember seeing you in the village before, Sheila. Have you only moved here recently?'

Sheila blew on her tea before taking a sip as if taking a moment to compose her answer. 'Yes, just a few years ago. I, er ... got divorced and decided I needed to move somewhere new with my son and make a fresh start.'

'I'm sorry to hear that. It must be nice to be near your dad, and for your son to be near his granddad too.'

Sheila's face fell, and Cara wondered what she'd said to upset her. 'It was nice at first, but my son's moved away now, to London, and I do miss him, even though I know he has to live his own life. London's such a long way away, though, and he hasn't managed to come back very often. Anyway, ignore me. I'm just being sentimental.'

'I felt a bit like that when I went away to Exeter to uni. I couldn't wait to get away, to be honest, but now I'm back, I realise just what I was missing. Perhaps it's just something he needs to get out of his system.'

'Maybe, but Joe can be very stubborn once he's made his mind up about something,' Sheila replied.

'Hang on – is your Joe the one who runs tech courses? I went to one over in Barnstaple just recently.' Cara couldn't believe Sheila was Joe's mum and that she'd been able to put all these family connections together at last.

'Yes, that's him. He didn't make it home that time either.'

Cara didn't know whether to say anything about Joe coming home again soon in case he hadn't discussed it with his mum yet, so they finished their tea in silence after that, and then Cara took the cups back to the kitchen, letting Sheila get on with her work and forcing herself to do the same. Despite feeling sorry for Sheila missing Joe, Cara was revitalised after talking to her, and she spent the afternoon working on a breakfast questionnaire for guests. It might mean daily trips to the butcher's and the bakery, but she hoped that would make more sense anyway, and it would certainly reduce the guesthouse's food waste.

Finally, exhausted at the end of another day, she climbed into bed and let her mind wander back once again to meeting Joe at the networking meeting. She'd warmed to him immediately, charmed by his kindness when he'd seen how nervous she was, but later, she'd been shocked by the thrill she'd experienced when he'd taken her hand to shake it. If she were being honest, she'd been attracted to him on the train, even though it was embarrassing to be caught staring. But while she was trying to be honest with herself, she was also sure she was crazy for being attracted to someone so soon after being let down by Phil. Hadn't she promised herself not to get involved with another man ever again? She rolled her eyes at herself in the dark.

She was just getting Joe's help with her business needs, that was all, she reasoned. Nothing else was going to happen. If she made a friend out of this, that would be great, and as he lived in London, that was all that could come out of it. And maybe that was for the best, she told herself as she slowly drifted off to sleep.

———

Joe was once again on the train from London to Barnstaple. He'd been nervous about running his courses last time but mostly confident in his ability to deliver some good training. This time, though, he had nerves of a completely different kind. He was a bit worried about seeing Cara again, because he'd really liked her and was hoping she felt the same, but mainly he was nervous about seeing his mum again after so long.

When they'd first moved to Devon from Leeds after his mum and dad finally divorced, he'd been looking forward to a fresh start, and to helping his mum achieve the same, but Watersmeet Bridge was so small after spending most of his life in a city, and there were no opportunities for him there at all. It wasn't long before he got bored and started planning his escape to London, much to his mum's dismay. She hadn't held him back when he'd told her about the job, but he could tell she was disappointed he'd decided to leave so soon after they'd arrived. And he felt guilty about not spending much time with his granddad either. The worst of it all, though, was that somehow, six months had passed since his last visit, and although he rang his mum every couple of weeks, it wasn't the same as seeing her face-to-face.

He rubbed his hands against his temples. He should have tried harder to visit – he knew that – but he didn't have a car, and it was a long train journey from London to Barnstaple, let alone getting from there to the village, and that would require some days off from work to make it worthwhile. So he'd stuck his head in the sand and not bothered to visit at all. It was ironic then that the thought of seeing Cara again had been the only reason for him to visit in all these months. It wouldn't take his mum long to work that one out.

Still, she'd been pleased when he'd called to ask if he could come and stay for a couple of weeks even though he'd be working. His mum was very forgiving, and he loved her for that. Maybe he should take the time to tell her that while he was here. He closed his laptop, which he'd had open for the whole journey on the table in front of him but had hardly looked at while his thoughts consumed him. He loved his work, but there was no doubt that the shine of moving to London had started to wear off. He was sharing a house with other professionals in Mile End, which was well-located and had lots going on but still left him feeling lonely and isolated. He'd tried socialising with his work colleagues and his flatmates, but they didn't really have much in common except the obvious, and he'd given up trying after a few goes at it.

He resolved to make the most of this visit to Watersmeet Bridge, and to come back more often in the future.

The train pulled into Barnstaple shortly afterwards, and once outside, Joe found a taxi quickly to take him the rest of the way. His mum had told him she was working that morning, so he was to let himself into the cottage, settle in, and she would see him later. He did at least remember the way to his mum's house despite only having lived there for a few months, and after the taxi dropped him off at the far end of the High Street, he started to make his way along the cobbled street, glad he'd brought a rucksack rather than a pull-along suitcase.

It was an overcast day, and there was a fine drizzle in the air, but he could still glimpse the harbour down the side roads as he walked along. There were a good few people around, and some of them even looked like keen tourists, given the weather and the time of year. Most of the businesses were closed for the winter, but he hoped that would work in his favour in terms of them finding time to talk to him about their digital needs. He was sure there were plenty of people who would welcome his help, and he was looking forward to helping as many of them as he could during his stay. His company had been strict about him only offering the first half an hour free, though before charging for his services. That made business sense, of course, but he didn't know how many of these small businesses could realistically afford to spend money on setting up websites and social media when they were all struggling to stay afloat these days.

He was almost at the end of the High Street now and coming up to his favourite view before the walk along the path to his mum's cottage. As he approached the bench that faced out towards the sea, he glanced to the right at the guesthouse located there. He marvelled at Cara's good fortune to be looking out over such a spectacular view every day. He sat down on the bench for a few minutes to breathe in the fresh sea air and resolved to make sure Cara had some pictures of the view on her website to help sell the location to prospective guests.

Before long, he was at his mum's cottage and letting himself in using the key from underneath one of the garden pots. He left his bags in the front room and made his way to the little galley kitchen to make himself a cup of tea. He opened the stable door to look out at the courtyard garden while he waited for the kettle to boil and was pleased to see how charming it looked after his mum had applied her magic touch to it. He was looking forward to seeing her, and to finding out more about her new life here.

Cara received a message from Joe early in the morning to say that he'd arrived and would like to come and see her later. Despite her immediate reply, she was anxious about seeing him again and wasn't able to focus on anything while she waited for him to turn up. Around eleven, she looked up as the door opened once again, and this time, Joe's head appeared around it. She put her hand on her stomach as a little flutter occurred at the sight of his handsome face framed by his unruly dark hair. She forced herself to ignore the feeling and to give him a bright smile. She was pleased to see him after all.

'Morning, Joe. It's great to see you again,' she said. 'Would you like a drink before we get started?'

'How about we start with a tour of the premises, and have a drink and a chat afterwards?' he said with a smile. 'I've put together a very basic website for you, but I've had to leave quite a few gaps for the moment, so it would be good to see how everything fits together for when we go back to it,' he explained.

Cara nodded, relieved she wouldn't have to deal with technology straight away. 'Okay, let's go.'

It didn't take her long to show him the ground floor of the guest-house as he'd already seen the reception area, and apart from that, there was only the kitchen and the dining area.

'I'm not much of a chef, but even I can see this kitchen is tiny. How do you manage to produce so many breakfasts in here?' he asked Cara as they walked through.

'It's hard – I can't deny it – but we're not that busy right now, so it's possible. It will be much harder if we get busier at any point, but I'm still sincerely hoping we will.'

'I admire your honesty and your guts for taking this on, you know.'

The unexpected compliment stole her breath for a moment. Her heart warmed at his praise. She led him back the way they'd come and towards what was obviously an extension to the original Victorian building.

'These are the owner's quarters. Penny, my grandma, has a

bedroom and a sitting room, and I have a bedroom too. We share the kitchen and the bathroom. My grandma's moved out now though.'

'Yes, of course. She's living with my granddad, I hear,' he said with a grin before focusing again on the matter in hand. 'There's the potential to do some reorganising of the space here, then, in due course. I know that would all come at a price, but just because there's no money to spare just now, you shouldn't be put off from thinking about the future.' He followed Cara back to the reception once again before she led the way up the stairs to the first floor.

'There's no lift, I take it?' he asked.

She turned to reply over her shoulder. 'No, and that doesn't always go down well with the guests either, especially the sort we usually see coming back here time and again.'

They arrived at a small landing, where the carpet had definitely seen better days and the wallpaper looked like it had been put up in the 1970s. Joe winced at the clash of colours, and Cara smiled at their shared dislike of it. There were two small double rooms on this floor, one of which also had the sofa bed in it, and a shared bathroom and a separate toilet. The next floor was much the same, and finally, there were three rooms on the third floor: two singles with a shared bathroom and toilet, and the family suite for three with its own bathroom.

'Would you like that drink now?' Cara asked as they made their way back down. 'I should think you need one after all that.'

They went along to the kitchen after Cara stopped in briefly at the front desk to check everything was as it should be. She gestured to him to take a seat while she put the kettle on.

Joe set his laptop down on the table and waited for it to boot up while Cara made their drinks.

After a couple of minutes, she joined him, putting two cups down on the table and taking the chair next to him. She tried not to sit too close, but she felt his presence even so. She could almost hear his mind whirring.

'Well, the guesthouse has lots of potential,' he began with a smile. 'And I've been wondering about how best to sell that on the website.'

Cara laughed, glad he could see the positives. 'It has indeed, which is why it's so frustrating that I haven't got the money to make the most of it just now.'

'I know, but still, with seven bedrooms, and one en suite, the separate owner's accommodation, nearby parking, a large garden, and spectacular views across the river and the sea beyond, there really are lots of things going for it.' Joe ticked all the plus points off on his fingers.

'But it also needs a complete overhaul decoration-wise and modernising to make it more attractive to new guests, and I have no idea how I'm going to do that with limited funds.' Cara swiped her hair off her forehead, frowning as she thought of all the problems she was facing.

'Well, let me show you what I've done with the website so far. It's only the first go at it, so it's pretty basic, and having done the tour, it's clear we'll need to make some changes.'

'Okay,' she said, taking a deep breath. 'Show me this new-fangled website and see if you can explain how it works to me.' Cara had an innate fear of technology despite having grown up with it, but she was also sensible enough to realise that she needed to get her head round websites and social media at the very least, if the guesthouse was to move into the twenty-first century.

She tried to keep calm while she waited for Joe to load the website, and then, suddenly, there it was before her. He'd used the glorious view of the bay as his background to the whole site, but there was a carousel of great pictures at the top as well.

'Wow! That's taken my breath away,' she said after a moment of stunned silence.

Joe released a long breath and mimed wiping sweat from his forehead. 'Phew! You had me worried there. Do you like it then?'

'I do. Did you take those photos?' When he nodded, she was even more amazed. 'You're a talented photographer as well then. That view of the bay has always been my favourite.'

'Mine too,' he replied, and they shared a smile. 'Until you can start redecorating, we'll need to be really careful with the photos we use on the site. We want to show the guesthouse to best effect, but we have to be honest too.'

'Yes, that's true. But we can take some new photos of some things now. There are a few you've used that are out of date. Hang on – let me make a list.'

Joe smiled. 'That's exactly the reaction I was hoping for. Let me take you through the pages I've set up so far so we can think about anything else that might need doing.'

'That's a long list,' Cara said when they'd finished going through the site. She was pleased with the overall effect, though, and grateful to Joe for all his work.

'I'll get cracking with taking and adding the new photos, and then we should be able to go live very soon.'

CHAPTER FIVE

After two weeks of running the guesthouse on her own, Cara was still finding it hard to settle into anything like a routine. Every day was such hard work, and although she had a bit more of a handle on what she was doing now, she still felt like she was drowning rather than making progress. Blowing her fringe out of her hair yet again, she considered how this morning's breakfast had flown by in a blur as usual. Even though she still only had a few occupied rooms, she was kept busy making and serving breakfasts for all the guests and then moving on to cleaning the rooms and changing the beds every day. And the paperwork just kept on piling up.

Penny had stayed away, as per her doctor's orders, although she was always available to answer questions whenever Cara needed her help. But facing each day alone was hard, and in her heart, Cara really wasn't sure she was up to running the business on her own forever.

She'd confessed her worries to Zoe in a panicked phone call just last night.

'I have no experience, and I don't know if I'm up to the challenge,' she'd told her friend wearily.

'Don't put yourself down,' Zoe had said. 'You might be surprised at how much you can do when you put your mind to it.'

'It's lovely of you to say that, but we both know just how much there is to do here.'

Zoe tsked. 'We've already talked about that. I believe you can do it. You just have to start believing in yourself. And Penny obviously has confidence in you, otherwise she wouldn't have handed control over to you, would she?'

Cara paused in the middle of changing the final duvet cover as she thought about Zoe's words. Perhaps she did have a point there about Penny trusting her to run the business. She gathered up all the dirty linen and bundled it into the bag for the laundry. At least she'd reduced their laundry bill by cutting down on the amount she was sending to them.

She made her way back downstairs to reception to find an unfamiliar man in a suit waiting for her at the desk.

'Hello. Can I help you?' she asked, depositing the laundry bag behind the desk as she focused her attention on him. He didn't look like their usual type of customer.

'I'm sure you can,' he said in an oily voice that made her immediately distrust him.

She rested her hands on the desk and waited to hear what he'd say next. He reached into his inside pocket and withdrew a business card, which he placed on the desk before her. Cara's eyes widened as she read it.

Jason Smyth, Estate Agent, Smyth, Brown and Co., Watersmeet Bridge, Lynford

She looked up at him in confusion. 'You're an estate agent,' she stated. 'I'm sorry, I'm still not sure how I can help you.'

'I think it's the other way round,' he said. 'I believe I can help you.'

'What do you mean?' It was like getting blood out of a stone, she thought, wishing he would come to the point.

He gestured around him. 'This is a lovely old guesthouse, but I'm sure you'd agree that it has seen better days. It's looking a bit run-down after, I imagine, some years of neglect.'

She bristled at the implication of his words. 'If you're trying to charm me, you're not making a very good job of it,' she retorted.

'My point is,' he went on hurriedly, 'I have a number of buyers who would be very interested in taking this property off your hands and restoring it to its former glory as an investment for the future. And then you'd have a tidy sum to go off into the sunset with, and you'd never have to worry again about running this place. I'm sure it must be tough-going for a young ... er, woman like yourself to be bearing all this responsibility.'

Cara gripped the edges of the desk. 'This guesthouse has been in my family for years, and although there is a lot of work to do, I'm perfectly capable of rising to that challenge. Watersmeet View is not for sale. Whoever told you it is was mistaken. So you've had a wasted journey here today, Mr Smyth. And I think it's past time for you to leave. Good day.'

She turned away, effectively dismissing him, and picked the bag of laundry back up while she waited for him to go. She heard the door close behind him and turned back to the desk, releasing the breath she'd been holding. His business card was still on the desk, and she picked it up, planning to throw it in the bin, but then she noticed he'd written something on it.

Do feel free to let me know if you should change your mind down the line. Jason :)

She couldn't believe the arrogance of the man and threw the card away. What or who had given him the idea the guesthouse was for sale, she couldn't think, but at least it had focused her mind. There was no question of her selling up now, even if things were hard at the moment.

She was going to get on with implementing her savings ideas, and it wouldn't be long before Joe got the website up and running. He'd also talked about helping her to set up a new booking system on the site, so soon there would be more customers, and that would give her the money to pay for decorating, among other things. It would come together – she was sure of it. She just needed to hold her nerve and keep going. Under no circumstances was she going to let Penny down when she'd placed her trust and confidence in her. Maybe if Cara started believing in herself the way her friends and family believed in her, she might actually start to think she could turn things around.

Joe had already been down in Watersmeet Bridge for a week and had quickly come to realise that a few weeks wouldn't be enough to help all the businesses that had contacted him as a result of Cara spreading the word. He'd been to see most of them, but half an hour really only scraped the surface as far as their needs were concerned. He'd need a good few hours with each of them to make a real difference. And, as predicted, none of them had the budget, let alone the time, to spend on learning how to do things for themselves.

His relationship with his mum had benefitted greatly from his stay so far, though, and he was glad about that. He didn't dare to think about how she'd feel when the time came for him to leave again.

He was meeting another new client this morning, a small gift shop on the High Street, and would be going past Watersmeet View on his way. Every time he went past, he wondered how Cara was getting on and wished he was going to see her as well. He was spending a lot of his time thinking about her, actually, and didn't quite know what to make of that.

A fine drizzle was coming down as he stepped outside the cottage, making him glad he'd taken a moment to put on a jacket with a hood, but it was fairly mild. As he walked down the hill, he saw some of his customers and called out hello to them with a smile. His work was enabling him to get to know so many people now, and to feel like he was part of the village community. He was surprised to find he liked that feeling.

Sadly, there was no view to appreciate today because of the

weather, but he was at least able to make out his mum working away in the guesthouse's garden. He stopped to lean over the wall for a quick chat.

'Hey, Mum. How's it going? The weather's not in your favour today.' He pulled a face.

'Oh, it's not so bad,' Sheila replied with a smile. 'I've worked in a lot worse than this.' She turned her face up to the sky for a second and quickly looked back down again to stop the rain from hitting her face. 'Still, not so nice when it's falling straight into your eyes though. Might be a good time for a break. Where are you off to?' She winced slightly as she got up from her knees.

'To that little gift shop on the High Street. They need some help setting up a social media page.'

'Okay, I'll see you later on then. I'm going to take refuge in the shed for a bit.'

Joe watched his mum as she walked towards the shed, worrying about her being out in all weathers. She'd told him his granddad had now pretty much retired, leaving all the work to her, and Joe was sure it was all a bit too much for her.

He turned to carry on along the High Street, not wanting to be late for his appointment. Today was meant to be his free thirty-minute session with the client, but there was a lot to get done in that time, and it all had to be done before their scheduled opening time. A few minutes later, he arrived at the shop's front door and gave a brief knock. He could see the owner inside, already working hard, and gave a quick smile and a wave as she looked up at him.

'Hello, Joe. Thanks for coming. Good to see you again.'

She showed him inside and led the way through the shop into a small back room with a kitchen area and a table and chairs. She motioned to him to have a seat while she went to put the kettle on. Joe got his laptop out, took off his coat, and sat down.

'So I've made a start on your page using the photos you sent me, and I wanted to check whether this is what you had in mind,' he said.

They worked solidly for the full half hour, by which time the owner had to go and open the shop.

'Thanks so much, Joe, for all your help. I really do appreciate it. I think I should be able to upload more pictures at least now. Whether I can do as good a job as you, I'm not so sure, but I'll give it a go.'

Joe made his way out shortly after, pleased with how the session had gone. He had some time before his next meeting, so he decided to stop for a coffee at the café opposite.

'Good morning. I'll have a latte please,' he told the woman at the counter once it was his turn.

'Of course. Can I get you anything else?' she said with a smile.

'No. That's it, thank you.'

She put his order into the till and then turned to make his coffee. Joe tapped his card against the machine and stood to one side to wait for his order to be served.

'There you go,' the woman said a few minutes later as she pushed his coffee across the counter towards him. 'I hope you don't mind me asking,' she went on, 'but are you Sheila's son, the one with all the tech knowledge?'

Joe laughed. 'Yes, that's me. Are you looking for some help?'

'I really am,' she groaned. 'I just don't know how to get the café's name out there to help me develop the business. Would you have time to talk to me early one morning, or at the end of the day? The café closes at 4 pm.'

'I could come back later today if that would work for you,' he said after a quick glance at the calendar on his phone.

'That would be brilliant. Thanks. I'm Helen, by the way.'

'Joe,' he said, extending his hand. 'I'll see you later on then.'

Joe took his coffee over to a table by the window overlooking the harbour. He got his notebook out to scan the list of clients he'd met or was due to meet this week. He couldn't believe that he was up to twenty different businesses. There really was demand here, but would any of them be able to pay his company's exorbitant fees after the first half hour?

It was a lovely spring morning as Cara set off from the guesthouse for her meeting with Finn and Olivia at The Bistro. Today, the sun was bright and warm on her skin, and she was delighted to see some daffodils coming through in the garden as she walked through it. There was no sign of Sheila or Hamish today, but she knew one of them would be back soon enough. Come to think of it, Hamish hadn't been around at all since Penny had moved in with him. She needed to go and see them both for a catch-up soon.

Everyone she passed as she strolled along the High Street said hello as always, renewing her love for the little village community. It was a wonderful place to run a guesthouse business, even if said guesthouse was a bit run-down and in need of some TLC at the moment. She hated to admit it, but that smarmy estate agent was right about that much.

In the distance, the sunlight glinted off the water as it passed underneath Watersmeet Bridge, and the boats in the harbour bobbed around in the light breeze. She was entranced by all the different colours – reds, blues, greens – as well as a whole host of catchy names. 'Justin Thyme' was her favourite for today.

Cara was delighted to see a queue outside the café as she passed by. She decided she'd pop in and buy her lunch there on her way back. All around, there were signs that spring was on its way, and that the village would get busy again once the season proper started. A few passers-by ambled along the cobbled street, exploring the individual gift shops and perusing the restaurant menus. There was a lot of interest in the menu at The Bistro, and Cara sincerely hoped she'd be able to eat there soon herself if she could get a table.

She stepped around the customers studying The Bistro's menu and pushed open the door to the restaurant. The bell tinkled, and Zoe appeared from the kitchen to greet her.

'Morning, you. How are you today?' she said as she came towards her.

'I'm pretty good, to tell the truth. The weather's lovely, and it's so good to be back home again.'

'And how are things going with the guesthouse?'

'It's hard, Zoe, I can't lie, and I still don't know if I can turn things round even with everyone's help, but I'm determined to give it a try. I'm not going to be selling up to any oily estate agents anytime soon, that's for sure.'

Zoe's eyebrows rose in enquiry, but before Cara could go on and fill her in, Olivia appeared.

'You must be Cara,' Olivia said when she reached her. 'It's lovely to meet you at last. Why don't we sit down here? Finn will be along in a minute. He's just dealing with a delivery.'

'I'll see you later,' Zoe said and disappeared behind the bar.

'Thanks so much for seeing me today,' Cara began. 'I know you must be busy, and probably very tired.'

Both women laughed. 'I am tired,' Olivia admitted. 'I should be putting my feet up more before the baby comes, but there's always so much to do.'

'Is this your first one?'

'No. It's our second. We have a three-year-old daughter as well. I have no idea how we're going to manage with another one. I guess we'll find a way, as we always do. Anyway, what can we do to help you? You've taken on a massive challenge.'

'I have, and I don't really know if I'm up to it, but I'm giving it a go. Right now, I need to increase the number of guests so I can afford to get the place redecorated, but I can't go too fast, because there's only me to deal with everyone, and if we get too busy, I just won't be able to handle it on my own. Joe Harris is helping me with a website, and eventually some social media, which should bring in more people, but I'd also like to join forces with some of the other small businesses in the village to share marketing and publicity ideas, which would benefit all of us in the long run.'

'Social media has been an absolute game changer for us. Have you looked at our Facebook page? It might give you some ideas for how to approach things. And there's a village group as well.'

'Okay, I'll do that, and would you be interested in me putting out some flyers in the guesthouse advertising The Bistro?'

'Sure, and we could offer your guests a discount on their first meal, if you like.'

'That would be great! Thank you. And would you be happy to have some flyers about the guesthouse here as well?' Cara hoped she wasn't asking too much of Olivia when she'd only just met her.

'Of course. That would be fine, and we'll be happy to recommend you if people ask. I'd like to come and see the guesthouse again before doing that, though, if you don't mind. It's been a long time since I was last there.'

Cara admired Olivia for her honesty and her principled approach to business. 'You'd be welcome anytime. Well, look, I won't keep you. Thanks again,' she said as she stood up.

At that point, Finn came into the dining room. 'Cara! Long time no see,' he cried as he came bounding forward. 'You probably don't remember me from school. I was a bit older than you. Sorry I'm late. Have you had a good chat?'

'We have, thank you. It's good to see you though.'

As Cara turned to go, the artwork on the walls caught her eye.

'Aren't they amazing?' Finn said, coming up alongside her. 'A local artist, Esme, asked us if she could have her opening night here a couple of years ago because there was no other venue left in the village for her to display her art. We agreed, and it was a great success, and since then, she's displayed her art here on a regular basis. She gets lots of sales from it, and we take a small commission. That's the thing about marketing – it needs to be fresh and different. Anyway, good luck with everything. I'm sure it will be fine once you get into your stride.'

Cara had just finished tidying up the dining room the next morning ready for their first guests when she saw the patch of water on the floor of the pantry.

'Shit. Where the hell did that come from?' She went straight to get the mop and wipe the mess up and then waited a few seconds to see if it would reappear. Sure enough, more water seeped out. Ideally, she'd turn the water off now, but she couldn't do breakfast without any water, let alone clear up afterwards. What was she going to do? She stood as if frozen by her indecision, and it was only the creaking of the back door being pushed open that snapped her out of her trance-like state.

'Morning,' Joe said. 'Sorry to interrupt, but I heard you from outside as I was about to knock. Is everything all right?' He frowned and cast a quick glance round the kitchen, trying to find the source of her distress.

'Joe! What are you doing here at this time of day?' she asked, although she was glad to see a friendly face.

'It's such a beautiful day I thought I'd get out early. I was just coming to say hello ...' He blushed slightly and then carried on. 'Is there anything I can help with?'

She sighed and was embarrassed to feel tears spring to her eyes. 'Not unless you know anything about plumbing. Something's leaking, and I don't know what it is. I can't turn the water off if I'm going to make breakfast for everyone.'

'Why don't I have a look at it while you get on?' he offered.

'Thank you so much. I'd be very grateful.' She couldn't believe he might be able to sort this problem out for her.

She went to put out the juices, and by the time she'd returned for the cereals, bread, and pastries, Joe was standing up again and wiping his hands.

'You do have a small leak,' he said, 'but I've found the source and put a bowl underneath it to catch the water until you can call someone out later to sort it out. Your grandma probably has someone she usually calls on.'

Cara breathed out a sigh of relief and smiled. 'Thanks so much, Joe. You've been a godsend this morning. Now all I have to do is to get through the whirlwind of breakfast service.'

'Do you want me to give you a hand with that too? I can be quite helpful in the kitchen.' He grinned, and she laughed.

'Oh my God. You are a lifesaver. If you're really sure, yes, please. Would you be happy to go and take orders when guests come into the dining room? I just need to get things ready for those who want full breakfasts now.'

Joe got straight onto it, and she soon heard voices in the dining room. Before she could go out and greet anyone, though, he came back in with the first order.

'I'll sort out the hot drinks if you're okay to carry on with the cooking,' he said.

Cara couldn't quite believe her luck in having met Joe. He just got on with things, and as a result, the breakfast service flew by. As soon as the last guest had been served, he moved on to stacking the dishwasher while she washed up, leaving them all done and dusted a full half hour earlier than normal.

'Thanks so much for all your help this morning, Joe. You made everything run like clockwork for once.'

'You've got a great system in place. All I did was give you an extra pair of hands so you weren't running round trying to do everything yourself. As soon as more guests arrive and more money starts coming in, you'll be able to hire someone in, and things will get easier for you.'

She nodded, but right now, she only wanted Joe to provide that extra pair of hands. She couldn't tell him that, of course, but she had to admit, she liked having him around, and that was a good feeling to start the day with.

Joe returned to his walk, leaving her alone with her thoughts and her usual long to-do list. She focused her mind on it to stop herself from spending too much time analysing her feelings for Joe.

First up on the to-do list today was to check Penny's address book for the name of a plumber, and then Cara wanted to call Ed, the decorator. She had to leave a message for both people, but she was hopeful they'd be able to come in later. She bounced up the stairs after that, full of renewed enthusiasm for the jobs of the day.

As she made her way back downstairs about an hour later, a deep voice called out from below.

'Hello? Anyone around?'

'Hi there. I'm just coming down.'

'You must be Cara,' the huge man in reception said as she came into view. 'I'm Ed.'

Cara greeted Ed with a big smile, taking in his enormous frame and cheerful face as she came down the last flight of stairs. She put out her hand to shake his, and his seemed positively bear-like when it closed over hers.

'Nice to meet you, at last,' he said. 'Zoe talks so much about you.'

'Same here. So, Ed, I want to have the whole place redecorated, but it's going to take some time for me to save up the money to have all that done. Will that sort of approach work for you?'

'Yes, sure. That's no problem. It might be tricky to fit your work in sometimes if you can only give me short notice, but I'll do my best to work something out for you.'

'Great. Why don't I show you the family suite up on the top floor then first? It's my best asset because it has its own bathroom.'

She showed Ed round, explaining she'd leave him to do the family room, only letting guests book the rooms on the lower floors until the top floor was finished.

Ed offered to quote for redecorating the whole of the top floor, including the other rooms as well, and to get back to Cara as soon as possible.

Once she'd said goodbye to him, Cara returned to the rest of her to-do list with fresh determination.

CHAPTER SIX

Luke Johnson judged that Cara Rafaelli had had enough time to wallow in her misery by now. Enough time that she'd be grateful to him for swooping in to save the day. He smiled to himself as he walked through the car park of the hotel he managed and across the small bridge that took him into the village. Today was the day that everything was going to change, and he was going to take another step towards his ultimate goal.

He made his way down to Watersmeet Bridge, taking in the bustling harbour on his way. There were fishermen on the quayside selling their morning catch, and he was satisfied to see the long lines of customers. There were plenty of boats bobbing about in the water too, but Luke barely gave them a glance. That sort of thing was for tourists, not for businessmen like himself.

Once he'd crossed the bridge, the residential fishing cottages were replaced by the cheesy seaside gift shops selling their usual tat, but also the more upmarket galleries and artisan craft shops, as well as higher-end restaurants. He gave them all nothing more than a passing glance, only checking they were still there, doing business, for the customers of his hotel to make use of.

If things went the way he hoped, he'd allow himself the one indulgence of stopping in at the village café to buy some lunch to take away. He would never stoop so low as to eat there himself, but he had to admit, they did make delicious crab and prawn mayonnaise sandwiches, and he would deserve a treat by the time he was on his way back.

He went through the guesthouse gate a few minutes later, not even bothering to look at the view it was named after, nor the garden just coming into spring as he went through. All he saw was how run-down the place looked. He rubbed his hands together, thinking about what a great deal he was going to get on this place before he demolished it and transformed it into lucrative second homes.

The door was open, so he pushed it and went inside, blinking a few times to adjust to the dimmer light. Cara Rafaelli was at the desk and looked up at him in surprise.

'Good morning,' she said with a smile. 'What can I do for you?'

'I'm actually here to do something for you,' he said, casting his eye around the dowdy-looking hallway.

Her eyes narrowed, warning him to tread carefully. 'And what might that be?' she asked, pulling herself up a bit straighter, all traces of the smile now gone.

'I should have thought that was obvious,' he said. 'I manage a very successful hotel here in Watersmeet Bridge, and I have literally years of experience, whereas you have none to speak of. And this place needs a lot of work doing to it from the looks of this reception area alone, so I've come to make you an offer. A very generous offer in the circumstances.' He gave her his most winning smile, but all he got back was a scowl.

'Just who do you think you are, coming in here and putting my business down? I'm not interested in anything you think you might have to offer me. I may not have your years of experience, but at least I have principles.' She folded her arms across her chest, and he forced himself to keep his eyes on her face.

'Oh, come on. You're not being honest with yourself. Your

grandma can't have been making any money from this ramshackle guesthouse for years. You must have debts to pay off, and how exactly are you going to do that, with so few guests coming through the doors, hmm? Wouldn't it all be easier if I just bought the place off you, and you disappeared into the sunset and left running the business to a professional like me?' He nodded, convinced she'd cave at any minute.

'My business is no concern of yours. I'm not interested in your offer, and I'm more of a professional than you'll ever be with an attitude like that. Now, if you don't mind, I'd like you to leave. I have lots of work to do, and right now, you're getting on my nerves and in my way.'

She skirted round him and went to the door, opening it wide for him to leave.

Luke stood his ground as a light breeze blew in and chilled the hallway. 'Don't you even want to know how much I'd offer you for this place? Not even a little bit curious?' He softened his voice in the hope of tempting her to ask him, but she simply waved her arm towards the door.

'I won't ask you again,' she said firmly.

He had no option but to move towards it.

'I think you'll regret this,' he told her, 'and my next offer won't be so good. You can rest assured on that front.'

Luke slipped out the door into the garden and tried not to wince as she slammed it shut behind him. His heart was pounding as he made his way back across the garden, the thrill of the chase boosting his adrenaline and making him feel better than he had in ages. She'd change her mind eventually – he was sure of it. It was only a matter of time, and for now, he had all the time in the world.

He spotted a woman gardening in the flower beds as he walked past, but she didn't turn to look at him, and he wouldn't have acknowledged her if she had. She was of no importance to him. He had to admit, he was shocked Cara had been strong enough to reject his offer. He hadn't expected that, but it simply meant victory would be all the sweeter when it finally came, as he knew it would.

Later that afternoon, Joe got to work again on the guesthouse's website. Cara had sent him some more up-to-date photos, and he wanted to add those in, as well as make the changes she'd suggested during their first meeting.

There was no facility to book directly on the site yet, which Cara felt to be crucial, so that she could cancel most of the expensive booking services Penny had been using. But while Joe knew his way around a content management system, he hadn't ever added a booking facility to a website before. Still, he was fairly confident that with a bit of research, he'd be able to work it out. At any rate, he was full of enthusiasm to be doing something for the guesthouse that would cost hardly any money but could have such a beneficial effect. It would save Cara so much and would allow her to offer guests a discount for booking direct.

Joe threw himself into his research, and within an hour, he'd registered with a free booking system and added their button to the guesthouse's website. Cara had told him the guesthouse needed to achieve an average of 50% occupancy all year round to stand any chance of making a profit, and this was an important step on that journey.

Next, he turned his focus to setting up some social media pages. He'd noticed the website was lacking in any real information about the local area, so he did a bit of research there as well before using that information to get their social media pages going.

He sat back in his chair at last and released a huge sigh of relief. It had been hard work, but it had also been satisfying. He decided he'd get out soon to take some more photos of the village and the area beyond it to add to the website and social media platforms as well in due course. He'd also have to teach Cara how to use social media at some point. He smiled to himself at the thought of the protests she'd make about that. He saved the work he'd been doing and stood up to go and help his mum with making dinner.

'Hello, love. How did you get on with that work you've been doing for Cara?' His mum was busy cutting vegetables for a pasta sauce, so Joe picked up his knife and started work on some mushrooms while they talked.

'I've managed to put a booking system onto her website tonight so people can book with her direct, which will save her a ton of money.' Joe swept his mushrooms into the pan to join the onions, celery, and carrots his mum had already chopped.

'That sounds good,' Sheila said. 'It also sounds like you've done more than half an hour's work for Cara, so shouldn't you be charging her now?'

Joe shrugged. 'I have, and I should. I've done it for some of the other businesses as well, but it's hard to have to ask them to pay when I know they're all so short of money. My company's charges are too high for them.'

Sheila added the tomatoes to the pan, gave it a stir, and turned to put some water on to boil for the pasta.

'If there's so much demand, couldn't you start your own business doing it here rather than going back to London?' she asked without looking him in the eye.

Joe sighed. 'If I could get enough regular work here, I might consider staying, but it's hard enough for all the businesses here as it is. And anyway, I already have a job in London.'

'We said when we moved here, though, that this could be a place for us to settle down after everything that happened, and I hoped that meant for both of us, not just for me. If you stayed, you'd have a better chance of getting to know your granddad as well. If you set up your own tech business and actually charged people a fair rate for the work you do, you'd be much better off and able to stay here for good.'

Joe shrugged. 'I don't think it would be that easy to make a living from the occasional tech job here.'

Joe had to admit his mum had a good point, but he didn't say anything. Instead, he busied himself by laying the table.

'I don't know whether I could make it work, Mum,' he said at last. 'But I have enjoyed being back here with you, and I'm really sorry I left it so long to come home.'

They sat down to eat, and no more was said, but Joe thought a lot about his mum's comments and whether he was really doing the right thing by planning to go back to London. He was enjoying spending time with his mum, but also with Cara, and he was really enjoying the work he was doing too. And he was beginning to feel like he didn't really miss his life in London. It paid well, but most of his earnings were going on his rent and bills. He hadn't managed to make any new friends to socialise with, and even if he had, he couldn't afford to go out anyway. He had a lot to think about, and soon, it would be time to go back to the city and decide one way or the other about his future.

'It would be good if you could go and see your granddad while you're here, too. He misses seeing you, you know.'

'I know, and I'd like to see him as well,' Joe replied. 'I've just been so busy since I got here, but I promise I'll go and see him tomorrow. How are you getting on with the gardening work on your own?' he asked.

'I enjoy the work, but there's too much for me, to be honest. And I'm so tired at the end of the day I don't have much energy left for anything else.' Sheila glanced ruefully across at her sewing machine, and Joe felt a pang of guilt that there was nothing he could do to share his mum's load.

'Maybe you need to reduce the number of customers you've got, or take someone else on to help you,' Joe suggested.

'If I reduce my customers any more, I'll struggle to pay the bills. I already considered whether to let some more of them go, but it's hard when you know they depend on you.'

Joe nodded, but he had no more ideas as to how to help his mum for now.

'Joe! You'll never guess what's happened.' Cara flung the front door open and stood in the entrance trying to catch her breath.

He looked up from his camera and smiled at the sight of her. 'I probably won't, no,' he said, laughing at her infectious excitement.

'We've had our first booking on the website! I just got an email. I can't believe you set it all up so quickly, nor that we've already had a booking just a few days later. It's so easy.'

Joe stood up and came round the shrubs he'd been standing next to. 'That is good news, and at least it shows it's working.'

They both took a step towards each other at the same time, and suddenly, Joe was aware of Cara's warm breath on his face. In fact, he was aware of every bit of her, and how well she'd fit against his body. He'd only need to reach out and draw her to him, but would she want that?

She looked up at him, and he could see her thick eyelashes brushing against her skin. He wondered if her mind was also working overtime. She reached out and took his hands in hers, giving them a gentle squeeze, the warmth of her skin soaking into his in a way that was even more pleasurable than he expected.

'Thanks so much for all your help in getting these things sorted out for me. I really appreciate it.' Her voice had taken on a husky quality, he thought, or maybe it was just that she was out of breath. And perhaps he was mistaking gratitude for something more.

He took a step back, and the moment passed, but his feelings didn't. 'No problem,' he said.

'There was something else I wanted to talk to you about, actually,' she said.

Joe released a breath and tried to ignore his feelings so he could listen to what Cara had to say. 'Go on,' he said, trying to keep his voice steady and his feelings hidden.

'When I was at The Bistro the other day, there was some art on the walls, and they told me how the artist had shown her last exhibition there. I was wondering how many other members of the community might have similar skills I could make use of here by offering courses for guests. So I could contact that artist – I think her name's Esme – to see if she'd be interested in running a painting course, for example. What do you think?'

Joe smiled at Cara's obvious nerves, knowing she was looking for his approval. 'I think that's a great idea, honestly. There must be loads of talented people here who'd love to run a course. How would you make money out of it though? Have you thought about that?'

'I'd agree a split between myself and the artist from the guests' booking fee so we both make a profit. And I think I'd have to ask people to pay upfront so that no money would be wasted on materials.'

Joe nodded. 'And where would you hold the courses?'

'That's the only potential sticking point,' she said. 'It would have to be the dining room, which is fine, but it would mean I could only offer one course at a time because of the lack of space. But I'd have to start small anyway to gauge how much interest there might be.'

'You've obviously given it a lot of thought, and it seems like it could work from what you've told me. I'd talk to Esme as soon as you can and see what she says. With people able to book on the website now, we could put something on social media about courses and start taking bookings straight away.'

'Have you set up social media as well?' she asked with a grin.

'I have, and I need to train you how to use it.' Now it was his turn to grin as she groaned.

'I knew this day was going too well. Okay, well, I suppose I have to learn sometime but not today, please.' She paused for a moment. 'Thanks for listening to my idea, and for being so positive.'

'You're welcome,' he replied. 'It's a great idea. You should be proud of yourself for coming up with it, and I think it could be a great development for you and the guesthouse.'

Once Cara had gone back inside, Joe took a moment to examine what had happened earlier. He was in no doubt now that he was developing feelings for Cara, but what was he going to do about them – if anything at all – given he was going back to London soon? He still knew so little about her, and he'd not told her much about himself either, but they were getting to know each other, and he liked her a lot. As he wasn't going to be staying in the village in the longer term, though, wouldn't it make more sense to maintain some distance? He groaned inwardly. This was why he didn't form attachments. Every time he'd done so in the past, something had gone wrong, leaving him with nothing but regrets. But for the first time, he was experiencing doubts about returning to his life in London and wishing he could stay and get to know Cara better. Right now, the thought of going back to the city was becoming less and less appealing.

He turned back to his photos just as he saw his granddad coming through the gate.

'Morning. I thought I'd better come and see you before you disappear again,' Hamish said with a wry smile. 'Do you want to take a quick break? There's something I want to talk to you and your mum about.'

Joe put his camera away and picked up his Thermos before following Hamish back out to the street to join his mum, who was already sitting on the bench overlooking the view the guesthouse was known for.

'I'm not going to beat about the bush,' Hamish finally said, dragging his eyes away from the view to look at them both. 'I want to give up my gardening business altogether so I can spend all my time with Penny now. And what I'd like to do is hand the business over to you both – by which I mean my current client list – and then all the money you earn will be yours. I don't know if it's the sort of thing you'd both like to be doing long-term, but I wanted to speak to you about it before I do anything else.'

'That's a bit of a surprise, Dad. I'll ... We'll need some time to think about it. Joe doesn't even live here after all.' Sheila looked stricken, and Joe felt for her, caught as she was between the two of them.

'Yeah, Mum and I will need to talk about it. But thanks Grand-dad,' said Joe. He wondered if his granddad was up to something, but he kept that thought to himself for now.

***

After saying goodbye to Joe and Sheila, Hamish took a long walk along the coastal path away from the village. He needed time and fresh air now to help him clear his mind. He'd talked things over with Penny before going to see them, and he knew she was worried about him. He'd so wanted to go home with a definite answer for her.

Since she'd come to live with him, he'd grown more and more sure of the way he wanted to spend the rest of his life. They were both in their seventies now, and he wanted to enjoy what time they had left by doing things together. They'd both worked hard all their lives, and he had some money put aside, as well as his army pension, and they both had their state pensions. It wasn't a fortune, but they could live well on it and just enjoy life.

He'd been banking on Sheila accepting his offer, because he knew she was struggling financially on her part-time wage, and with Joe in London, she had no one else to help her pay the bills. Sheila was good at the job, and with Joe's help, she could develop the business further, he was sure, so he was surprised they'd not been more interested in taking it over together. He didn't understand what there was to think about. He heaved a sigh, knowing that he was being impatient and perhaps just a bit unreasonable in expecting them to decide so quickly.

He reached the top of the cliff and turned to look out to sea. It was a breezy day, and the sea looked choppy underneath a brilliant blue sky. He shuddered involuntarily, glad he wasn't out on the water today. He breathed in and out deeply a few times, trying to calm his mind, before turning to make his way back down again to the village. The way back was quicker, and he was soon back home.

Hamish lived in a former fisherman's cottage, with walls of stone and a bright red front door. He'd been here for years now, and he loved the community he'd adopted when he retired out of the army. He could have gone back home to Scotland, but there was nothing left for him there since his wife had died, and he'd always liked Devon.

He kicked off his boots and left them by the door before going inside. Penny was sitting in her chair by the window reading a book. He still hadn't quite got used to the thrill of seeing her in his cottage when he came back in.

'Hello, sweetheart. Sorry I've been so long,' he said taking the seat opposite her.

'What did they say then?' Penny asked in reply.

Hamish filled Penny in on the conversation. 'Sheila was grateful for the offer, I think, and she said they'd give it some thought. I suppose that's all I can ask, and there's no rush for them to say yes, but I was surprised they didn't jump at the chance.'

'Well, maybe for Sheila, but Joe's life is in London. You're asking him to move back here again and change his whole life, when not too long ago, he couldn't wait to escape.'

'Yes, that's true, but I did think he might have had enough now and would want to come back. There is also the fact that the work here is seasonal and not very dependable in the winter months, so maybe Sheila's worried about that.'

Hamish helped Penny with her coat before they set off for the village together to get some lunch.

'But Sheila does have other skills she could make use of when she can't do the gardening. Maybe she's just not very business-oriented though,' she said, finally slipping her arm through Hamish's once they'd reached the cobblestone High Street.

'I've done all I can for now. They'll just have to make up their own mind about where their futures lie. But I don't mind saying that I hope they take me up on my offer and won't make us wait too long before they make their decision.'

'Now, where are we going to go for lunch?' Penny asked with a smile.

'Maybe we should go back to the café again and see what's on the menu today,' Hamish said.

'This is why I love you, Hamish Ferguson.'

Hamish felt like the luckiest man alive to have fallen in love again at his age. He was a romantic soul, and his heart was full of the love he felt for Penny.

'Have you noticed how well Cara and Joe seem to be getting on?' he asked after a couple of minutes had passed.

'I have,' she replied with a twinkle in her eye. 'And I'm glad. I think they could be very good for each other.'

'Me too. I wouldn't want to get my hopes up too much, but Joe might well have some good reasons for settling here now.'

'Agreed,' Penny replied. 'Cara's not had much luck with men, though, it has to be said.'

'Well, maybe she just hasn't found the right one yet and her luck is about to change.'

They arrived at the café a minute later and hurried inside, out of the cold. It was just getting busy for lunchtime, but they were still able to get their favourite table by the window. Hamish settled Penny into her chair and took off his own coat.

'Now then, what can I get you, my dear?'

Penny giggled at the posh voice he tried to put on, and his heart soared.

'You must know my order by now,' she laughed. 'But I'll have a crab sandwich on brown bread and a cappuccino, please.'

Hamish set off for the counter and joined the short queue. Helen, the owner, seemed harried but glad to be busy. It looked like a lot of work for one person, and Hamish sympathised with her. It was hard running your own business, as he knew only too well, and a fine balance between doing well and finding yourself overwhelmed. Hopefully, his days of doing that were nearly at an end so he could look forward to an easier life with Penny.

CHAPTER SEVEN

Joe had been working from home for most of the day while his mum was out gardening. He'd found it almost impossible to think about his work, though, after the bombshell his granddad had dropped the day before. It was a great opportunity for his mum, but she'd already told him she could barely manage on her own as it was, which left him feeling obliged to stay and help out. But gardening really wasn't his thing at all, even if he did want to help his mum.

He had no idea how to make his granddad's offer work for all of them, and of course, he hadn't even made up his mind about his own future. He certainly had plenty of clients in Watersmeet Bridge right now, but whether they'd stay with him and be able to afford to pay him in the future remained to be seen. If he did agree to help his mum in the gardening business alongside his digital work, he could make a living of sorts, but was that what he really wanted? He'd have to compromise about the gardening, and also make do on a much smaller salary, as well as returning to live at home. His ego kept reminding him that he'd feel as though he'd failed in London and was returning home with his tail between his legs.

He stood up and stretched and went out to the kitchen to make a cup of tea. Staring out the window while he waited for the kettle to boil, he went over the pros and cons for what felt like the hundredth time since their talk with Hamish. On the plus side, he'd be able to get to know Cara better, and that really was a plus. He could start his own business, and there seemed to be enough clients for him to at least make a start on that. He'd also be able to see more of his mum and granddad, which being here had made him realise was important to him, and it was also something he'd missed. But as for the cons, he'd have to do gardening work, which didn't appeal that much to him. He'd also have to give up his life in London and move back home to live with his mum when, by rights, in his late twenties, he should have moved on from her by now. There definitely seemed to be more cons every time he thought about it all.

Behind him, the door to the kitchen opened, and his mum appeared with her wellies in hand.

'Ooh, has the kettle just boiled?' she asked with a pleading look.

'I swear you can hear it boiling from wherever you are,' Joe laughed, getting down another mug from the cupboard. 'How's your day been?'

'Not too bad,' she said. 'It's been milder and brighter today, so it was good to be outside. How about you?'

'I haven't got much work done, to be honest, because I keep thinking about granddad's offer and getting distracted.'

Joe put the two mugs of tea on the table, and they sat down opposite each other.

Sheila sighed. 'I've been thinking about it a lot too, and I'd really like to take over the gardening business, but I can't take on the whole client list on my own. I've already had to put quite a few customers off for the time being since I haven't got time for them all. Your granddad doesn't really seem to have thought through all the practicalities, does he? I know you don't want to do gardening work, Joe, so don't you dare feel like you have to say yes just to help me out. I'll just have to come up with some other way round it.'

'You don't think granddad has done it on purpose, do you, Mum, to encourage me to stay and not go back to London?'

'Oh, no, he wouldn't do that. He's just trying to look out for us both.'

Joe pushed his hands through his hair. 'Look, Mum, I have been thinking about the future since I've been home and wondering if I could make a go of my own business down here. I've enjoyed being in London, but it hasn't met all my expectations, so it wouldn't be a bad thing for me to move back here. But I would find it hard to live at home again after having my independence for so long.'

'Well, I understand that, of course, but we've got along okay while you've been home, haven't we? I try not to fuss around you and just let you live your own life. Obviously, I'd be delighted if you decided to move back here permanently but it has to be your decision. It looks like there could be something growing between you and Cara as well.'

'There are some real pluses to moving back, certainly, but what about the gardening? I really don't see myself doing that.' Joe pulled a face, and his mum laughed.

'Well, I've invited your granddad and Penny round for dinner this evening, so we can talk it over then. You'd be welcome to ask Cara along as well, if you'd like.' With that, Sheila stood up. 'That said, I'd better have a shower and get changed so I can think about what to cook.'

Joe wasn't sure he was ready to discuss it with anyone other than his mum yet. They'd hardly had time to come to terms with it them-selves. He put the cups in the dishwasher and went back to his room, trying not to feel overwhelmed by how much his life had changed in just a few short weeks. Still, meeting Cara had to be the best change by far, and if he did move back to Watersmeet Bridge, he'd see her much more often. As he packed away his laptop, he let that thought settle in his mind and tried to imagine a new relationship developing between them. And he decided there was no better time than right now to give it a try.

Delighted by Cara's acceptance of his late invitation to dinner, Joe decided to go and meet her at the guesthouse before bringing her back to join everyone else at the cottage. He'd got ready quickly and was on his way out the door when his nerves kicked in and he began to worry about how the evening would go.

What if Cara didn't like him the way he liked her? Well, it would be better to know sooner rather than later, he guessed. And in his heart, he was sure there was something between them. He just needed to be honest with her, and then he'd know how she felt. He made his way along the gravel track towards Watersmeet View. It was quite dark already at 6 pm so he couldn't really appreciate the view across to the sea, but he saw it in his mind's eye all the same.

As he approached the front door of the guesthouse, he took a deep breath to collect his thoughts. He pushed open the door and stepped inside to find Cara waiting for his arrival, and looking almost as nervous as he felt.

'Hi,' he said softly. 'You look lovely.'

She brushed at her hair self-consciously and gave him a sweet smile. 'Thank you. You look great too.' She paused for a moment. 'I'm really nervous,' she blurted.

He stepped closer and took her hands in his. 'So am I,' he replied. 'I'm sorry it was such late-notice, but I wanted you to come and join us.'

He held her hand as they walked through the garden, only letting it go when they passed through the gate. Once they were through it, she took his hand again, and he was comforted by that. Before he'd managed to think of something reassuring to say, they were outside his mum's cottage.

'Oh, this is beautiful!' Cara exclaimed. 'I had no idea this was where your mum lived.'

He opened the front door and led Cara straight into the front room, calling out to his mum as they went. Sheila appeared a moment later, waving from the kitchen with floury hands.

'Welcome. Come on through when you're ready.'

Joe took Cara's coat and followed her into the kitchen.

'Thanks so much for inviting me, Sheila. I haven't brought you anything though. I'm so sorry.'

'Don't be. It was very last-minute,' she said. 'But I'm very glad you were able to come. Joe, why don't you get Cara a drink and show her the garden room? I've almost finished making my pie, and I'll be with you in a minute.'

Joe led the way to the garden-room extension at the back of the house, which also doubled up as a dining room. His mum had laid the table and switched on the fairy lights, and the effect was magical.

'Goodness, it's beautiful in here,' said Cara as soon as they went in. 'The garden looks wonderful too. How lovely that you can sit in here and study it during the day.'

'Mum's done wonders with it – she really has. You'll have to come back another time and see it in daylight,' Joe replied. 'Now, would you like white or red?'

'White for me, please.'

Joe poured two glasses and held one out to Cara. They clinked them together. 'I'm really glad I was able to come home and get to know this place better,' he said.

'Me too,' said Cara with a smile. 'Will you be able to come back again soon, do you think?'

'I'd really like to,' he said. 'I've enjoyed getting to know you while I've been here as well.'

'I have too. I'll be sorry to see you go.'

Before he could talk with Cara about the future in any more detail, they heard the doorbell go.

'I'd better get that. I'll be right back.'

Joe went back towards the kitchen only to meet his mum on her way to the door.

'I'll get it, Joe. You go back to Cara,' she said.

But the time for discussion had passed, and they were soon joined by Penny and Hamish, and his mum a few minutes later, after she'd taken off her apron and washed her hands.

'Hello, Cara, sweetheart. How are you? I haven't seen you for a while,' Penny said as she leaned in for a hug and a kiss.

'I'm fine, Grandma. Just busy, that's all. You look much better too.'

'I feel wonderful, and now Hamish is going to be with me all the time, everything's falling into place.'

'What's happening with the gardening business?' Cara asked. 'Is he giving it up?'

'That's the plan,' Hamish said as he joined them.

Joe and Sheila turned to them, and suddenly, everything went quiet.

'My granddad's offered his business to me and my mum, Cara, but no decisions have been made as yet.' He gave his granddad a warning look, which was met with what sounded like a mischievous chuckle from both Hamish and Penny.

'Anyway, dinner's ready, and everyone has a glass, so let's go and sit down,' Sheila said, steering the conversation away from business.

Joe guided Cara to the seat next to him on one side of the table, with his mum on her other side, and Penny and Hamish opposite them. Sheila served the chicken, ham and leek pie she'd made to everyone before sitting down.

'Help yourselves to vegetables, everyone, and there's plenty of gravy. Enjoy!'

'Mmm, this is delicious, Sheila. Thank you,' said Cara after her first mouthful. 'It's been a while since I had a proper homemade dinner.'

'It's easier when you have more people to cook for, isn't it?' Sheila said. 'Not so much fun cooking for one. And I expect you get quite fed up after cooking breakfasts every day.'

'It is full-on, that's for sure, and I'm so exhausted by the evening, usually. I don't know how you managed it for so long, Grandma.'

'It is tiring working at our age,' Hamish interrupted, but Penny nodded in agreement. 'And that's why I want to retire as well.'

'That all makes sense, Granddad, but Mum can't manage your client list on her own, and my life is currently in London, so it's not an easy decision for us to make. We need some time to think about it.' Joe glanced at Cara, hoping she understood where he was coming from.

'Why don't you just move back here then, Joe?' Penny asked, with a contrived look of innocence.

And Joe didn't know what to say to that.

After dinner, Cara and Joe walked back together to the guesthouse. It was much colder now, and Cara wrapped her arms around herself, trying to keep the warmth in.

'I had a lovely evening, Joe. Thanks for inviting me,' she told him as they walked slowly back along the path. 'I have the feeling you didn't enjoy it quite so much.'

'It was great to spend more time with you, but I could have done without my granddad pushing us for a decision. That was pretty frustrating I must admit.'

Cara opened the front door and led the way into the kitchen before putting the kettle on. She'd kept her coat on for the time being because there was no radiator in the kitchen, and it had grown cold in their absence. She switched on the little convector heater they had instead and hoped it wouldn't take long to work its magic.

'Yes. My grandma's been the same,' she said. 'Once they get a bee in their bonnet, they don't waste any time in making sure they make it happen. I love my grandma very much, but I do feel like she's dropped me in it a bit.'

'It's hard not to feel a bit manipulated by it all, really,' Joe said, taking the cup of coffee she passed him with a smile of thanks.

'So, have you got any idea what you're going to do?' Cara hadn't said much at dinner when they were talking about it, but she was starting to like him – to depend on him even – and that felt like dangerous territory if he hadn't decided on his future plans.

'It's a great offer for my mum, I know, but I would obviously have to stay here and help out for it to work. I could try to build up my tech work on the side, and I'd be able to spend more time with both my mum and my granddad.'

'I sense a "but",' Cara replied.

'Well, my life now is in London. That's why I moved away, because I preferred living in a city.'

Cara's heart sank. 'And how do you feel now? Are you happy there?'

He didn't answer for a long moment. 'Well, I thought I was, but if I'm honest, since I've been back home, the idea of leaving again is becoming less appealing. I've found that I like the community here, and, well, this is what I wanted to talk to you about. I don't know if I'm going out on a limb here, but I enjoy being with you particularly.'

He gave her a shy smile, and her heart performed a little somersault at the thought of what that might mean. She swallowed and waited for her heart to settle, and for her common sense to kick in. While she'd been delighted when Joe asked her to come to dinner, and she was heartened by his words now, she needed more than that from him. 'So what are you thinking about the future? Because as much as I like being with you too, and it would be great to spend more time together and get to know each other better, I can't cope with any more uncertainty in my life.'

'I understand that – I really do – and the last thing I want to do is to make your life more difficult. But I just don't know what to do for the best.'

'It's a risk that only you know whether you're prepared to take, Joe. But from what you've said, you're not as happy in London as you expected to be. And you have the offer of a job here if you take up your grandad's offer with your mum, which would be a strong business to start with. Your tech skills are definitely in demand as well, so if you moved back here to give all of that a go, we could see where things go between us too.'

'Okay,' he said, blowing out a long breath. 'Well, it looks like I'll have a lot to think about when I go back to London then. But I'm really glad you'd like to give things a go between us.' He smiled and reached out a hand to her, which she took and squeezed.

'You must be sure, though, Joe. You have to do this for yourself, not for your granddad, or your mum, or even for me. You have to do it because you want to.'

'You're right. Thanks for talking it all over with me, but look, I'd better get off. You've got an early start in the morning.' He let go of her hand reluctantly and stood up.

Cara stood too and led the way back to the front door. 'It's your last day tomorrow, isn't it?'

'It is, yes, but hopefully, I'll be back before you know it. Would you like me to come round to do some social media training for you before I go?'

'It would be great to see you, even if I do have to learn about social media,' she laughed, with a gentle roll of her eyes.

Joe leaned forward then and kissed her gently on the cheek. 'I'll see you tomorrow then. Good night.'

She was thrilled that Joe was going to give his own business a try. She would do everything she could to help him as well so he could stay for the longer-term. She liked him, and it seemed to be mutual, and he was so different from the other men she'd had relationships with, so maybe she should let down her guard and see where things might go between them. She could tell he had his own doubts about trusting in a new relationship as well, though, so it would be a big commitment for both of them to start something new.

As she went to bed, she kept remembering that kiss and wishing it had been a proper one. If she could learn to trust again, she was certain there'd be a lot more kisses on the horizon – and with that lovely thought, she drifted off to sleep.

Joe wandered through the village early the next morning, saying hello to one or two people he knew on his way. He was increasingly surprised by how much he'd come to like the Watersmeet Bridge community after a few years away. He'd helped so many small businesses sort out their digital set-up now, and word of mouth was helping him to get new customers all the time, some of whom were even starting to pay him. Although all the money was going to his employer at the moment, he saw that he could make a business of his own from this if he moved back.

He finally reached the lookout point in front of Watersmeet View guesthouse and turned to admire it. He loved this view so much and had really enjoyed fitting in a quick walk every morning to see it before he started work. It was nice to have a moment to himself before he got busy. He'd miss it when he went back to London. He fired off a few shots with his digital camera, sure they'd come in useful for the guesthouse's new website at some point.

When he turned back round to face the guesthouse, though, he was saddened to be reminded of how run-down it looked. Cara really had her work cut out with all that would need doing. It had obviously been a stunning building once, he thought to himself, and he knew it would be again.

He'd been honest about wanting to help Cara, but he was sure she'd come into her own and turn the guesthouse's fortunes round without any real need of help from him – or anyone else, for that matter. He'd sensed that strength about her straight away. All she needed to do now was to believe in herself.

He'd done quite a bit more work on her website now, and he wanted to go through it all with her before he left to make sure she could work on it on her own. His own enthusiasm for the guesthouse project was already fired up, and he'd love to see it restored to its former glory, not only for Cara's and Penny's benefit, but also for the benefit of the whole village – the one he couldn't wait to escape from not so long ago. The small community was coming to mean something to him, and that was a new experience compared to just a few years ago. Now it was starting to feel more personal.

But he still wasn't sure whether he was really ready to give up his life in London after having worked so hard on it for the past few years. He did like Cara, and she had said it was mutual, but they were still at the very beginning of their relationship and had no idea whether things would work out between them. And if he came home, he'd be back living with his mum again, which seemed a bit of a backwards step even though he enjoyed her company. And gardening was really her thing, not his. He loved his tech work but had no real idea about running his own business. Could he really make it work?

He made his way to the front door of the guesthouse and stepped inside, where he found Cara working at reception.

'Morning,' she said, standing up to greet him.

'Morning,' he replied, following her along the corridor to the kitchen.

He set his laptop down on the table and took off his coat before taking a seat and switching everything on.

'Since our conversation last night, I've been thinking. If you do decide to set up your own digital business,' Cara said, a twinkle in her eye, 'you'd need to toughen up a bit and not keep taking pity on other poor business owners. You must charge people, including me,' she laughed.

'I know. You're right. It would all be a very steep learning curve for me.' He paused, not really wanting to get into it all again when he was already starting to doubt himself. 'So what made you change your mind about the social media training?' he asked.

'It's just that I want to get on with offering these courses, and I can't afford to waste any time now. A smarmy hotel guy, Luke, came round yesterday to try to get me to sell the guesthouse to him, and I just have a bad feeling he's going to keep on pestering me until I give in.'

'Really? What an arsehole,' Joe said.

Cara laughed. 'I couldn't have put it better myself. Anyway, he was keen to tell me all the things that are wrong with this place, and sadly, everything he said to me is true, despite the unprofessional way he went about it. The guesthouse needs a ton of work doing to it, and I have no money to do it with. But I do want to turn things round here, and even if I have been wavering a bit, his rude offer made me realise just how much this all means to me. And I don't want to let Penny down either.'

'I don't think you could ever let Penny down. And you're strong enough to make a go of this. You didn't let him browbeat, you and you can be proud of yourself for that. It would have been the easiest thing in the world to accept his offer.'

'My grandma's lived in Watersmeet Bridge all her adult life, you know,' she said. 'She and her husband bought the guesthouse just after they got married, and she took over the running of it on her own after he died.' She paused for a moment to collect herself. 'My mum was only ten then, and I know it was hard for Grandma, trying to be a mum and a dad for her, as well as trying to keep the business going. But she did it, and when my mum died, she looked after me as well.' Cara sighed, and Joe's heart felt like it might break for her. 'I so want to keep it going for her now, after all she's done for me. I'm not afraid of the hard work that's going to take, but there are so many demands to running a business these days, and I'm afraid those things might stop me from getting the guesthouse back on its feet.'

'My impression of you so far is that you're stronger than you think, you know. What you're going to do is hard – there's no doubt about that – but I'm sure you're up to the challenge of bringing the guesthouse back up to scratch. And I'm happy to help you as much as I can, starting with teaching you all about social media.'

Cara groaned. 'I know I need to learn about it if I want to start advertising and selling these courses, but I honestly think they could be the key to the future of the guesthouse now. And I so want to show that patronising Luke just what he can do with his stupid ideas.'

CHAPTER EIGHT

Luke had arranged to meet Jason early that morning in an effort to avoid being seen by anyone he knew. There were bound to be questions if he was seen going into the local estate agents. He pulled his coat collar up against the cold wind, pulled his scarf a bit tighter, and made his way briskly along the High Street, keeping his head down as much as he could. There were only one or two other people out at this time of day, and no one he recognised, so by the time he arrived at the door of the agency, he was confident he'd not been seen. He cast a quick glance from side to side before opening the door and stepping through.

A young receptionist looked up at once and gave him a bright smile. 'Good morning, sir. How can I help you?'

'I'm here to see Jason Smyth,' he said. 'I'm Luke Johnson.'

She picked up the phone to call Jason, although how she managed it with her long, painted nails Luke had no idea, and he turned away to look outside and make one final check that no one was watching him.

'Jason will be out in just a minute. Please take a seat. Would you like a drink?' the receptionist asked.

'No, thanks,' he replied, undoing his overcoat and perching on the end of a very squishy, battered sofa that was less comfortable than it looked.

'Luke. Great to see you, mate,' Jason said to him a moment later.

Luke gritted his teeth at the use of the over-familiar word. They definitely weren't mates – not even close – and anyway, Luke would never use that word. He stood up, sticking his nose in the air, and shook Jason's extended hand as briefly as he could get away with.

Jason led the way to his office, and Luke breathed a sigh of relief that they were going to be able to talk in private. He took a seat in front of Jason's desk as Jason shut the door behind them.

'So what's the latest?' Jason asked as he sat down. 'How did your meeting go with the stubborn Ms Rafaelli?'

'I didn't get anywhere with my offer either, but I made my point well. Still, we can't afford to waste any more time. I want that place, and I want it at a knockdown price. She's a fool if she thinks she can turn its fortunes around when it needs so much work doing to it.'

'Yes, and I've double-checked their financial situation. There's no mortgage on the property, but there are some debts to be paid off.'

Luke didn't ask him how he'd found that out. He'd rather not know, so then he couldn't be blamed for doing anything nefarious.

'Maybe it's time for you to go back again and say you've got an interested buyer this time. You won't give her my name, of course, but you could outline the kind of offer I'd be willing to make.' Luke tilted his head to one side as he considered what kind of offer he might be talking about.

'How much are we talking?' Jason asked, narrowing his eyes at the thought of a big commission.

'Well, what do you think it's worth?' Luke was here for the man's professional opinion before making any commitment of his own.

'It's easily worth £800K, but it needs a lot of work doing to it to bring it up to scratch, so if I was going to market it for them, I'd advise starting at £750K, I think.'

Luke's eyebrows shot up. 'There's no way I'd consider offering that. I want to get this place at a bargain price, not pay what it's really worth. It would cost a lot of time, as well as money, to demolish it and then build on it. No. The most I would offer would be £600K, and she's already rejected two offers, so I think you should go in with an offer of £500K.'

Jason's jaw dropped open momentarily before he regained his composure. 'I don't think even she's naive enough to accept that, to be honest with you.'

'Maybe not, but that's her lookout,' Luke replied smoothly.

'Okay. Just as long as you understand before I go in with that offer that it's likely to be rejected straight away.'

'You won't know until you try. It's worth taking a risk on this, because dependent on how hard she's finding it to run the place, she might be more open to offers than you think. When can you go and visit her again?'

'Later this week, probably. I've got a lot on this end of the week.'

Luke stood up, and Jason joined him, shaking his hand once again.

Luke was back on the street a few minutes later. He kept his head down as he walked back to the hotel, but the street was much busier now. Still, after a couple of minutes' walk, no one would know where he'd been or what he'd been up to.

He smiled to himself at the thought of his plan to convert the guesthouse into holiday homes for well-to-do tourists with more money than sense. When he'd first taken over as manager of the hotel, two years ago, there'd only been the hotel itself to think about. But now, due to his careful budgeting, his plans to build his own empire were coming to fruition, and it was only a matter of time before he could resign and make his own way.

He just had to hope Jason could make this plan come good for him so that he could get started on building his little empire. He'd need to get on to the bank soon about getting a mortgage for when the time came. He was sure it wouldn't be a problem – the hotel was one of their best customers after all, and they'd give him a reference – but it was important to do the groundwork so that there'd be no surprises. He made a mental note to add that phone call to his to-do list.

As soon as the breakfasts were over and she'd cleaned the kitchen and put everything away, Cara planned to escape the guesthouse for the rest of the morning so she could catch up with Zoe. She wanted to see her friend, but she was also missing Joe and needed something to take her mind off him.

The sky was a bit dark and gloomy as Cara set off for the village, but it was warm enough, and she filled her lungs with sea air as she walked. The view of the harbour and the sea beyond it lifted her spirits as always, and she was looking forward to a break from the guesthouse for a bit, as well as to hearing Zoe's news to take her mind off everything else – most importantly, when Joe might be coming back.

They'd agreed to meet in the café, which was only a short walk from the guesthouse, and Cara was delighted to see that Zoe was already installed at a table, with two flat whites in front of her.

'Oh, you angel,' Cara said, almost falling into her seat. 'I've never needed a coffee as much as I do this morning.'

'Tell me all about it,' Zoe replied with a chuckle.

'Absolutely not. I want to hear your news first.'

'Okaaayyy.' Zoe rolled her eyes, and Cara knew she'd pour everything out to her friend in due course. For now, she just wanted to listen to someone else's life for a moment. 'Well, everything at The Bistro is just great. I love my job, and Olivia is fabulous to work for. And the combination of Finn plus Olivia is a match made in heaven, both for them as a couple and for The Bistro itself. I don't think we've ever been so busy, and it's great.'

'That is great news. I'm so pleased for you, and for them both. And how about you and Ed?' Cara sipped at her cooling coffee, relishing the smooth taste of the foamy liquid.

'I have good news on that front as well,' Zoe said, and then she paused dramatically.

Cara nudged her. 'Go on then. I can see you're bursting to tell me,' she laughed.

'We're moving in together at last. And I just can't wait after going out with him for all this time.'

'Fantastic! Whose house will you be living in?' Cara asked, happy that her friend was finally getting what she most wanted.

'I've been renting, and Ed has his own place, so he's asked me to move in with him. And we've been talking about the future too.' Zoe smiled a dreamy smile.

'What? Like getting married?' Cara could hardly contain herself at the thought of attending Zoe's wedding.

'Well, engaged first of all, and then saving up for the wedding for a bit. We wouldn't want anything flashy, but we'd need to save even for the small do we have in mind.'

'Olivia and Finn would surely allow you to have the reception at The Bistro, wouldn't they?'

'Yeah, I think so, but we couldn't expect them to offer it to us for free. They could lose out on a lot of money if they did that.'

'I'd still ask them about it. I bet they'd be happy to help you out, as would lots of other businesses in the village, I'm sure.'

'I just want to move in first, and then we'll see where we go from there, you know.' She took a mouthful of her coffee, and Cara sighed, happy for Zoe but still envious of her happiness.

'And now I suppose you want to know what's been happening at the guesthouse.'

'Of course. I've waited long enough. Come on, it can't be all bad.'

Cara filled her in on the latest developments. 'So I do obviously want to keep the guesthouse going, but that Luke guy and the estate agent have been very persistent. I know I haven't seen the last of them, and I just worry that one day, they'll turn up when I'm feeling vulnerable, and I might give in.'

'You don't think they're working together, do you?' Zoe asked, eyes wide as she considered the possibility.

'That is a distinct likelihood.' Cara put her elbows on the table and let her head fall into her hands. 'How can I have been so stupid as to not have worked that out for myself?' she asked.

'It's not stupid. You have hundreds of things on your mind. But at least you'll think about it next time. Anyway, how's business going?'

'It's going pretty well for the moment. We're getting more and more bookings in via the website system Joe set up for me, but there's something else I want to introduce as well.'

Cara told Zoe about her idea to host courses at the guesthouse.

'That sounds great. I can easily put you in touch with Esme.' She checked her phone quickly and sent across the contact details for the artist. 'And what about Sheila? She could teach gardening, and Joe really knows his tech stuff. You should ask them to help as well.'

'That's a good idea. I think guests would really like to be able to do something creative while on holiday. Maybe Finn would be prepared to do a cookery workshop too.'

'The possibilities are endless,' Zoe said. 'And there's no harm in asking anyone.'

'We all need to try and help each other more.'

'What about asking the café if they could do the catering for guests attending the courses? That would be a really sensible extension to their business.'

'That's a fabulous idea,' Cara agreed, her eyes sparkling with newfound enthusiasm.

'And how are things between you and Joe?' Zoe asked, expertly changing the subject and catching Cara off-guard.

'He's been a real help to me, Zoe, and I have to be honest and tell you that I really like him. But I do worry about taking another risk with someone so soon after the failure of my last relationship – if you can even call it that. And I can hardly have a relationship with him if he's not even here.'

'If you like him, it's always worth taking that risk. And he'll be back soon, you know.' Zoe shrugged. 'What have you got to lose?'

Cara thought she had a lot to lose if she got close to Joe only for everything to fall apart, as it had done for her before. Her heart couldn't take that all over again.

Joe had already been back in London for a few days and still hadn't worked up the courage to give in his notice. It was as if returning to London had made him forget all the good things he'd experienced down in Devon. He'd got straight back into his job and was enjoying it again, which was also making it hard for him to see the benefits of leaving to set up on his own.

Still, he did want to go back to Watersmeet Bridge to continue helping the business owners he hadn't been able to get round to on his first visit, so he wanted to speak to his manager about that. He had a meeting scheduled with him this morning, so he was going to bring it up then.

His morning journey to work took him past a little bakery where he usually stopped to get his breakfast. His mind jumped back to the café in Watersmeet Bridge, where Helen always greeted him by name and with a warm smile. He approached the counter smiling about that memory and found himself in a queue of people all glued to their phones as they waited their turn. Not a single person looked up while they waited. They all just shuffled along in the queue as if frightened to make eye contact with a stranger.

'Morning,' he said to the barista when it was finally his turn. 'Please could I have a latte and a chocolate croissant to go? Thanks very much.'

'Name?' the barista asked, with no hint of a smile.

'Joe,' he replied, and as the barista turned away, he gestured wordlessly at the card machine in front of Joe.

Joe paid, and sensing the next customer at his heels, he took his packaged pastry and moved down to the end of the counter to wait for his drink. What a soulless exchange, he thought to himself, realising he missed the social interaction in Watersmeet Bridge. He couldn't blame the barista or the other customers. It was just how life was in a big city, and for him, the novelty of it was clearly wearing off.

He found the café experience repeating itself throughout his journey into work – on the street jostling with other walkers, many of whom were on their phones; on the tube, where it was an unwritten rule never to look anyone in the eye; and even in his own office building, where the security staff looked more suspicious of anyone carrying a bag than the staff working in an airport. It was maddening and depressing, and hardly the mood he wanted to be in for his meeting with his manager.

He dumped his rucksack by his desk, changed out of his trainers into his work shoes and grabbed his laptop before heading towards the largest office on his floor, where his meeting was due to take place.

His manager, Stefan, was on the phone as he reached the door, but he waved to him to come in and sit down. Joe waited patiently, using the time to boot up his laptop, trying not to eavesdrop on the conversation Stefan was having.

'Hey, Joe. How's it going? Looking forward to your update, mate, especially the financials.' His boss was loud and over-friendly, and despite not being much older than Joe, he had a self-confident air about him that Joe didn't think he'd ever achieve.

'Well, the visit was a success, I would say. I managed to build a list of about thirty customers, and to give them their free half hour, but because they're all small businesses, very few of them could afford our fees, so they didn't agree to meet with me again after that.'

Stefan frowned dramatically and took off his expensive designer glasses. 'Damn. That doesn't sound so good. I was expecting you to have done two more hours' work with each customer so your two weeks down there would have paid for themselves.'

'I'd like to go back, though, because I think there are even more small business owners in need of help.'

'Oh, no. That's not going to happen, mate. You needed to bring in significant cash from this trip before you could even think about another one. I need you to prepare to run some more courses that'll bring us in some actual money.'

'Where would they be?' Joe's mouth had gone dry. This wasn't the way he'd been expecting their conversation to go at all.

'One in Sheffield, another in Bradford. They want you up there next week.'

'I can't do that,' Joe said. 'I promised I'd go back to Watersmeet Bridge.'

'You had no business promising that, Joe,' Stefan snapped, all smooth talk now off the menu. 'Now, you need to get back in the loop and read your emails so you can be ready to leave on time.'

Joe closed his laptop and stood up, leaving the office without another word. He returned to his desk, cleared it of the few personal things he kept there, and then opened his laptop to find the resignation letter he'd been half-heartedly writing since he came back to London. He read it through one last time and sent it off to Stefan before picking up his bag and leaving. He had plenty of unused holiday days, so he was going to take them now.

Back on the street, he blew out a long breath. He was shocked at the way he'd been able to make that decision without any debate. Stefan's obnoxious attitude had done Joe a favour, and now everything else would just fall into place.

He made his way back home without even noticing other people this time. He had a greater sense of purpose than he'd had for ages, and he couldn't wait to pack up his stuff, hand in his notice at his flat and be on his way back to Cara and Watersmeet Bridge.

As Zoe had to get back to work, she said goodbye after she and Cara had finished their coffees, and Cara wandered back through the village towards the guesthouse. She'd pick herself something up for lunch from the bakery today, she decided, and she could hopefully renew another one of her friendships at the same time.

She said hello to several people as she wended her way along the cobbled street towards the bakery, and her heart warmed at just how good it felt to be back home. There was a queue outside the bakery as always,, but she didn't mind, and anyway, it was a good opportunity to chat with the other villagers while she waited. She was pleased for her old school-friend, Rosie, and for all the good luck she and her husband, Ewan, had created for themselves and their family since setting up the bakery.

'Hey, Cara. It's great to see you. What can I get you?'

'That tomato and mozzarella tart looks wonderful. I'll take two slices, please. How are things here?'

'We're so busy, but, you know, we can't complain about it. It's all good for business. It's so lovely to have you back here to help Penny. And we're so grateful for the guesthouse's continued business as well. It's really important to us.'

'I know, and it's important that we local businesses support each other. I love being back, and I hope we'll have a chance to catch up properly at some point.'

Cara said goodbye and let Rosie carry on serving. She was glad they were busy, but she knew how hard it was to get the business and then to maintain it. She left the shop and carried on walking back home, wondering if the bakery might want to offer a course to her guests at some point.

That reminded her about asking the café if they'd be interested in catering for guests who attended the courses, so she popped in there as well, emerging a few minutes later with a business card.

As Cara arrived back at the guesthouse, her mobile beeped with a notification. She stopped to look at it and was delighted to see she'd had a booking and an expression of interest in a painting course. It was time for her to contact Esme to see if she'd be interested in running a course for her.

After checking everything was okay at reception, she opened her email inbox to find a further five bookings, along with several other enquiries about courses.

'Whoopee!' she yelled, unable to stop herself from doing a little dance around reception as well.

She checked her phone for the message from Zoe that contained Esme's contact details and quickly typed out an email. Now people had expressed an interest in the courses, she could think about getting the decorating done, because she'd finally have the money to pay for it.

Cara took a deep breath and released it. Maybe she did have a chance of turning things round after all. Her confidence was starting to grow, and things were improving with the guesthouse finances all the time, and if these courses took off, things would really start to change for the guesthouse and its fortunes. She finally felt she had some good news for Penny.

While she was lost in her thoughts, another email came in. At the ping from her computer, she looked at the screen and saw a reply from Esme. She quickly scanned the contents and was delighted to read Esme's positive response and a request to call her about it whenever it was convenient.

'Hi, Esme. It's Cara here. Thanks for coming back to me so quickly. I don't suppose you'd be free to pop round now, would you? It would be great to meet you and talk this over in person.'

'Sure. I'll be there in about ten minutes.'

While she was waiting for Esme, Cara started an email to the café asking if they'd be interested in catering for the courses.

The guesthouse door opened just as she was finishing off her draft, so she saved it, planning to come back to it later. The woman who appeared had the classic look of an artist about her, with red hair pinned up on top of her head, held in place by what looked like a pencil, and she was wearing a beautiful vintage multicoloured dress.

Cara came round the desk to shake her hand. 'You must be Esme. It's wonderful to meet you.'

'And you. I'm so interested in these courses you're planning, and it sounds like your guests are too.'

'Thank you. I'm delighted you're interested, and I already have enough people for a first course for you. We'd have to limit it to six people because of the space in the dining room, but let me show you, and you can tell me what you think.'

She took Esme through to the dining room and showed her the available space.

'This is great. It's about the right size for when we're working indoors, and six people is fine. When do you think you'd like to run the first course? And how will we sort out fees and payments?'

Cara liked Esme's straightforward approach, and they soon reached an agreement.

'I can't stay too long today,' Esme told her as they made their way back to reception, 'because my sister's staying with me, and I need to get back. But we can email and message to get everything sorted, if you're happy with that.'

'Of course. Do your family live in the village?'

'Yes. We moved here when I was still at school, and we're all still here, although I moved out to my studio a few years ago now, and my younger sister's looking for a job after finishing uni. Listen, do you want me to spread the word among my friends about your courses? I know a few other creative people in the village.'

'Yes, sure. As long as they're in the village, that would be great.'

Cara waved Esme goodbye and smiled at the end of a very satisfying day.

CHAPTER NINE

Today was the day Ed would make a start on redecorating the top floor of the guesthouse. Cara had made sure not to accept any new bookings there until the work was done, which meant the loss of a week's earnings, but she planned to put the prices up slightly afterwards to help compensate for that. She'd had to warn the other guests as well, but she was confident Ed would be discreet and wouldn't get in anyone's way.

By the time breakfast was over and she was able to go upstairs for the first time, Ed was all set up, with dust sheets and ladders in place, and raring to go.

'Morning, Ed. Is everything all right?'

'All good,' he said with a smile.

'Would you like a drink?'

'No. Not just yet, thanks, but maybe later.'

She left him to get on and made her way back downstairs to check on reception. She intended to speak to their laundry supplier to reduce the number of their weekly cleans again while the work was being done, and also to her toiletries supplier to see if they could reduce their order. They were still ordering new supplies on the basis of being fully booked, which meant they had enough stock to last them for quite some time to come.

She also finished typing her email to the café about catering for her courses and sent it off. She'd realised when speaking to Esme the week before that she might actually be able to run more than one course at a time, because sometimes Esme would want to take her students outside. And with that in mind, she went outside to talk to Sheila.

'Morning, Sheila. How was your weekend?' she asked when she found her in the barn cleaning her tools.

'Pretty good, thanks. Joe's been helping me to advertise my dress-making services on social media, and I've already had a few enquiries, which I'm amazed about.' She smiled. 'He told me you were thinking about running courses here, which I think is a brilliant idea.'

'Thank you,' Cara replied. 'I'm only just starting out with the idea, but it would be great if it took off.'

Sheila studied her for a moment before taking a deep breath. 'I'd be very happy to run a course for you, if you think people would be interested.'

'That would be fantastic! Thank you. I really think they would be interested.'

Cara filled Sheila in on the details of how they'd split the profits once the course was in place.

'That all sounds great. I really appreciate you giving me the opportunity.'

'Have you decided whether to take Hamish up on his offer?'

'I think so, although I haven't confirmed that to my dad as yet. I can definitely carry on doing what I'm doing, but I'm not sure if I could manage the whole business on my own. And it would obviously mean a big change for Joe to give up his new life in London. I'm not sure his heart is in gardening anyway, so we'll have to see.'

'It is difficult, especially with the gardening work being seasonal, but I'm sure you'll make the right decision for you.'

Cara said goodbye a few minutes later and went into the kitchen to make a cup of tea for herself and Ed. As she was free after that, she decided that a visit to Hamish and Penny was overdue, and today would be a good day for it.

She sent a quick message off to her grandmother and then went upstairs to give Ed his tea.

'How's it going?' she asked after putting down his cup safely out of the way on a bedside table and casting an appreciative eye around the suite.

'Pretty good. I've done the ceiling and the coving in here, and I'm making a start on the walls now. Once I've done as much as I can in the family suite, I'll move on to the other rooms.'

'Great, thank you. I'm just going to pop out to see Penny and Hamish. I'll be back after lunch at the latest, but you can message me if you need anything. I won't be far away.'

Her phone pinged with a reply on her way downstairs, and she was delighted to see it was from Penny telling her they were home. She grabbed her coat and bag and made her way through the garden to the street.

She enjoyed the walk out of the village and up the hill towards the coastal path where Hamish's cottage was located. The views were stunning, despite there being some very nasty-looking grey clouds in the sky, and she determined to come this way more often.

A few minutes later, she knocked at the front door to the cottage and waited for someone to let her in.

'Hello, sweetheart. Come on in,' her grandma said a moment later.

Cara put her arms out to her for a hug. 'I'm sorry I haven't seen you for a bit. I wanted to leave you to rest, and then suddenly, a couple of days had gone by. That's why I'm here now. I missed you.'

Penny kissed her on the cheek and turned to lead the way through to the back room, where Hamish was waiting for them. Cara shared a quick hug with him as well before taking a seat.

'How are things going at the guesthouse, lass?' he asked as he poured her a cup of tea.

'Really well, actually. Ed's started redecorating the family suite today, and soon, I'll be offering guests my first painting course.'

Penny clapped her hands together in delight. 'I knew you could do it,' she cried.

Cara proceeded to fill them in on all the developments, proud of how things were progressing.

'It really does feel like I've turned a corner now, although that awful Luke man and his estate agent have also been pestering me.'

'What?' Penny and Hamish chorused. Hamish waved his hand at Penny, deferring to her.

'This smarmy man, Luke, came into the guesthouse the other day trying to get me to sell up. He's even sent an estate agent over as well. Luke's the manager at the big hotel at the other end of the village, across the little bridge.'

'Well, we'll see about that,' Penny said, and Cara felt a tiny smidgen of pity for Luke in that second. He had no idea what Penny's wrath could be like.

Esme was going to run the first day of her painting course today, and the six new guests had all arrived over the Easter weekend and settled in. Cara had made sure she was up early and completely organised for breakfasts so she could whizz through and get everything done and tidied up in plenty of time before the course started at 10 am.

Fortunately, all the guests were attending the course, so they all had the same idea of coming down early to breakfast, which was a great help. Cara was just finishing stacking the dishwasher when Esme arrived to set up the dining room.

'Morning, Esme,' Cara said, coming through from the kitchen and casting her eye around the room. 'Is everything okay for you?'

There were only six full-sized tables in the dining room, which was just enough to run the course, and Esme was clearly used to setting up her equipment.

'Yes, it all looks good. It must have been a rush for you to get things tidy though. I'm sorry,' she said as she moved the final table into place.

'It's been a busy morning – that's for sure,' Cara replied. 'But it's so good to see you here, and to know we're going to be running our first course. Do you have everything you need for today?'

'I think so. I'll just need to get some water for the brushes, and some jugs of water and glasses for everyone as well. What time did you want us to stop for lunch?'

'I'll get the jugs and glasses, but you can go through to the kitchen for your other water. I think the café's going to deliver the food about 11.30 so you can break for lunch whenever works for you.'

'As it's such a nice day, I thought we might go out this afternoon. Will it be okay to leave everything set up here while we do that?'

'Yes, of course. We'll just need to clear the room at the end of each day, which I know isn't ideal, but we can store your stuff in the corner of the room ready for the next day, if that's okay.'

Esme patted her on the shoulder. 'Don't worry, really. It will all be fine. I've worked in much more cramped and unfriendly places. Perhaps we can just see how this course goes and get feedback from the guests before deciding how we can do things better next time.'

Cara was relieved at how sensible Esme was, and she hoped everything would go well for the two of them. Getting this first course right was important to both of them, but it was even more important for the guesthouse and the future of the course programme.

The rest of the morning flew by, and then, at 11.30, a young woman arrived from the café bearing two trays of food.

'Here you go, Cara. Food for your guests. Made by my own fair hand.'

'Oh, that's amazing. The food looks delicious. I'm sorry, have we met?' Cara wondered how the young woman knew her name.

'We haven't met, but I'm Esme's sister, Sophie, so she's told me all about the courses. I've just started working at the café. It's great fun, actually. I hope we get to do it for more courses as well. How's every-thing going so far?'

'It's lovely to meet you, Sophie,' Cara said with a smile. 'Fingers crossed, everything has gone according to plan. It's already shown up where there might be a few problems in the future, but I'm trying not to think too far ahead at the moment, just trying to go with the flow.'

'That's a good idea. I hope the day goes well, and the rest of the course. I'll probably be back tomorrow with the food again, so I'll see you then.'

Cara smiled as Sophie left, grateful for her encouraging words. She picked up the trays and went towards the dining room, slipping inside to deposit the trays on one of the smaller tables that wasn't being used. She stood for a minute taking in the calm atmosphere in the room. Everyone was busy painting, talking softly to each other every now and then. It looked like they were all having a good time.

Esme looked her way before coming over. 'Ooh, that food looks lovely. The café's done us proud.'

'I think it's mostly your sister's work. She said she'd quite enjoyed it. It was lovely to meet her. How's it gone this morning?'

'Great, actually. They're all enthusiastic to learn, and they're all getting on well together, which helps a lot.' Esme laughed, and Cara was relieved.

'I'll just go and get some plates for you all,' she said before edging her way round the artists to get to the kitchen. She made a mental note to put some plates in the room before the start of the course the next day.

After lunch, Esme took the artists out along the coastal path with their sketchbooks and pencils, leaving Cara free to tidy up the room and refresh the water. All things considered, the first course had gone well. The only immediate difficulty was the cramped space in the room and the issue of only being able to run one course at a time. Even though the artists had gone out this afternoon, Cara couldn't really let anyone else use the space while their course was still running, and ideally, she needed to run several courses at once if she was going to make a decent profit from doing this. But for now, she couldn't see any way of doing that.

By the end of the afternoon, Cara was exhausted from the tension of being on hand all the time, even though Esme had borne most of the burden.

'It's been a great first day, Cara. They're all looking forward to tomorrow.'

'It's been an amazing day, but exhausting, I must admit. Thank you for all you've done.'

'It's been my pleasure, but I can see how run off your feet you've been making sure everyone's been happy. You've been a great host, but if the courses become any more popular, you're going to need some help round here, aren't you?'

'I am, and I've been looking for someone who might be able to help me on a part-time basis to start with, but so far, I haven't had any luck.'

'I'll ask around, if you like. There might be someone I know who's looking for a job.'

Cara's eyes lit up at the thought of finding someone to help her at last. 'That would be wonderful.'

She said goodbye to Esme, and after tidying up, she called it a day, knowing she'd need a good night's sleep before they did it all again tomorrow.

Joe had arrived back in Watersmeet Bridge after texting both his mum and Cara to update them on his plans. He hadn't wasted any time and had left London the following day. The landlord wasn't worried about his departure – he'd have no trouble re-letting the room. Joe might even get his deposit back if the landlord found someone to replace him quickly.

He'd settled straight back in at home and turned all his attention to setting up his own tech business doing exactly what he'd been doing before, but this time for his own benefit. He'd already contacted all the customers he'd met previously, explaining he was now working for himself and detailing his services and charges. He was able to charge far less per hour than his old company, and he was hopeful that he'd get business as a result. But for now, things were quiet while he waited for people to respond.

It had given him the chance to do some gardening work with his mum, though, who definitely needed the help now that his granddad had pulled back. He thought they'd have to accept his granddad's offer, especially as neither of them had any other regular work to speak of as yet. But the gardening wasn't part of his long-term plan, and thankfully, his mum understood this, so they were being careful not to take on too much work in case Joe had to focus on his tech work and leave his mum to her own devices.

It was his turn to work at the guesthouse garden today, so he'd got up early to fit in a walk before he had to get started. He was just finishing mowing the lawns now, and he planned to go in and give his invoice to Cara afterwards for the work he'd done since her free half hour, as she'd insisted. He pushed the mower towards the barn, leaving it to one side while he heaved open the doors. He'd always thought how wasted the barn was, with so few tools in it and lots of empty space, and today, it seemed even more so. He and his mum kept it very tidy and there was tons of unused room inside.

He made his way to the front door of the guesthouse and took off his boots before going in. Cara had her head down at the reception desk and was obviously focused on her work. He coughed gently to get her attention without surprising her.

'Joe! It's good to see you,' she said, and his heart lifted. 'How is everything? Have you got time for a cup of tea?'

'Sure,' he replied and followed her down the corridor. 'You'll be glad to hear I've brought your invoice, as requested. Well, sort of glad,' he added.

'No, I am. That's good. And I presume you and your mum have

decided to accept Hamish's offer, as I saw you mowing the lawns just now.'

'Well, we've not told him officially, but I don't think we have much of a choice, really. It's mum's only job at the moment, and my tech work is still quiet for the time being, which I'm hoping is only temporary.'

Cara stopped in the middle of making the tea. 'You could always run a course for me,' she suggested with a gentle raise of her eyebrows.

Joe laughed but then paused to think about the suggestion. 'That's actually a very good idea, because it would work out a lot cheaper for my customers to come all together.'

'Of course! I'm full of bright ideas.' They both laughed then.

'It would definitely make a lot of sense for me to offer courses to my potential clients.'

'Why don't we advertise a course and see if anyone signs up? I'd be happy to help you, if you like.'

'Okay then, but I will hold you to that offer.'

'I'm glad you're back,' she said then, with a smile. 'I think you and your mum make a good team, and if you can both develop your other businesses as well, you'll have those to keep you busy over the winter.'

'Thank you. I hope that's how it all works out. How has your first course been going?' he asked as he accepted his cup of tea.

Cara filled him in. 'I am worried about how I'll provide all these courses, though, with just the one room available.'

'Yes, that could become difficult if there's a lot of interest, but that would also be a good problem to have.' Joe paused, not wanting to cause Cara any further worries but knowing he should tell her what was on his mind. 'I wanted to mention to you about the barn in the garden as well.'

'Not a problem, please? I can't deal with falling-down barns right now.'

'No, nothing like that. It's just that it's half-empty even with all the tools in it, and I wondered if you could store something else in there to make better use of it. Or perhaps you could store what's in the barn in the shed instead and find another use entirely for the barn.'

'Hmm. I can't think of anything else I could use it for at the moment, but I will give it some thought.'

'Is there anything else I can help you with tech-wise? I know you've taken some more photos. Are you okay with how to upload them to the website?'

'I have no idea how to do that. In fact, I could probably do with some training on using the website. I've been doing okay with social media, I think, but I'd like to put up some videos as well. Do you know how to do that?'

Joe smiled. 'Look at you go,' he said. 'There's no stopping you now. But yes, I can show you how to use the website, and also how to upload videos. That's no problem.'

'I took some photos of the course yesterday as well, and I want to put those up so the guests can see how they're run.' She took a sip of her tea.

'If I did run a course, and you were happy for me to, I could use the guesthouse's website and social media for some of my examples.'

'That's a good idea. You should also see whether you could pitch running a course for any beginners at the next networking meeting. I'm sure they'd be up for that, and they'd probably be prepared to pay you for your time as well.'

'That would generate some new business for me as well, I'm sure.' Joe sighed. 'It's great being able to discuss all these things with you, Cara. You know exactly where I'm coming from. I'm glad to be back too, so we can pick up where we left off.' He drained the rest of his cup of tea and stood up just as Cara did.

The two of them came face-to-face, just a hair's breadth between them, and suddenly, it was the obvious thing for him to take a step closer, and for them to kiss. But their lips had hardly met before the two of them were forced to step back at the sound of the bell ringing for Cara from reception.

'Joe, God, I'm sorry,' Cara blurted out before dashing away without so much as a backward glance.

Joe was sorry too, but only because their first kiss had been so awkwardly interrupted. He waited a moment before retreating back out to the garden, wondering when he might get the chance to kiss Cara properly.

It was the last day of the course, and Cara had a full guesthouse of people to contend with. Ed was finishing off decorating upstairs, and all the guests were with Esme in the dining room, finishing off their masterpieces so they could take them home with them the next day. And on top of that, she was expecting someone to come and see her to talk about the possibility of working with her.

She was just about to go and check on the course when the front door opened. Instead of a young woman appearing, though, as she was expecting, it was the smug hotel manager, Luke. Cara couldn't keep the look of disgust from her face. She'd only recently rejected yet another ridiculous offer from the estate agent, who she was now convinced was working on Luke's behalf, so why on earth was he here again?

She came straight to the point. 'I'm very busy, so if you're here to waste my time by making me a pointless offer, you can just turn around and leave. I don't have the time for you or your smarmy estate agent to keep hassling me on this.'

Luke's eyebrows rose in surprise, but he regained his composure quickly. 'I have come to make you an offer, but this one is more in keeping with the value of the business you have here, seeing as you wouldn't listen to me last time,' he told her, glancing around the reception area as if to see what she'd been up to since he was last here.

She walked round him and opened the door. 'As I told you the last time, as well as just now, I'm not interested, and I'd like you to leave.'

'Not even in £550K? Are you sure about turning that much money down?'

'I don't need your money, because my business is doing very well, thank you, and I'm not interested in selling it to you or anyone else.'

Luke sneered at her momentarily before replacing it with the same bored look he normally had on his face. 'I really can't believe your business has picked up that much in just a few weeks. You really should consider this offer, because it's the final one I'm going to make.'

Cara closed her eyes briefly, trying to find the strength to deal with this persistent and annoying offensive. 'I came up with a great idea, and I've put it in place. And now my guests are loving it. So yes, business has picked up, and I expect that to continue.' She folded her arms, unable to keep the bragging sound from her voice.

'And what great idea is that?'

And Cara told him, proud of how well she'd done and all the bookings that were coming in from guests wanting to attend the other courses she'd booked in. 'So, as I said, I don't need your offer to bail me out. I've succeeded on my own terms,' she finished. She gestured once again to the door, and this time, he moved towards it.

'Suit yourself,' he said, 'but I bet this will just be a blip. Your "success" won't last,' he said, making little air quotes around the word, 'but by the time it all goes wrong, my offer will no longer be on the table.'

He disappeared through the door before she could say anything else, leaving her with only the pent-up anger he'd caused and a slight worry that perhaps she shouldn't have told him so much. She closed the door behind him and tried to put her doubts out of her mind. It was too late now, and what could he do to spoil things anyway?

She hurried into the dining room, where the guests were hard at work, chatting excitedly as they finished off their activities from the week. In no time at all, her spirits were lifted, and she'd almost forgotten Luke's rude intrusion into her day.

'It looks like everyone's enjoying this last session, Esme. Are you pleased with how it's all gone?'

'I really am, Cara. It's been so much fun, and I've even sold a few of my own pieces to some of the guests, which has been a bonus. Has my friend Lily been to see you yet? She was really enthusiastic when I mentioned the job to her.'

'Not yet, but I'm sure she'll be here soon. I'll just go and check whether your lunch has arrived.'

As she reached the door, it opened to reveal the young woman Cara had been waiting for, and she was bearing the lunch trays.

'Hello, I'm Lily,' she said. 'I've brought the lunch in, as it's just arrived. I hope that's okay.'

'Of course,' Cara said with a smile, already appreciating Lily's initiative. She showed her where to put the trays and then guided her back to reception so they could chat.

'Thanks so much for seeing me today. I was really keen to meet you after Esme told me you were looking for someone. I don't know if you know, but I used to help Penny out once in a while when I was younger, before I went off to uni. I think you must have been away at uni yourself then.'

'I didn't know, but that's good news. It means you know something of what we're doing on a day-to-day basis. I have to be honest and tell you that at the moment, I can only afford to take someone on part-time, but if the courses take off, as I hope they will, I could offer you more hours then.'

'That's fine. And what sort of thing would you want me to be doing?'

'A bit of everything, really, except for breakfasts, which you won't be able to do. I need to be freed up to check on courses and arrange more, but I'm happy for you to learn everything that needs doing. What did you study at university, by the way?'

'Marketing,' she replied. 'I always thought I'd have to move away to get a job, but I really want to stay here if at all possible. And marketing might come in handy here.'

Cara beamed. 'It most certainly will. How about you start next week? If we start with four hours a day, Monday to Friday, would that work for you?'

'I can't wait,' Lily replied. 'Shall I come for nine o'clock?'

Cara was delighted that the morning had ended better than it began and tried to forget about Luke and instead concentrate on the positives.

CHAPTER TEN

Now they were moving into the season proper, bookings were up, and Cara was busy from the moment she got up, with an increasing number of breakfasts to prepare single-handedly. This morning, she had six fried breakfasts on the go and hungry customers waiting. She stared at the three fried eggs cooking in the frying pan, willing them to hurry up so she could get on with the next batch. Her eyes began to glaze over as she became mesmerised by the frying eggs, and the next thing she knew, an insane beeping had started above her head.

'Damn that thing,' she cried, waving her tea towel at the smoke alarm above her head while simultaneously trying to take the pan off the gas. By the time she'd got the alarm to stop beeping, the eggs were ruined. She was almost in tears at the thought of having to cook them all over again. She took a deep breath, knowing there was nothing else for it but to start again. She dumped the burnt eggs in the food-waste bin and then opened the back door to help the smoke escape.

'Right,' she said to herself. 'How many eggs do I need?'

She'd soon finished the first three breakfasts and was ready to plate up. She kept the remaining eggs warm while she went off to deliver the first three and apologise to the customers for the delay before returning to plate the rest up. Cara took the last three breakfasts out and smoothed the ruffled feathers of some of the customers before returning to the kitchen to tidy up.

She spent the next half an hour cleaning the kitchen and clearing the empty plates from the dining room before loading the dishwasher. She checked she'd done everything before moving to the reception area to see what else she needed to be doing that day. Thank goodness Lily was starting today and she'd be able to hand some of her to-do list over to her.

'Morning, Cara,' Lily said, poking her head round the front door a little while later. 'How are you this morning?'

Tears bubbled up as she thought about the disaster in the kitchen once again.

'Sorry, Lily. I've not had a very good start to the day.' She wiped her tears away and tried to smile at her, mortified that this was the image she was presenting to Lily on her first day.

'Would you like a cup of tea? Then maybe you can tell me what I can do to ease your load a bit.'

She nodded and pointed Lily in the direction of the kitchen.

Lily returned a few minutes later with two steaming mugs of tea. Within half an hour, she was answering the phone and dealing with bookings and enquiries, leaving Cara free to get the dining room set up for the creative writing course that was starting that day. This one was being led by a local author, and there was very little for her to do really, but she wanted to make sure everything was clean and tidy. The guests and attendees had all arrived the day before, and the course was due to start at 10 o'clock.

She'd just finished everything when she heard voices in reception and went out to see if Lily needed a hand.

'Cara, this is Mrs Evans. She's interested in running a course for you,' Lily told her with a smile.

Cara put out her hand to the older woman and smiled. 'Hello, nice to meet you. Which course would you be interested in running, and when?' she asked.

'Beginners' crochet, and as soon as you can fit me in, please. I've heard so much about this from other villagers, and I'd love to do something with you.'

'That sounds perfect. But at the moment, I can only run one course at a time, because my space is limited, and I'm fully booked until June. Would that be of interest to you?'

The woman's face fell. 'Oh, I had hoped to get going sooner than that. That's a real shame. I hadn't realised you could only run one course at a time. Perhaps you could put me down provisionally, and I'll get back to you.'

She said goodbye, and Cara sighed. 'I knew this was going to happen,' she told Lily. 'Now she'll go and tell her friends, and then the interest might well dry up. I really don't know what I'm going to do about this. Anyway, how have you been getting on out here?'

'Really well. I've taken a few bookings, and the system's really simple. The post has arrived, and there's a linen delivery here as well. Do you want me to deal with that while you sort the post out?'

Cara was relieved to have Lily working with her but saddened by the disappointment she was feeling at having to let Mrs Evans down. She had no idea how to resolve that problem at all. When she took a quick look at the bookings, though, she could see that more and more courses were getting booked up, and that could only be a good thing. The post contained a few invoices, and she taught Lily how to deal with those before escaping outside into the April sunshine for a breather and to get some lunch.

She went and looked at the view for a long while to get some of her balance back after a difficult morning. She would have loved to talk this development over with Joe, but after their stolen kiss and her subsequent embarrassed apology, she no longer knew how he was feeling. When she allowed herself to think about it, she was surprised by her lack of regret at kissing him back, and she'd wished she'd been able to take full advantage of it. Deep down, though, she also knew she still had some doubts about getting involved with someone else so soon after the disastrous relationship she'd just come out of, but she didn't want to send mixed messages to Joe either.

She cast one final glance at the view before making her way to the café to pick up some lunch for herself and Lily. Two more villagers stopped her along the way to ask about courses and both times when she had to explain she had no space before June, they changed their minds and left her feeling like she'd already become a victim of her own success.

'Have you heard anything more from Sheila and Joe?' Penny asked Hamish later that morning as they walked up the coastal path, away from the village.

'No. I've not even seen either of them since Joe came back, to be honest, but the fact he has must be a good sign, I'm thinking. They must be so busy with the gardening now the weather's getting better, so it's probably no wonder we haven't bumped into each other. Why do you ask?'

'It's just that, as Cara's doing so well, I've decided I want to hand Watersmeet View over to her now rather than wait. And if Sheila and Joe would make up their minds and take over your gardening business, then we'd be free to get on with the rest of our lives together.'

'I think it's a grand idea to make Cara the official owner sooner rather than later. It would boost her confidence as well because she'd know you trusted her to make a good job of it.'

'Oh, I've always known she would, but these courses are a fantastic idea, and I can really see that gaining traction as she goes on. I just want to hand over the responsibility, though, and not to have to worry about it all any more.'

'Have you been worrying then?' he asked, taking her hand.

'I can't help it, Hamish. I dare say I'll continue to worry even when it no longer belongs to me. It's the habit of a lifetime, I suppose.'

'Oh, sweetheart, you should have said something earlier. You should go and see your solicitor then.'

'I've spoken to them already, and it would be very quick to do, but I haven't told Cara of my plans. I just worry she won't want it either.'

'Maybe you should go and talk to her first then,' Hamish suggested. 'And perhaps I should follow up with Sheila and see what they've been thinking.'

Penny decided to go and see Cara that afternoon, but when she got to the guesthouse, she found Lily at the front desk instead.

'Hello, stranger. How are you?' she asked, hugging the young woman to her.

'I'm really well, Penny, thank you. And you? Are you enjoying your retirement?'

'I am enjoying the rest, certainly. I'm not quite retired yet, but hopefully it won't be too much longer. Is Cara around?'

'She's just in with the course, but she'll be back in a minute, because I finish soon.'

'I'm very happy to see you working here with my granddaughter, Lily. She needs the help, and you know the business, so that's worked out well for both of you.'

'It has, and although this has only been my first day, I've really enjoyed it. Cara's asked me to think about new marketing ideas as well, so that will give me something else to do.'

'Oh, Grandma, I'm sorry to keep you waiting. I didn't know you were coming today,' Cara said, emerging from the dining room a minute later.

'It was an impromptu visit, sweetheart, and I've had the pleasure of catching up with Lily as well after all these years.'

'You must get off, Lily. Thanks so much for today. I'll see you in the morning.'

Lily went on her way after saying goodbye, and Cara guided Penny to the kitchen for a cup of tea.

'How are things then? Are you missing this old place at all?' Cara asked with a grin.

'Not really. I have to be honest. I miss you, but that's about all. But everywhere I go, all I hear is compliments about how you're turning things around here, and I'm so proud of you,' Penny said as she sat down at the table.

'I miss you too – not least to talk things over with. But I'm glad to hear there are compliments, although that might not last after today.' Cara filled Penny in on her course problem.

'I'm sure you'll come up with a solution,' Penny said. 'It's wonderful that so many people are interested in running and attending these courses. I knew you could turn things round, and that's part of the reason why I wanted to see you today.'

'It is?' Cara frowned as she put down the teacups and took a seat.

'Yes. I think it's time I handed the guesthouse over to you officially.'

Cara gasped. 'Oh, Grandma, I don't know if I'm ready for that yet.'

'If you're not ready now, when will you be?' Penny countered. 'You're doing an incredible job, and I don't need to have anything to do with the business any more. I want you to have it and to make the most of it while you're young. And I want to make the most of the time I have left doing all the things I've always wanted to, with Hamish by my side.'

Cara stared at her grandmother. 'I understand that, I really do. It's just such a big step, and I've only just started.'

'And you're doing brilliantly. This would mean that you'd have the freedom to make decisions on your own without having to consult me. It would truly be your business.'

'But what will you do for money?' Cara asked after taking a sip of her tea.

'I have a good pension, don't you worry. And I'll always be here to talk things over with, even if I'm not here at the guesthouse. What do you say?'

Cara blew her still long fringe out of her eyes, stalling for time. 'Well, I don't know what else I can say. You seem to have made up your mind, but I do have my doubts as to whether I'm up to running the business completely on my own.'

'Your trouble is that you have no self-confidence, and I blame your last boyfriend for that partly. I have confidence in you, though, and I know it will be hard for you taking the business over, but I was just as inexperienced when I took it over, and I still managed to learn what to do and make a go of it. Hamish and I both think you'll do fine.'

'And if I don't, I'll only have myself to blame,' Cara muttered, certain of impending disaster.

It was back to the grindstone again the following morning as Cara stumbled out of bed at 6 o'clock to prepare breakfasts for her guests. She was going to bed late completely exhausted and waking up every morning feeling exactly the same. The only good thing about being so physically worn out was that she had no time to think when she was asleep.

This morning, though, breakfast went like clockwork, and as she had very little to do in terms of setting up for the course, she was ready and waiting for Lily when she arrived at nine.

'Morning, Lily. How are you today?'

'I'm great, thanks, and glad to see you looking a bit happier today. What would you like me to do this morning?' she asked.

Cara set Lily to work on cleaning some of the bedrooms, giving her time to do some paperwork. She'd cleared her backlog in no time, and as she had a few minutes, she decided to call one of the villagers who'd expressed an interest in running a beginners' photography course to see if they'd like to book in for June.

'Hello, is that Sarah Hughes? This is Cara Rafaelli from

Watersmeet View. I'm ringing about the photography course you wanted to run.'

'Oh, hello. It's good to hear from you, but unfortunately, you're too late. I've found somewhere else in Watersmeet Bridge to run my course.'

'Really? Where's that?' Cara couldn't believe her bad luck just when everything seemed to be going so well.

'I don't know if I should say. They have asked me to be very discreet about it, because they don't want to be inundated with people wanting to run courses.'

'I see. Well, that's a shame. I think my guests would have loved to attend your course. Do let me know if you change your mind, won't you?'

Cara gritted her teeth. Who could be doing this? Before she'd started running courses, there was nowhere else to go, and now, suddenly, somewhere else was offering it. She stared out the window pondering who else could be offering the same service. Sophie was crossing the garden as she considered the issue, and shortly afterwards, she appeared at the door, forcing Cara to focus on the course she was running right now.

'Morning, Cara. I've got your lunch delivery. How's everything going?'

'Morning, Sophie. Really well, thank you.' She would have loved to confide in Sophie but felt it was better to keep this problem to herself for now.

She took the food trays from Sophie, thanked her, and then delivered the food to the dining room. After checking everything was okay, she went in search of Lily. She found her on the first floor finishing the cleaning of the final room.

'How are you getting on?' she asked.

'Not too bad. I hope I've done it properly.'

'I'm sure you have. I really appreciate you doing this today. I've been able to get my paperwork done in record time. But I won't leave you to do this every day. I just think it's worth you knowing how all aspects of the business work.'

'Absolutely. I'm enjoying it even if it is cleaning.' They both laughed.

'I was just thinking this morning about whether the café might also be up for offering a discount on their meals to guesthouse customers in exchange for some publicity. The Bistro has already agreed to do it. If we go ahead, I wondered if you could create a flyer for me, please.'

Lily's face lit up, and Cara understood that was where her real interests lay. 'I would love to do that. I have all the software and could come up with something really smart for you. I'll bring my laptop in tomorrow, if you like.'

'Great. Now, would you like a cup of tea after doing all this hard work?'

Cara made her way back downstairs to put the kettle on, and Lily joined her in the kitchen a few minutes later.

'I've just found out somewhere else in the village is offering courses. I contacted someone who wanted to offer a course before, but they're now going elsewhere to run it, instead of here. She wasn't prepared to say where it was.' Cara frowned as she thought about this new development

'That's annoying. Any ideas who it might be?'

Cara shook her head. 'I should have thought I'd have competition. It was naive of me not to.'

'Try not to let it get you down. Just focus on what you're doing. It's going so well, and I've heard some good comments around the village.'

As the kettle finished boiling, Cara remembered boasting to that smarmy hotel man about the success of her courses. She slapped her hand against her forehead, sure she'd unwittingly given him the ammunition to compete against her.

'Damn. I think I've worked out what might have happened.' She told Lily about smarmy Luke and how she'd boasted to him about her great idea. 'I suppose he would have heard about the courses at some point, but I can't believe how I went and gave him the heads-up early, and now I'm probably going to lose the people who wanted to run courses for me as a result.'

'Well, I honestly think the ones who've already run courses for you, or who are booked in, will stay faithful to you, and maybe the others will regret their decision down the line when they find out what a horrible man that Luke character is.'

Lily went back to reception, leaving her with her thoughts. Cara had never even been to Luke's hotel and wouldn't be able to now without being recognised, but she worried about exactly what was on offer there. She decided she'd look it up on the internet and then take a walk through the village later to see what the hotel was like from the outside. He may have all the facilities, but did he have the right personality for liaising with all the people needed to run the courses?

As Lily said, she had to hope she had her good personality on her side – which she could definitely say was not the case for him.

Joe hadn't seen Cara for a few days, and he had to admit, he was missing her. He'd tried really hard to stay away, to distance himself after their attempted kiss, but in the end, his need to see her became too much. And now he had an idea which he wanted to share with her, and he was eager to see her and tell her.

He finished getting dressed and found his mum in the kitchen eating her breakfast.

'Morning, Mum. I'm off to see Cara, so I can do the guesthouse's gardening work this morning, if you like, and then I'll see you after lunch.'

'Okay, love. Take care, and I'll see you later.' Sheila looked up briefly from the slice of toast she was buttering, gave him a smile, and then carried on.

Joe set off through the village, glad to see it would be another beautiful day. He quite enjoyed gardening in the spring. The weather was usually fine but not too hot, and life was bursting anew from the soil, as evidenced by the daffodils bobbing in the breeze by the side of the street. April was the best time of year, in his opinion. He stopped for a moment to take in the view of the bay, and to inhale the sea air, before turning to enter the guesthouse garden and find Cara.

When he reached reception, though, there was no sign of her. Instead, someone else was manning the front desk.

'Hello there. Can I help you?' The young woman's smile was bright, and Joe was pleased that Cara had obviously found someone to help her.

'I'm Joe, the gardener, among other things,' he said with a smile. 'I was looking for Cara.'

'Oh, hi. She's just in with the course people at the moment, but she'll be back in a minute.'

'I need to get started on my work. Would you mind letting her know I'm here, please? I'd like to have a word with her about something.' He paused. 'I'm sorry, I didn't ask your name.'

'I'm Lily. Good to meet you, and I'll let her know.'

Joe went out to the barn to collect his tools but spent a good few minutes appraising the barn before he got started. He was just about to go back outside when Cara appeared.

'Hello, you,' she said. 'Haven't seen you for a few days. I thought you might have abandoned me.'

'I know, I'm sorry. I've been busy, but I've had an idea, and I wanted to tell you about it. So here I am, at last.'

'Okay, I'm all ears.' She tilted her head, and he thought about kissing her again. He gave his own head a little shake and tried to concentrate on what he wanted to say.

'Well, as I mentioned the other day, this barn is currently wasted as a storage place for tools, and I think it could easily be converted as another place for you to run courses in. And what's more, I'd be happy to help do some of the work for you.'

Cara swayed a little in surprise before grabbing the hand he reached out to her. 'My God, Joe, I can't believe what a brilliant idea that is. But you can't be serious about being able to do that work for me, surely? Where did you learn all these skills?'

Joe laughed. 'I've had a lot of different jobs over the years, and skimming plaster was one of them.' He led her inside the barn again and gestured round. 'All it really needs is a good clean-up and then replastering. It's even got a concrete floor. It wouldn't be very warm in the winter, but you've got plenty of time to do something about that later if you want to. And there's lots of light from the two windows, as well as these two main doors,' he added, pointing at them for extra emphasis.

'You're right. I can't believe I haven't thought about this before. It's perfect.' And suddenly, she threw her arms around him.

He stepped back as she fell against his body and closed his arms around her to stop either of them from falling any further. He pushed her gently upright but not completely away and then brushed her hair out of her eyes. And it was the easiest thing in the world then to lean in and gently brush his lips against hers. He went to move back, not wanting to kiss her again if it wasn't what she wanted too, but she pulled him back towards her, and they kissed again – this time more deeply, and with obvious sounds of pleasure.

Joe had no sense of time passing as they prolonged their kiss further, and he enjoyed the sensation of her body being flush with his. In the end, Cara pulled back first, her eyes alight with passion and her cheeks flushed too.

'I'm really sorry I didn't have time to do that the other day,' she said. 'I was a bit unsure too, but I've regretted it ever since.'

'I'm glad you're sure now,' he said, knowing his feelings must be equally well-written all over his face. He glanced around, hoping no one had seen them giving in to their desires.

Cara smoothed down her top and then her skirt and patted her hair back into place – not that any of that was necessary. 'I'm a bit lost for words, to be honest. I'm sorry for throwing myself at you like that.

I was just so pleased with your idea, and then one thing led to another.' She shrugged helplessly.

Joe took her hand. 'Don't apologise, please. I'm pretty confident about this idea, though, and if you're sure about it, I can get it done in no time for you.'

'Look, shall we meet up later to talk about it some more?'

'Sure,' he said. With one final smile, she left him on his own to debate where things would go from here.

CHAPTER ELEVEN

Cara and Lily had already settled into a nice rhythm working together after just a week, and Cara was pleased by the easy way Lily had started to share the workload at the guesthouse with her. Now she was confidently checking people in and helping with their queries about the village, which made the two of them a good team to welcome people to Watersmeet View.

Not only that, but Lily had arrived this morning bearing some initial flyers she'd created at home over the weekend, which Cara could present to the café and The Bistro to advertise a discount on meals for customers staying at the guesthouse. Both businesses had agreed to offer the discounts in exchange for a recommendation from the guesthouse, knowing the publicity would do them the world of good.

Cara was keen to get out and run some personal errands today, but for that, she'd have to leave Lily in charge. She'd have had to do it at some point, she reasoned with herself. She couldn't stay at the guesthouse all the time, and she had no worries about trusting Lily. It was just that it was a big responsibility for her new employee, and a big step for Cara as her employer.

'All the beds are changed and the rooms cleaned now, Cara. What would you like me to do next?' Lily asked mid-morning.

'That's great, Lily. Thank you. I need to pop into the village this morning for an hour,' Cara said, making her decision at last, 'so I'm going to leave you in charge while I do that. You can cover the desk and take any phone calls, put on bookings, as you've been doing. If there are any other jobs you need to do, you can do those at the same time as keeping an eye on the desk. Are you okay with doing that?'

'Yes. I'll be fine. I'll see you in an hour then.'

'Obviously, if you have any problems, you can message me,' Cara said with a smile. She grabbed her bag, said goodbye before she could change her mind, and set off for the village, making a careful note of the time so she could be back within the hour.

It was another beautiful spring day, although still a bit chilly, so she pulled her jacket together and zipped it up against the breeze. She was so glad to be out for the first time that week that she almost forgot how nervous she felt about leaving Lily on her own.

Her first stop was the doctor's. She needed to re-register now she was back in the village, and she'd been putting it off for ages. She made an appointment for a check-up as well before heading off to the dentist to do the same. Her last stop was the Post Office, leaving her with just enough time for a quick coffee at the café.

'Morning, Helen. I'll have a latte, please, and I wanted to drop these flyers in to you too.' She handed over a clear pocket envelope with some of Lily's flyers in.

'These are lovely. Did you do them yourself?'

'No. My new employee, Lily, did them for me. She's a bit of a marketing whizz.'

She took her latte to a table by the window facing onto the street and tried to enjoy the rare free time she had. She wondered if she might see Joe in the café but was almost glad not to, because now she had some time to think about him as well. While she sat there people-watching, she wondered if Lily might be interested in running a marketing course, perhaps for some of the other small business owners. And maybe that would tie in nicely with something Joe could offer. Her mind whirred with possibilities.

Cara finished her coffee and glanced at her watch. She only had ten minutes left before her hour was up, so she left the café and walked alongside the wall overlooking the river and the bay below it for a bit, filling her lungs with fresh sea air and letting the wind blow through her hair. That would have to do for now, until she could get out again. Reluctantly, she turned back towards the guesthouse, crossing her fingers that everything had gone all right in her absence.

She went through the little gate and strolled up the garden, taking in the sea of daffodils now dominating the flower beds, their golden heads nodding in the sunshine. Oh, how she loved them. Sheila had planted little blue Scilla underneath them, and the blend of colours was fantastic. The guests often commented on how beautiful the guesthouse's gardens were, and she knew it was such an asset for them. They had a lot to be thankful to Hamish – and now Sheila and Joe – for.

She couldn't see Joe anywhere in the garden, which was just as well, because they'd only get talking, or even kissing, and she didn't want to be late going back in – although she hoped there'd be more kissing soon. She took a deep breath as she stepped inside the doorway and looked around. All was calm. Lily was waiting for her with a smile.

'Hey, Cara. Did you have a nice break?' Lily asked as she approached the desk.

'I did, thank you. I got lots of jobs done, and it's such a beautiful day too, so I made the most of it. The café was very impressed with your flyers. I didn't have time to stop in at The Bistro as well, but I'll get round to that as soon as I can.' Cara glanced down at the reception desk, noticing how organised everything was, and breathed a sigh of relief. 'How have things been here anyway?'

'All fine. I took a few more bookings, and there were a couple of calls asking questions about the courses, but I was able to answer them all. Thank you for trusting me to be here on my own.'

'I trust you completely,' Cara replied. 'I just didn't want to over-load you with responsibility too soon. But you've passed with flying colours, as I knew you would. I did want to talk to you about whether you might be interested in running a marketing course at some point, but for other small business owners in the village. Have a think about it, and we can talk some more tomorrow.'

'Sure, and I can drop those flyers off at The Bistro on my way home, if you like.'

Cara watched Lily go, reassured at just how well things had gone.

Joe woke early the next day and went downstairs to enjoy some quiet time to himself before the day got started. All he'd been thinking about in his spare time was how wonderful it had been to kiss Cara and when he might have the chance to do it again. He smiled as he sliced some bread to make toast for breakfast. He still couldn't quite get over the attraction between them, but he sensed Cara was nervous about starting something new. He understood that, of course, but he hoped to reassure her that he was committed to their relationship over the coming weeks.

He and his mum still hadn't told Hamish their decision about whether to take over the gardening business or not, but they really couldn't leave it any longer. Now that he'd decided to come back and had taken on the gardening with his mum, it would give the two of them a regular income over the summer and ensure his mum could keep paying her rent. But if his own business picked up and he needed to concentrate on that, his mum would lose out as well, because she couldn't run the business on her own. So he was just hoping they could both build up their other businesses alongside the gardening work.

His tech work was only just getting going, but there was the possibility of running some courses for Cara. Whether all of this would add up to enough of a stable income year-round, he had to wait to see. And his mum's dressmaking was only just getting off the ground, so it was all going to take some time. He sighed and told himself to be patient. He'd made his decision, and he had a roof over his head so there was nothing urgent to worry about for the moment.

By the time he'd finished making the toast, his mum had joined him, ready for the day ahead.

'You must have got up early this morning, Joe,' she said. 'You've had a bit of an air about you these past few days. I wonder what's brought that on,' she added, with a twinkle in her eye.

'I don't know what you're talking about,' he replied, trying not to grin. 'Shouldn't you be getting on with making your own breakfast? I'm sure you have somewhere to be pretty soon,' he said, trying to distract her.

'I'm just about to do it, cheeky. Anyway, where do you fancy going first today?'

'Well, I wondered if we ought to go and see Hamish about the gardening business. We still haven't given him our final answer.'

'Are you sure about it then?' she asked, popping her bread into the toaster.

'Yes. I want to help you run the gardening until our other businesses take off.'

Sheila stared at her son in surprise. 'Do you really mean that? You're not just being soft because I need help?'

'Well, look, don't get your hopes up, but I really enjoy working here with you, Mum, and if I carried on helping you with the gardening, you'd be able to keep trying with your dressmaking, and I'd carry on with my tech stuff, and hopefully, by the time winter comes, we'll both have established our other businesses to help get us through. What do you think?'

Sheila put her arms round him then, and he laughed, as she was the second woman to have done that in just a few days. 'Oh, son, I'd love it if you decided to stay here and settle in the village. You could really make a go of your tech stuff, and your help with the gardening would allow me to try to make a go of the dressmaking too.'

'Well, we'd better speak to Hamish then today as our first step.'

'Of course. Let's go and see him straight after breakfast.'

The sky was overcast as they made their way along the path, but Joe was pleased they'd finally made their decision, and that he'd committed to his own decision as well.

They arrived at Hamish's cottage shortly afterwards and waited for him to open the door. Joe was nervous. He didn't know why.

'Morning, both of you. This is a lovely surprise. Come on in.' Hamish greeted them a moment later when he opened the door.

Joe followed his mum as Hamish led them down to the kitchen, where Penny was sitting at the table finishing her breakfast.

'Morning, Sheila, Joe. Help yourself to tea,' she said, pointing to the pot sitting in the middle of the table.

Joe shrugged his jacket off and sat down next to his mum, who was already pouring out two cups of tea. When he looked up, they were both staring at them expectantly.

'Well, it's probably best if we get straight to the point,' Sheila said. 'We're going to accept your offer and take on the gardening business between the two of us.'

Hamish's face cracked with a broad smile. 'That's great news, but are you both sure?'

'We are.' His mum glanced across at him and he nodded at her, giving her some reassurance. 'We've given it a lot of thought and decided we can do this together through the summer while we try to build up our other businesses.'

'Businesses?' Penny asked, looking from Joe to his mum. 'I know you do the tech stuff, Joe, but what's your other business, Sheila?'

'Joe's helping me set up a dressmaking business,' she said – with a hint of pride, he thought. 'And Cara's asked me to run a course for her as well.'

'Oh, that's marvellous,' Penny said, leaning back with a smile. 'Didn't I tell you, Hamish?'

Hamish nodded. 'You didn't have to, love. I knew Cara was up to the job all along.'

'What do you mean?' Joe asked.

'Well, I'm handing the guesthouse over to Cara officially now. And once you two take over the gardening business, Hamish and I will be free to retire fully, and to live the rest of our lives together with no other responsibilities except to each other.'

Hamish took her hand and gave it a gentle squeeze. 'You've made me very happy, both of you, and I know you'll do well with the business, and with your other businesses as well.'

Joe breathed out a sigh of relief, pleased at how things were working out for them all.

After being rejected by the last tutor she'd contacted, Cara had been wondering who to try next to see if she could find someone who hadn't been poached away. Although she'd been thrown to find out Luke was running courses – which she'd confirmed by looking at the hotel's website – she wasn't about to give up on hers. She looked down at the list of tutors she'd drawn up initially and came across someone offering a course in ceramic art. She remembered the tutor was quite new to the idea of running courses, so maybe she was a good one to try, as it would be a while before there was a space.

'Hello. Is that Harriet Woods?'

'Yes, that's me,' a soft voice replied.

'This is Cara at Watersmeet View. I'm getting in touch to see if you'd still be interested in running your ceramics course here for some of my guests, please?' Cara crossed her fingers and hoped.

'I'm definitely interested, but when would you be looking at? I still need time to put a course together, and I'm a bit nervous about doing my first one.'

'My next space isn't until June, so hopefully that would give you enough time to plan something. I could even put you in touch with another artist, Esme, who's run a painting course here, if that would help you out at all.'

'Oh, I know Esme, but I didn't realise she'd run a course for you. I'll speak to her and pick her brain, but I would love it if you could put me down to run something in June. Thank you so much.'

'No, it's me who should be thanking you. My guests are loving the courses I've put on so far, so this will be another lovely addition to my list.'

'I am glad you've got back in touch, because I've been hearing you've got some competition, and I didn't know if you were still running courses up there.'

'Apparently, I do, yes, and I'm pretty sure I know who it is. Do you know, Harriet, if you don't mind me asking?'

'I do. It's that awful man from the posh hotel at this end of the village. Luke something, I think his name is. He contacted me, but I just didn't like his tone, and I wanted to stay loyal to you, because you understand I'm not ready yet. I think you need to watch out for him. He's up to no good, I'm sure of it.'

'Ah, I thought as much. He's been pestering me to sell the guesthouse to him – can you believe it? And I think this is another attempt to put me out of business. I know his tricks, but thank you for being loyal. I appreciate that. And thank you for the warning about him, too.'

'You know, Cara, he's contacted some of my other artist friends, who've been stupid enough to go with him, and some of them are already saying he's being very underhand about paying them their cut, so you may find people come back to you when they realise what a chancer he is.'

Cara rang off a few minutes later, amazed by this latest information. What a nightmare of a man Luke was, she thought. She had no idea why he was so hell-bent on buying the guesthouse when it was nothing like his hotel. And what if Harriet was the only tutor not taken in by him? What might that mean for Cara's fledgling courses business?

She went to make herself a cup of tea while she thought about what she was going to do next. She still had a number of tutors on her list to call, and that was all she could do, really, and she'd just have to hope some of them might still be interested in working with her. In the meantime, she'd ask Joe to get started on converting the barn, and she'd ask Ed to decorate it when the time came. The finances were already looking a lot better, and she could now afford to pay both Ed and Joe for the work they'd done. And she'd had another idea for the barn as well.

Since speaking to Joe about it, she'd considered transforming the barn into a sort of community hub as they no longer had a village hall. That way, she could run courses there in the day, but she could also hire it out for social events in the evening, which she thought might be a better approach. There would be a lot of work involved, but with Lily's help, she thought she could do it, and she was sure it would pay for Lily to become full-time. She hoped it would also help out other small businesses, such as Helen's, and perhaps even The Bistro, depending on the event. And it would give her no end of pleasure to be able to give something back to the community in the form of a meeting place for everyone.

It had been a quiet afternoon, with Lily gone for the day and this week's history course out roaming the South West Coast path in the capable hands of their tutor, so there was no better time for Cara to continue working her way through her list. She wandered back to reception with her cup of tea ready to contact the next tutor. She checked the number and gave them a call.

'Hello, this is Cara Rafaelli at the guesthouse,' she began.

About half an hour later, she'd gone through her whole list and was pleasantly surprised at the number of people still interested in working with her. But most of them had repeated what Harriet had told her, leaving her full of resentment for Luke's interfering by the time she'd finished. There were a fair few people he'd managed to lure away from her, and she was disappointed they wouldn't be able to run courses for her guests now. Those guests would maybe even decide not to stay with her now, she thought, and that left her feeling even more despondent.

Cara was delighted when Ed called her upstairs the next morning to see the result of all his hard work. The family suite now looked modern and fresh, and the two single rooms had been transformed into light, airy rooms with a feeling of more space about them. Ed had even found the time to redecorate their shared bathroom and toilet.

'Ed, I can't thank you enough for all your hard work. You really have transformed this whole floor. I'm so grateful, really, and the guests have hardly been disturbed at all.'

'No worries, Cara. It's been a really lovely job, actually. It's made a nice change to work here when there are guests around, rather than doing it in the winter season as I have in the past.'

'You'll be pleased to know I've had more bookings than expected as well, so you can submit your invoice to me straight away for immediate payment.'

'Oh, that's brilliant, Cara, thanks. And when do you want me to move on to the next floor?'

'As soon as we can arrange it. I think we might have to do it room by room from now on, so we don't disrupt the guests any more than necessary. Although, as I said, we hardly knew you were here. But by doing that, I'll only have one room out of action at a time, and that's the most important thing.' Cara paused before bringing up the next subject she wanted to discuss. 'There is something else I wanted to ask you about as well. Do you have time to look at the old barn with me outside?'

He gave her a smile. 'This sounds intriguing, but yes, I've got time.'

Cara helped Ed to carry his things to his van, and then they went round to the barn together.

'So we've had an idea to convert this into a kind of community room where I can run courses in the day but hire out the space for events or meetings during evenings and weekends. I wondered if you could do the conversion and the redecorating afterwards, please.'

'That's a great idea. We could really do with somewhere like that. I can do the conversion, the replastering, and the decorating too. It would be easy for me to do all that. I can get you a quote together for it and drop it back to you later today.'

'That would be wonderful,' she told him.

Ed went on his way shortly after, just as Joe was arriving to do some gardening. Cara gave Joe a shy smile as he drew closer, and he returned it before he went to drop his bag in the barn.

'So, how've you been?' Cara asked when he returned.

'I've missed you,' he said, looking up at her and briefly touching her hand.

'I've been thinking about you such a lot,' she said with a laugh.

'I know we haven't had time to talk, but maybe we could try and get out together at some point.'

'That would be nice,' she said. 'What did you have in mind?'

'How about a walk and a sandwich lunch sometime?'

'That sounds perfect. I'll see if Lily could stay longer one day. I'm sure she'd be up for that.'

'Mum and I went to see Hamish yesterday to tell him we're happy to take on his gardening business.'

Cara's hands flew to her cheeks. 'So you've decided to give it a go?'

'Yes! We're going to give the gardening a go and try to build our side businesses at the same time.'

'Oh, that's fantastic news. I'm so glad.'

'You've been a great help as well with offering us both the chance to run courses too.'

She waved away the compliment. 'It's no more than you both deserve. You're so talented.'

'Have you had any more thoughts about the barn?'

She told him her thoughts about making it a sort of community space, and about her conversation with Ed.

'I can still clear the barn out for you if you want me to. I think that's a great idea you've had, and it will be lovely for the village to have that space.'

'That's great, thank you. I think it will be a good thing for the village – and for me – to have that extra space for courses. I found out yesterday it is Luke who's offering courses in competition with me, but there are still a lot of tutors who want to stay with me rather than go with him.'

'I should think they only need to meet him the once to get the measure of him. It's good you're not letting him put you off. What you're offering is great. You should be very proud of it. And I hear from Penny that you're now the new owner as well? Pretty talented yourself, I'd say.'

Cara blushed. 'Well, I haven't definitely confirmed it as yet, but I'm thinking that I will now.'

'Well, I'd better get on with some gardening, but let me give you my number, and you can let me know what Lily says.'

He read out his number to her, and she put it into her phone before sending him back a quick text. He reached out to touch her face gently before turning to go into the barn.

'See you soon.'

Cara headed back to the guesthouse to get on with yet more paperwork. She couldn't wait until she could see Joe again and spend more time with him on their own. She was delighted he'd moved back to Watersmeet Bridge and hoped that everything would work out for him and his mum. She knew she was already in danger of falling for him, and if he were then to change his mind and leave again, she'd be left broken-hearted once more.

The door opened, and suddenly, the room was full of hungry walkers looking for their lunch. She turned her attention to them and their food, reluctantly leaving all thoughts of Joe behind for a while.

CHAPTER TWELVE

Cara took one last look at herself in the mirror and decided she looked presentable enough for dinner with Penny and Hamish. They'd invited her round that evening, and she was looking forward to getting away from the guesthouse for a while, although they were sure to spend some of the evening talking about it.

She left her contact details on the desk at reception before grabbing the bottle of wine and the flowers she'd bought and setting off for Hamish's cottage. It was only a short walk, but she was glad of her jacket, as the evenings were still quite cool.

'Hello, my darling,' Penny said a few minutes later as she opened the door.

'Hello, Grandma. These are for you from the guesthouse garden,' Cara said, handing over the flowers as she stepped inside.

'Oh, they're lovely. Thank you.' Penny took the mixed bunch of daffodils and tulips from her granddaughter. 'Come on through to the kitchen. We're almost ready.'

Hamish was in front of their ancient cooker, stirring something in a pot that smelled wonderful. Cara put the bottle of wine on the table and went over to have a look.

'It's some French recipe Penny made me tackle, but basically, it's just a stew,' he said with a laugh.

'It looks and smells amazing,' Cara said, giving him a quick peck on the cheek, which made him blush.

'So, how's everything going at the guesthouse?' Penny asked as she finished laying the table.

'Pretty well. Bookings have picked up since I introduced the courses, and I've run about three now, with some more to come. But I've also had it confirmed that Luke's offering courses as well.'

'Oh goodness, I'd quite forgotten about that with everything else that's been going on,' said Penny, handing Cara a glass of wine. 'I was planning to go and see him and give him a piece of my mind.'

'He just doesn't seem to take no for an answer, and now he's trying to ruin me instead,' Cara said. 'But I don't think you should get involved, Grandma. It'll only stress you out.'

'Agreed,' said Hamish with a look at Penny. 'You're not going to just give up and let him win, though, are you, lass?' Hamish asked.

'Absolutely not,' Cara confirmed, and they all laughed. 'No. I've rung all the tutors who were interested in working with me, and a fair few of them still want to. He has enticed some of them away, but that's their lookout. I'm just going to keep going with the ones who want to stay with me.'

'That's the spirit,' said Penny. 'Now, you sit down, Hamish, and I'll serve.'

Hamish took his seat and poured wine for himself and Penny, and soon, they were all tucking in to the 'stew' and roast potatoes on the side.

'Oh, this is so delicious. Thank you,' said Cara. 'I never have the time or the energy to make a proper meal for myself any more.'

'I know it's hard work, love, but you must make sure to look after yourself properly, especially if you're in this for the long term.' Penny studied her granddaughter to see if she'd tell them whether she'd decided to take the guesthouse on.

'Well, of course I am,' Cara confirmed. 'I'm already invested in the place, and now these courses have been going so well, I want to carry on making it work. That was one of the things I wanted to tell you tonight. If you're still sure about handing the guesthouse over to me, I'm happy to do it.'

'Oh, that's great news,' Penny said. 'Let's toast to that.' She raised her glass. 'I've already got the paperwork,' she added. 'You could even sign it tonight.'

Cara grinned. 'Why doesn't that surprise me?'

'We know you'll do a grand job there,' Hamish told her.

'I hope so. It means as much to me as it does to you, Grandma. And Joe has given me another good idea as well.'

Penny raised her eyebrows and exchanged a look with Hamish, which Cara caught but chose to ignore.

'Tell us more then,' Penny said before eating another mouthful of her dinner.

'We're going to convert the barn into a community space so I can run courses there during the day and rent it out in the evenings for events and the like. What do you think?'

'That's a great idea. The village really needs somewhere like that,' Hamish said. 'Will it be expensive to convert it?'

'I don't think so, not with Joe and Ed helping me.'

'You've mentioned Joe quite a lot,' Penny said. 'Are you two officially an item now?'

Her grandmother didn't beat around the bush, and she wouldn't be able to get away with anything other than the truth. 'Not really an item, but we like each other,' Cara said.

'Well, that's grand,' said Hamish with a smile. 'I think you two go well together. And you know Sheila and Joe have agreed to take over my gardening business?'

Cara nodded. 'He has told me about that, and I'm really glad he's going to give it a go.'

'Yes, me too.' Hamish sounded relieved.

'You will go slowly with Joe, though, won't you?' said her grandma.

Cara pushed away her plate and looked up into their worried faces. 'I'll be careful before giving my heart away again,' she said, answering their concerns. 'It's just that sometimes, it's hard not to fall. Sometimes, you don't have a choice,' she said.

'I hope things work out for you both,' said Penny. 'But you need to be prepared for the fact they might not.'

'I know, and he has been honest with me, I think, which is important. But I'd be very sad if things didn't work out, obviously, as I know he would too.' That didn't even remotely describe how devastated she'd be if they didn't, but there wasn't a lot she could do about it. She'd just have to see how things went between them and hope her leap of faith was justified.

Joe finished packing the sandwiches he'd made into a small cool bag and popped in a couple of drinks as well before grabbing his jacket and making his way out to the High Street to meet Cara. She'd arranged for Lily to stay till two o'clock today, so they had a couple of hours ahead of them to get to know each other better.

Cara was waiting for him by the garden gate when he arrived, and his heart warmed when he saw her beautiful face.

'Hey. You look keen to go,' he said with a smile.

'I just don't want to get drawn into anything and then not be able to go after all,' she said. 'I've been looking forward to this.'

'Me too.'

She joined him on the street, and they set off for the coastal path, walking away from the village. It was a clear spring day with hardly any clouds in the sky, and there was even some warmth from the sun.

'It feels so good to be outside,' Cara said. 'This is the first time I've been on this path properly since I came home.'

'Is it? Well, I'm glad I suggested it then. It's one of the best things about Watersmeet Bridge, being able to walk this path above the sea.'

'It is – you're right. So you're glad you decided to come here, you and your mum?' Cara asked then.

'Yes, definitely. It was always going to be a good idea for Mum to be nearer her dad after so many years away in Leeds, and there were just too many reminders of her life with my dad, so it was a good idea to have a fresh start.'

'That's how I feel about being back here again too. The chance of a fresh start.' She paused for a moment. 'Do you still see your dad?'

'No, and I won't, not after the way he treated my mum.' His certainty was definite, and he wasn't going to change his mind about it.

Cara surprised him by taking his hand then, and it felt so right to hold her smaller hand in his. They followed the path as it wound up past the few remaining houses and then onto the cliffs above the village. They stood at the edge looking out over the sea for a few minutes before turning away and wandering down towards the river and the woodland on the other side.

After a while, they found a good place to stop and have lunch and sat down on an old bench to eat.

'Mmm, this is delicious,' Cara told him after taking the first bite of her egg mayonnaise sandwich.

'It's pretty tasty, isn't it?' Joe agreed. After a pause, he continued, 'What happened to your mum, if you don't mind me asking?'

Cara closed her eyes briefly, and he felt guilty for bringing the subject up.

'She died from breast cancer when I was young. As my dad had already left us to go back to Italy, my grandma brought me up after that. There's hardly a day goes by when I don't think of her,' she said, her eyes shining with tears.

'I'm sorry. That must be hard.' Joe didn't know what else to say.

'It's still so raw after all these years, and I really miss her sometimes, you know.'

Joe nodded. 'Do you ever hear from your dad?'

'God, no. I wouldn't want to either. My grandma's enough for me now. I wish I'd kept in touch with her more when I was away at uni in Exeter, but I got distracted by the relationship I was in, and then that all fell apart, and I realised she was the most important thing to me. And so here I am, and it feels good to be back home here again.'

'It's a real community here, and it's the first time in my life I've felt like I really belong somewhere. I like to keep myself to myself, though, so I have found it hard when everyone seems to know your business. That's the great difference between life here and life in a city.'

Cara laughed. 'Oh yes, I know that feeling only too well. But most people here mean well and want the best for you once they know you. And you and your mum have settled in well here, I think.'

They finished their sandwiches, enjoying each other's company and not feeling the need to talk for a while.

Joe glanced at his watch. 'Well, I suppose we ought to start walking back soon,' he said.

'I know, but can we stay for just a little bit longer?' She gave him such a sweet smile that he would have found it hard to refuse under any circumstances.

'Of course.' He didn't really want to leave either. He packed the lunch things away and then put his hand out to Cara, pulling her up.

And that was the perfect moment for another kiss. They were both lost in their embrace, with only the feel of the wind in their hair, and nothing else to worry about. Joe curved one hand around Cara's waist and rested the other lightly on her back. He never wanted this perfect moment to end.

Cara was the first to pull away, but she didn't let go of him. 'Joe, I...' she began.

He stepped back. 'What is it, Cara? Is everything okay?'

'It's perfect, Joe. But I'm just a bit frightened by all these new feelings. It's not been that long since I was nursing a broken heart.'

Joe sighed. 'I know. I'm finding it hard to deal with everything too. After my parents split up, as well as a few failed relationships of my own, I vowed never to get involved with anyone again, because all it seems to do is bring heartache. But then I met you, and suddenly, I wanted to try again.' He took her hands in his. 'If we don't try, we'll never know if we could make things work, and we might miss out on the best relationship ever.' He smiled as he looked down at her.

'Okay,' she said. 'That's a good enough reason for me.'

They packed their things back into the bag and started the walk back towards the village. Joe was glad Cara had been honest with him about her fears. He only hoped that they could make things work, and that taking the risk would be worth it.

The paperwork from Penny's solicitors was delivered the following Monday. Cara took it from the courier knowing instinctively what it was and understanding that the future of the guesthouse now lay completely in her hands. She took in a deep breath and then released it slowly, trying to calm herself before opening the envelope and reading the contents.

As she read the papers with her name now inscribed as the owner, her heart beat a little faster. Was she really up to this? Perhaps it wasn't too late to change her mind. Then she looked up and out into the garden, and beyond it to the sea in the distance. If she was going to stand any chance of making a go of this business, she needed to have confidence in herself – otherwise, how could she expect other people to believe in her? She'd already achieved so much with the courses, and now she had the barn conversion to look forward to as well. There were lots of positives.

She put the papers in her desk drawer and tried to remember what she was doing before the courier came. The door to the dining room opened then, and it all came back to her.

'Hi, Cara. We're all done for the day. Thank you again for all your help.' Esme's first course had been so popular she'd offered to run another one, and this one was also going well.

'No problem at all. I'm glad everything's going so well. Is there anything else you need before tomorrow?'

'No, thank you. It's all good. I'll be back early to set up again in the morning. Have a nice evening.'

She made her way into the dining room and started to clear the tables. There was very little to do, because Esme was so organised, but she took the time to make sure everything was ready for breakfast in the morning. She was just on her way back to reception when her phone rang.

'Hello, Cara. This is Eileen Evans. I called you the other day about running a beginners' crochet course for you.'

'Oh yes, hello. What can I do for you?'

'Well, I'm afraid I'm ringing to say I won't be able to run a course for you after all. It's just that I've been offered more money to run my course at the hotel at the other end of the village, and they've also got so many more guests and facilities that I'd be mad not to take their offer. I hope you understand.'

Cara listened in a daze, and before she could even ask any questions, the woman had rung off. She couldn't believe how this had happened. But then her phone rang again, and so on, for the next half an hour. It was as if it had been orchestrated for them to all call her one after the other. By the time the phone finally stopped ringing, everyone she'd called the other day – with the exception of Harriet – had called her back to cancel their agreement with her.

And suddenly, Cara found herself in tears. She had never felt so vulnerable. Hardly was the ink dry on her signature taking over the ownership of the guesthouse and she was facing disaster. She sank onto the chair behind reception and sobbed, letting all her emotion out. That swine Luke ... Why was he doing this to her? She swiped at her tears as they were replaced by anger at his underhand behaviour. How had he even got to those people? Surely someone must have given him their names.

There was nothing she could do. She couldn't force the tutors to change their minds. It was their decision who they chose to work with, and money was often the deciding factor for people who were looking for work. And she understood that, she really did, but she was saddened by the lack of loyalty from so many villagers who she'd known for so many years.

She'd already advertised the courses on their social media, so she'd now have to go back and cancel all those courses, probably losing customers as a result.

And the tears fell again. It was all so unfair. And then she realised Luke had probably seen her adverts on Facebook and simply found out who could run those courses. Well, that was a lesson learned for the future – if the guesthouse even had one.

She sat there dabbing at her tears for ages, completely at a loss for what to do. Finally, she called Zoe for help and reassurance.

'Christ, what an arsehole that man is!' she exclaimed when Cara told her. 'Listen, stay where you are. Put the kettle on, and I'll be right round.'

That was the motivation she needed at last to get up and do something. She made her way to the kitchen and put the kettle on, as requested, before nipping to the loo to check the state of her face. When she was satisfied she looked vaguely presentable, she went back out to reception.

Zoe arrived a minute later and pulled her straight in for a hug. 'God, Cara, I'm so sorry about all this.'

Cara tried hard not to start crying again but felt better after the hug Zoe gave her at least. 'It's a real nightmare,' she told her friend. 'And I've just received the paperwork today saying I'm the new owner as well. Fat lot of good I am. I just don't know what I'm going to do, Zoe. He's there everywhere I turn, waiting to bring me down no matter what I do.'

They went through to the kitchen, and Zoe took charge of the tea-making.

'I know it's awful right now, but you're still doing really well, and you have some other ideas up your sleeve. Maybe you just need to be careful about who you tell them to from now on, so he doesn't get wind of things so easily. I know you can pull this back, Cara. I have every confidence in you. You just have to have faith and keep going.'

Joe had been steadily clearing out the contents of the barn at the guesthouse since early that morning. The weather forecast for the day was good enough for him to be able to stack everything on the lawn and the gravelled area outside the kitchen, which was just as well, because there was a lot of stuff. He'd need Cara to confirm which things she wanted to keep and what she wanted to get rid of, but they'd need to hire a skip at some point, he was sure of that.

He was pleased Cara was pressing on with the conversion of the barn, even though she'd had a setback with so many tutors going off to work with Luke instead. He admired her guts and her refusal to give up in the face of Luke's underhand tactics to try to force her out. Joe really hoped things would turn around for her, and soon.

The trouble with working on the barn was that he had lots of time to think, and now he was in danger of overthinking everything about his life. Although he and his mum had plenty of gardening work now, he worried whether they'd be able to build up their other businesses enough to support both of them through the winter. His tech work was taking a while to pick up, and he was worried if it didn't happen soon, he might not be able to make a decent income after all.

He sighed to himself as he threw yet another box of rubbish onto the pile. He stood back to assess the situation and was relieved to see the barn was now almost empty. There wasn't very much to be kept, he realised, and he was sure it would all fit into the small shed on the other side of the gravelled area. Once the barn was empty, he'd move all the stuff they were going to keep into the shed and then ask Cara about booking a skip for the rubbish.

'Hello, Joe. How are you getting on?' Cara appeared from the kitchen door and gave him a broad smile.

Still lost in his thoughts, it took him a moment to respond and to stop frowning. Her smile wavered, and he felt terrible.

'Sorry, Cara, I was deep in thought there. Anyway, yes, getting on fine, actually. The barn's nearly empty, and when that's done, I'll put the stuff I think we want to keep in the shed.' He gestured towards the 'keep' pile, and she nodded. 'Then I think you should hire a skip to get rid of the rubbish,' he finished, pointing to the larger pile.

'That sounds like a good idea. And when will Ed be able to start work on the inside, do you think?'

'I should be able to sweep it all out today as well, so anytime you like, really.'

'Would you like to stay for some dinner when you've finished?'

'Yes. That would be great, thanks. I'll see you later.'

Cara went back inside, and he returned to his task. Within half an hour, the barn was empty and swept out, and he turned his attention to moving all the items they were keeping to the shed. By the time he'd finished, the grass was clear, and the rubbish was all stacked neatly on the gravel.

He grabbed his jacket and his bag and made his way across the garden, and out back onto the High Street, to go home for a quick shower before coming back later. He was tired after a long day of physical work but satisfied all the same. On his way, he admired some of the gardens he passed, some of which were gardens of their clients. He'd been surprised at how much he was enjoying the gardening work, and he found it balanced nicely with the digital work, which mainly kept him indoors. Maybe it was time to ramp up his efforts to expand his digital work to stop him from worrying about the future so much. He could start planning some courses for Cara, which would help both of them, and perhaps contact the networking people, as Cara had suggested. By the time he got home, he was feeling a lot more relaxed about everything.

'Hey, love. How's your day been?' his mum asked as he went through to the kitchen.

'Not bad. I emptied out the barn for Cara. I'm just back for a shower before going over there again for dinner, if that's okay?'

'Yes, of course. I haven't started on anything yet, so that's no problem. Are you okay? You look like you have a lot on your mind.' His mum looked him in the eye in that special way she had, but he didn't want to offload all his problems onto her.

'Yeah. I've just been worrying about my digital work not picking up yet. I just need to step up my efforts a bit, I think.'

'You've not been back that long either. It's going to take a while. Try not to fret too much.'

'I'll try.' He rolled his eyes and went off to the bathroom.

Half an hour later, he was back on the path to the guesthouse and looking forward to seeing the sun going down on his favourite viewpoint. He had to focus on the positives of this new life he'd committed to, and this was one of them. Cara was another, of course, and he definitely wanted to explore things with her. He was also enjoying answering only to himself rather than being at the beck and call of a company, even though it was still very early days. Living here in Watersmeet Bridge had every chance of changing his life for the better, and of making him happy. He just had to believe in it, and to throw himself into it in every way possible. He owed it to himself, to his mum, and to Cara to give it his best shot and make it work.

CHAPTER THIRTEEN

Cara still couldn't quite put her finger on it the following morning, but she was sure Joe had had something on his mind when he'd come over for dinner with her the night before. She'd tried to jolly him along during the evening, but he was quieter than usual, and of course, that was leading her to think the worst. Today, this feeling had transformed itself into irritation at the mixed messages he was sending her, and she was determined to get a straight answer from him about it.

After finishing the breakfasts that morning, she tidied the front desk while waiting for Lily to arrive, thinking through what jobs she could ask her to do that day. One of them would be to find the best price for getting rid of the rubbish from the barn. Cara planned to contact Ed herself to see when he could make a start on decorating the barn, and she was also going to spread the word about her intention to turn it into a community hub.

'Morning, Cara. How are you today?'

'Morning, Lily.' Lily was right on time as always, and Cara was reminded once again of her good fortune in finding her.

Cara filled her in about the rubbish from the barn that needed getting rid of, and the other things on her to-do list.

'Okay. I'll get right onto that,' Lily said. 'Are you going out?'

'Yes. I want to spread the word about the barn being converted into a community space, but I want to speak to people face-to-face, rather than using social media, so I can control who knows.'

'That sounds like a good idea. And I think a lot of people will want to book the barn for events and the like.'

'That's what I'm hoping. Okay, I'll grab my coat. I'll have my phone with me, so do ring if you have any worries about anything. Esme should be fine. I'm sure she'll tell you if she needs anything anyway.'

Cara set off for the village, stopping in at a few places along the way to run some errands, but also to let the people she trusted know about her plans. It took about an hour before she arrived at the café for a well-earned break.

'Morning, Helen. I'll have a cappuccino today, please. How's everything going with you?' she asked.

'Much better, thanks, in large part to you.' Helen smiled.

'Oh, I'm glad. In fact, I hope to be sending even more work your way, if you're interested.'

'That sounds good. I'll have to talk to you properly when I'm not working, but thank you for thinking of me again. I really do appreciate it.'

'No worries.'

Cara thanked her and went to take a seat at a table in the window. She wanted to call Joe but was steeling herself for what she needed to say. The café was bustling enough that no one would overhear her conversation, so before she could change her mind, she dialled his number.

'Hey, Joe,' she said when he picked up a few minutes later.

'Hello, Cara. What can I do for you?' He sounded surprised to hear from her.

'Have you got a minute to talk?'

'Well, not really, if I'm honest.'

'That's just what I want to talk to you about, this blowing hot and cold on me. I want to know where I stand with you. I think you owe me that at least.'

Joe was silent for a few seconds, but then she heard him release a breath and compose himself. 'I do owe you that. I'm sorry. But now's not the best time – and that's not me trying to avoid the conversation. I felt bad after being so preoccupied last night, and I do want to explain that. Look, can you give me half an hour to finish what I'm doing, and then I can take a break and talk to you properly?'

'Okay. I'm having a coffee in the café, so I'll wait for you.'

And with that, they said goodbye. Ordinarily, Cara would have enjoyed the view, but she was distracted, wondering what Joe would say. At least he'd admitted that his mind had been elsewhere last night, and that he owed her an explanation.

By the time Joe finally joined her, she'd long since finished her coffee and was beginning to give up on him.

'Cara, sorry I've been so long. We're just so busy.'

'I really need to be getting back to the guesthouse. Could you walk with me so we can talk that way?'

'Okay, sure.' A frown flitted across his face but then disappeared just as quickly, and he shrugged his coat back on.

The High Street was busy with villagers as well as tourists, and she was glad to see that. She just hoped the guesthouse would be able to benefit from the increased traffic as well.

'I'm sorry about yesterday,' Joe said again as they started a slow walk back to the guesthouse.

'I don't mind you being preoccupied at dinner,' she said. 'It's just that I don't really know what's going on with us. When we went out for lunch last week, things were really good, but now it seems like a distant memory. Something's changed, and I don't know what it is.' She glanced sideways at him and saw him wince.

'It's just that I'm worried my tech work isn't taking off yet, and that makes me nervous about the future,' he said. 'We're busy with the gardening right now, but what about when the season ends? What if we don't manage to get our other businesses off the ground because the gardening is taking up all our time? I haven't even had the chance to talk to you about running a course, and neither has Mum. But I really do want to make this work, and you're a part of that, of course.'

'I understand that, but you should try to tell me when you're worrying rather than leaving me to get the wrong impression and start thinking you've changed your mind about moving back here.'

They were back at the guesthouse now, and they stopped outside the gate and turned to face each other.

He reached out to touch her face gently. 'I know, and I'm sorry. I've been on my own too long, and I'm used to keeping my thoughts and feelings to myself. I didn't mean to make you worry as well.'

She stepped closer and brushed his lips lightly with hers, and his arms went round her, pulling her against him. It was a relief to know there was nothing else on his mind, but it had unsettled her, and she hoped that he'd trust her with his thoughts next time.

While Cara was pleased to have had some phone calls about her plans for the barn, she was frustrated by how long it was going to take to finish the conversion. This was partly because Ed was now so busy with other work, but also because her bookings had dropped off a little since Luke had started offering courses too, and so she didn't have lots of money to spare to pay for the work to be done. She was in a catch-22.

On top of that, she still had this lingering doubt about her relationship with Joe, and she was sad that things between them seemed to have already faltered. It was time for her to focus on the guesthouse, but saying it was one thing, and doing it was another.

She'd been able to offer a couple more courses in the coming months though. Lily had agreed to offer a marketing and design course, which had been eagerly taken up by guests, and one of Harriet's friends, Sylvia, had contacted her about offering a knitting course, which made up for the one that had been lured away by Luke. She'd just have to wait awhile for these courses to take place for the money to come through.

So things had gone quiet for now and that worried her. She really didn't want to have to let Lily go when she was such a godsend, but without any courses on the go, and with bookings down, things were once again looking bleak. Then she got a phone call from Finn at The Bistro.

'Hi, Cara. I've heard from Zoe about the trouble you've been having recently, and I've got a proposal for you. I wondered if we could rent your dining room as a spare space for some of the catering events we've been asked to do. As you have a kitchen there as well, it would be perfect for us to use for some of the special events we do when the restaurant's closed. At the moment, we're having to turn people away, you see.'

'Oh my goodness, that's a brilliant idea,' Cara replied. 'Would you like to come over and take a look at the kitchen and dining room?'

They agreed Finn would come over that afternoon to check the space out and to discuss fees, etc. Cara couldn't believe her good luck. This was just what she needed to get her back on track for all her other plans. The Bistro events mainly took place in the evening, Finn had said, although his other chef would need access to the kitchen beforehand, which meant she might need to reorganise her courses so they wouldn't be affected, but she thought she could do that.

Lily had taken over responsibility for the website now that Joe had set it all up and she'd been working on that all morning in the dining room. Cara went in to tell her the good news.

'That sounds fantastic. What a great idea. And the website's really looking good now, I think,' she said, showing Cara some of the photos she'd put on.

'Maybe today's not going to be such a bad day after all,' Cara said.

'Hello?' a voice called from reception.

Cara recognised Zoe's voice and went out to greet her, leaving Lily to the website work.

'This is a nice surprise,' she said, giving her friend a quick hug.

'Well, I'm on my way back to work after running some errands, but I wanted to ask you something quickly. We do need a proper catch-up and soon, but this couldn't wait.' Zoe's eyes were bright, and Cara wondered what she was so excited about.

'Go on then. It's always good to see you, even if it's briefly.'

'Well, I wondered if I'd be able to book the barn for a party once it's all finished.'

'A party?' Cara frowned, but only in thought, as parties hadn't occurred to her as something she might offer. 'What sort of thing do you mean?'

'Well, like … an engagement party?' Zoe smiled again.

'An eng— Oh my goodness! Are you and Ed getting engaged?' Cara let out a squeal.

'We are,' Zoe confirmed, and this time, she beamed.

'You know I'd do that for you both, with pleasure. And what's more, it's a great idea for the barn to be used for events like that.'

'Is it okay for me to tell people then? I know you've had problems, so I don't want to cause you any more.'

'It is, but keep it face-to-face if you can for now, please. I'm trying to keep my plans off social media for the time being so Luke doesn't work out what I'm up to.'

'Sure. Well, that's great news.'

'It certainly is. Congratulations to both of you. I'm so pleased for you.'

They shared another quick hug before Zoe had to leave, and Cara was left smiling for a long time afterwards, pleased things had worked out so well for her friend. She hoped that this would give Ed the incentive to get on with the work on the barn as well.

If she was going to be working with Finn, that, together with the new courses she'd be running, would give her the money to pay for the work on the barn, and then she could start using the barn as well.

She was relieved she could see a way out of this storm, and then she could stop worrying about Luke and his nefarious plans, because she would have managed her own future.

She only wished she could sort things out with Joe as well. She really wanted him to settle in Watersmeet Bridge for the long term, but she had no real influence over that. He needed to get there on his own. She just hoped he'd reach the same conclusion as her and his mum, and soon. His future was here, and she was sure he could make a go of things.

It was now mid-May, and Cara had been managing to keep running courses most weeks as they went into summer at the guesthouse. Ed was also supposed to start work on the barn today, and he said it should only take a couple of weeks to complete. Money was coming in quite steadily, so Cara hoped to be able to keep Lily on, and to pay Ed for the work on the barn. After that was done, she planned to ask him to continue with the decorating work.

And as if she'd conjured him up by thinking about him, Ed popped his head round the front door.

'Morning, Cara. Am I all right to go straight round and make a start?'

'Yes, of course. The way's clear for you. It'll be great to see it transform.'

Ed disappeared again, and a few minutes later, Lily arrived. Cara was on cleaning duty today while Lily managed reception and updated the website and their social media. They'd settled into a good routine, and Cara was grateful for it.

She blitzed her way through the rooms, cleaning and changing beds in no time, glad of something to keep her mind from wondering about Joe. He'd popped in a couple of times with questions about the garden but hadn't stopped for a chat. Why did everything have to be so complicated? It wasn't the first time she'd wondered this.

She finished cleaning the last room and made her way back downstairs to reception.

'You did that in super-fast time today,' Lily laughed. 'It feels like you only went up about five minutes ago.'

'It was a bit longer than that, but I guess you've been busy too.'

'We've had some more bookings in today via the website, as well as via Facebook, so we're doing well,' she said.

'Thanks for all you're doing, Lily. It's just as well you know how to manage it.'

'No problem at all. I enjoy it, so it's easy for me.'

'I wish I could say the same. How's the course going this morning? It sounds like they're having fun.'

The knitting course was happening this week, and so far, it all seemed to be going well.

'All fine. I went in and checked a little while ago, and they were all so busy chatting I don't think they even noticed me.'

'Okay, that's good. I'm going to go and take Ed a cup of tea. Shall I make one for you as well?'

'Yes, please. I'd love one.'

After making the tea, Cara went out the back way towards the barn to see how Ed was getting on. He was standing outside the barn with a frown on his face when she reached him and handed him his cup of tea.

'Everything all right?' she asked.

'No. I think we might have a bit of a problem with the roof in that it's not watertight. I found a small leak at the back, which would have been hidden by all the stuff Joe cleared out. I don't think it's major. It just means I can't get started on plastering the walls until that's been sorted and the wall has dried out.'

'Oh, damn. And is that going to be expensive?'

Ed glanced across at her. 'I really don't know, Cara. Don't go thinking the worst. I know someone I can call in, and we'll wait and see what he says. But I'll have to give up for now, and that means it might be a while before I can come back again. I'm sorry.'

Cara went back inside a few minutes later, sure that the world was conspiring against her. Then Joe popped in, but this time, he stopped to talk.

'Hey, Cara. How are you?' He gave her a smile, but he looked tired.

'Not great, to be honest. I just found out that the roof of the barn has a leak, so Ed can't get started until that's been fixed, and worst of all, I have no idea how much it's going to cost.'

'Oh, that's awful news.'

'And to make matters worse, I overheard some people talking in the café the other day saying how much they'd enjoyed the course they attended at Luke's hotel recently. It sounds like everything's going really well for him.' Bitterness seeped through her every pore. She couldn't imagine how things could get any worse. 'Well, it was my fault for giving him my great idea, I suppose.'

Joe rolled his eyes in sympathy. 'I'm sorry to hear that, Cara. You weren't to know he'd be so devious.' He gestured towards the barn. 'Is Ed going to get someone in to look at the roof for you?'

She nodded, already worried sick about the potential expense. She wanted to pour her heart out to Joe and have him console her, but he'd been so distant of late that she didn't feel comfortable doing that. She couldn't even bring herself to chat with him.

'Anyway, it's not your problem,' she said. 'I'll let you get off. Thanks for popping in.'

His face fell at her dismissal, but he turned away, taking her very strong hint. Cara had a quick word with Lily and then escaped to her office to be on her own with this latest setback.

She collapsed into her desk chair and put her head in her hands, unsure of what she was going to do next. She glanced across at the calendar. It was two weeks until Finn wanted to host his first catering event in the dining room. They'd agreed she'd take a 25% cut of the profits from each event, and with the courses she had booked, there was still a fair amount of money coming in, but she had nothing put by for emergencies. And fixing the barn's roof definitely fell into that category. She had no idea how bad the damage would be, nor how much it would cost to fix it.

For now, she'd just have to wait and see. But her mind was doing insane things, imagining the worst and she just didn't have it in her any more to keep calm and rational about it all.

To Cara's surprise, Ed's roofer friend turned up later that afternoon to assess the situation, jolting her right out of her pity party. She was still worried about what he would say, but at least it would be over quickly.

'You must be Cara,' he said as he came through the door. 'I'm Brian. Ed told me you've got a problem with the roof of your barn. Can I take a look?'

She stood up quickly from the desk and came round to shake his hand. 'Of course. Thanks for coming out so quickly.' She led the way to the kitchen and out the back door to the barn.

'Oh, that's only a small leak,' he said after putting his ladder up against the wall and studying the roof for a few minutes. 'And the good news is, it's only in one section, so it won't be too costly to replace that piece of membrane. Shouldn't take too long either. I should think you're looking at about £150 for materials, and just a couple of hours' labour, so with VAT, that'll be just over £300. Does that sound all right?'

Cara released a breath. 'Yes, that's all right. Thank you. And when do you think you'll be able to do the work?'

'I can come back before the end of the week and fit you in, if that's okay.'

'That would be fantastic. Thanks so much, Brian.'

Brian left, and Cara went back inside to reflect on what had happened. All in all, she'd been lucky. It wasn't going to cost too much to repair the roof, and she could get it done quickly. But this was a lesson in having an emergency fund to hand for this sort of thing in case it happened again in the future. And she was certain it would. She'd probably overreacted to the situation as well, so she needed to toughen up a bit, because there were always going to be problems, and she'd have to deal with them as they arose.

She heaved a sigh of relief as she went to make a cup of tea. The crisis had been averted, and now she had to move on. When she reached the front desk again, she got her phone out to give Ed a call.

'Hey, Ed. I was just ringing to thank you for sending your friend, Brian, round to look at the barn. He's just gone, and it wasn't as bad as we first thought, thank goodness.'

'Well, that is good news. Unfortunately, I'm not going to be able to get back to you for a while, because I'm really busy next week, and the one after. I wondered, after all that's happened, whether it might be an idea to speak to Joe and see if he can make a start for you after all.'

Cara's heart sank. She already felt bad about being so cool to Joe that morning, but now she'd really have to eat humble pie. 'Oh yes, that makes sense. Okay, thanks again, Ed. I'll speak to you soon.'

She stared at her phone, willing herself to call Joe, but every time she got ready to press the button to dial his number, she chickened out, unsure about how to even start the conversation. She was over-thinking things again, she knew, and she badly needed to get this work done. She finally dialled his number.

'Hi, Cara. What can I do for you?' He had his professional voice on, and she couldn't blame him.

'Hi. I wondered if you'd be free to come over again this afternoon. I want to talk to you about a couple of things if you've got time.'

'I could come back now, if that works for you?'

'Sure, thanks. See you soon.'

Cara tried to practise what she wanted to say, but the more she tried, the more the words stuck in her throat. She wanted to apologise on the one hand, but on the other, she felt like he'd brought it on himself by being so distant with her. He couldn't really blame her if she'd reacted to that by being cool to him too. It was petty of her, she accepted that, but that was how she felt. Now, though, she needed his help so maybe she had no option but to apologise.

Joe turned up about ten minutes later and for a long moment, neither of them said a word.

Then they both spoke.

'Look—,' she began.

'Cara—,' he said. 'Sorry, you go first.'

'I'm sorry I was cool to you this morning. I've just been upset by the way you've been so off towards me lately.' She bowed her head in embarrassment.

'I deserved it, Cara. I know that. I'm sorry too. I've just got so much on my mind, and I don't want to burden you with it, that's all.'

'Look, you've been honest with me, so I know the situation. I can make up my mind about whether you're not being fair to me. I just wish you'd give me the chance to do that and not keep shutting me out like this.'

Joe's face brightened. 'I'm sorry. I guess I was trying to protect you – and me – from more heartbreak, but I can see that was wrong.'

'Good. So can we try again? And can I ask you a massive favour as well?'

Joe laughed, and she joined in. 'I'd like it if we tried again,' he said. 'As for the favour ... well, that depends on what it is.'

She came round the desk, and she reached for him this time, and he pulled her gently into his arms for a kiss. Never had a kiss felt so good, and she poured everything into it, wanting him to know how important he was to her, and how much she hoped to persuade him to stay. It was several minutes before their kiss came to an end, and she was so out of breath and anything resembling sense that she just took him by the hand and led him to the barn to tell him more about the favour she had in mind.

CHAPTER FOURTEEN

Joe had been working on the barn all morning, filling in holes in the plasterwork in preparation for skimming all the walls afterwards. That was a way off, though, because there was so much filling to do, and it was painstaking work. Cara had been taking him cups of tea and biscuits, and she'd also made him stop for lunch, but he was still at it mid-afternoon.

Lily had left for the day, so Cara hadn't been able to go out so often, but things had quietened down a bit now, so she made her way to the front door to go out and check how he was getting on. But when she went outside, there were two men in black suits standing in the garden with clipboards.

'Excuse me,' she said, marching up to them. 'Can I help you?'

'We're from the planning department, Miss. We've come to look at the work you're doing on this barn to see whether it meets with the council's planning regulations. According to our records, you haven't applied for planning permission.'

Cara's mouth dropped open in surprise. She had so many questions she didn't know which one to ask first. Joe had come out to listen to the conversation, and he stepped in instead.

'Can we see some ID, please?'

The man who'd spoken to Cara narrowed his eyes. 'Why would you question who we are? I've told you, we're from the council.'

'You've not even given us your names,' Cara said, finding her voice at last. 'We'd like to see your ID, please.'

The other man came forward then, flashing his ID card hanging on a lanyard round his neck. The other man did the same.

'Hang on a minute. I can't see your names or your company from that quick flash. Can you take them off for me, please?' Cara's impatience was growing.

They both took off their ID passes and handed them to her. Once she'd looked at them and judged them to be authentic, she nodded at Joe.

'Now, why are you here?' Joe asked.

'You need planning permission for a change of use, sir, and it is our understanding that you don't have it.'

'And how did you come by that "understanding"?' Joe went on. 'Someone must have given you that information.'

'That's none of your business, sir. All that matters here is keeping to the law, and at the moment, you're not doing that.'

'As you don't know what we're planning to do with this barn, I fail to see how you can conclude that we're breaking the law,' Joe stated quite calmly.

Cara was amazed by his articulate delivery in the face of these two drones from the council. And as he'd said, someone must have put them up to this.

'What are you planning to do with it then? Why don't you just tell us that?'

'We're planning to—,' Cara began, but Joe reached out and put his hand on her arm to stop her.

'You need to write to us to formally explain what it is you think we're doing wrong. Then we will reply formally, with a solicitor's letter if needs be, to explain our intentions. But you can't just turn up here like this.' Joe folded his arms and flicked his head towards the front gate, encouraging them to leave.

'We'll set that in motion as soon as we get back to the office,' the younger man said. 'Good day.' He turned on his heel, pulling the other man with him, and set off towards the gate.

'What the heck was all that about?' Cara asked when the men had gone back onto the High Street and were safely out of earshot.

'I don't know for sure, but if those two really work for the council, I'd be surprised. Still, I think they've had the intended effect. We'll need to check out what they said and make sure we're not going to fall foul of the law.'

'Joe, you were amazing, but you're right. We'll need to check. I can't believe I didn't even think about it.'

'I didn't either. It didn't even occur to me, and I feel stupid for not thinking about that.'

'Come on. It's a setback, but I'm kind of getting used to them now,' Cara replied with a chuckle. 'I'm sure it will be okay.'

She wasn't sure. In fact, she was worried, and if it turned out to be true, it was the last thing she needed on top of everything else.

'Well, look, I'm going to carry on working. There's no harm in carrying on while we try to find out.'

'Good plan. I'll ring the council to see what they say.'

Cara went back inside wondering what on earth she'd done to deserve all these mishaps. She went straight online to get the number for the council, and before too long, she was on hold waiting for someone to answer the phone. But the number just rang and rang, intermittently disrupted by awful music or automated messages. She checked her phone after what seemed like an eternity but was only five minutes, in fact, and carried on holding.

'Hello. How may I help you?' The employee on the other end sounded as bored as Cara felt after waiting for nearly twenty minutes to get through.

'Could you put me through to the planning department please?'

No further words were needed, and Cara was soon listening to a ringing tone again. Then she was answered by a machine asking her to leave a message, which she did in the absence of anything more useful.

She put her phone down on the desk and returned to the council website to see if she could find anything helpful there, but there was very little to go on. She had no idea how long it would take the council to get back to her, and as the end of the office day was approaching, she wasn't expecting to hear from anyone today anyway. She heaved a sigh, frustrated beyond words at this latest turn of events.

Joe had offered to help Cara by researching the problem they were now faced with. As their own council had very little information, he started by looking at other council websites instead, reasoning that the laws must be the same or similar across the whole of England. It was a complicated process, and time-consuming as well. As he'd been the one to suggest the barn conversion in the first place though, he owed it to Cara to try and help her get some clarification on the subject.

The first thing he investigated was whether what they were planning to do to the barn constituted a change of use. Previously, it had just been used for storage, but it didn't need to be approved for that, or for anything similar to that. However, he could see that if people were going to be using it, there'd be some health and safety considerations. But did that really add up to a change of use, or not?

He'd been staring at the computer screen for a good couple of hours when his mum interrupted him with a cup of tea.

'Come on, love. You need to take a break and do something else for a bit.'

Joe rubbed his eyes and nodded in agreement. 'I know. It's just so frustrating, and I haven't made any progress yet either.'

'Maybe you should get out for some fresh air. Perhaps go and talk it over with Cara even. I'm sure you can sort this out between you.'

Joe stood up and stretched his legs and his back out before picking up his tea. He'd love to go and see Cara, but only when he had some good news for her, and there was no sign of that yet. He stared out at the sea in the distance, noting how choppy it was today, which seemed like a representation of everything that was happening. He was mortified this had all been his idea, and that he hadn't had the good sense to check whether they needed permission before going ahead with it. They needed someone who knew about this sort of thing to check it for them. He couldn't keep wasting time on the internet.

After finishing his tea, he decided to find out if there was a local firm of architects he could speak to. He found one over in Barnstaple, Cahill Jones Architects, who also happened to have a very helpful website with FAQs on it. As he scrolled through the popular questions, he found one about barn conversions and discovered a link to 'permitted development rights' – a recent change in the law. As he read through the details, his mood lifted immensely. If he was right, this was exactly what they'd been looking for.

He stood up again and threw on his coat. Now it was time to go and find Cara to see what she thought about this. He called goodbye to his mum as he went through the hallway and hurried along the High Street towards the guesthouse. He'd spent the whole morning researching this which had stopped him from carrying on with his work on the barn but if this new information proved to be correct, it would have been worth it.

He strode up the garden path towards the front door, noting the flower beds needed tidying up as well, and worrying that that work was falling by the wayside with all these other issues cropping up all the time. He pushed the door open but found the reception area empty. He glanced at his watch, knowing Lily only worked till lunchtime.

'Hello?' he called out, not wanting to go searching through the rooms in case he disrupted a course. He didn't want to intrude.

The kitchen door opened a minute later, and he saw Cara make her way back to reception. She looked wrung out, and he felt for her.

'Hey, Joe. Sorry, I was just making myself a drink. Do you want one?'

'No, thanks. I'm fine. Are you okay?'

'Not really. I'm worn out by the way all my plans seem to come to nothing. I can't even find the energy to look into this latest problem. Have you had any luck?'

'I think I might have found something after hours of looking.'

He told her about the permitted development rights regarding barn conversions.

'That does sound good, but how are we going to confirm it?'

'I'll try calling the council again this afternoon, if you like. They close for lunch, so I can give it a go when they reopen. I just wanted to tell you that there might be a light at the end of the tunnel after all.'

'Thank you. I appreciate that. I hope there is, but I'm all out of ideas otherwise.'

'Have you got a course on today?' he asked.

'No. Nothing this week. Most of the tutors have left and gone to work for Luke instead. He hasn't got any worries about planning permission, I'm sure.'

'Well, don't worry. We'll get this sorted, and then you can pick up with your plans. It will all come together in the end. Try not to worry.'

She grimaced. 'I'm trying to toughen up, but it's not easy, especially now that I'm the official owner of the guesthouse. Did I tell you I've signed the paperwork?'

'No, you didn't, but that is good news.' He gave her a quick smile and squeezed her hand. 'I noticed the garden's looking a bit sorry for itself. Do you want me to give it a tidy tomorrow?'

'Yes, that would be great, and you can tell me if you make any progress with the council then as well.'

'Okay. Well, I'll let you know if I find anything out today, but I'll come round tomorrow morning anyway. Try to get a good night's sleep, and tomorrow, everything will look better.'

Joe walked back across the garden and out onto the footpath towards home. He sincerely hoped he was right about the barn conversion, for Cara's sake, because otherwise, it was going to be hard for her to come back from this.

After another bad night, Cara got up early the next day to see to breakfast for the few remaining guests. They were now midway through May, and they should be full, but without the courses to entice guests in, their fortunes were failing once again. Cara refused to give up, though, while there was still a chance of turning things round, despite her weariness and lack of sleep.

At least breakfast always went well, and there were no hiccups this morning. Similarly, there were very few rooms to clean and tidy. She went off to do them herself even though it was Lily's turn, preferring to do something physical to keep herself busy. Joe had turned up early and was making a start on the front garden first. He'd put a call in to the council the day before and was waiting for someone to call him back so there was no news for the moment.

She made her way back downstairs after cleaning the rooms and changing the beds.

'Shall I put those things away, as you've done all the hard work?' Lily asked as she reached the bottom of the stairs.

'Oh, yes, please. That's kind of you.'

'I'll stick the kettle on after that as well.'

'Thanks. Could you make one for Joe as well, please?'

Lily disappeared, and Cara took the seat behind the front desk. She glanced out of the front window but couldn't see Joe anywhere, so she guessed he must have moved round to the side or back gardens. At least that would all look nice when he'd finished. She was just checking the bank balance to make sure she'd be able to pay him when the front door opened. When she looked up, it was all she could do not to groan at the sight of Luke standing before her once again. He was there to taunt her – she was sure of it – from the smug look on his face.

'Good morning, Cara. How are you today?' he asked, his too-white teeth gleaming.

'What do you want, Luke? I distinctly remember telling you not to come back again after your last visit.' She pulled herself up straight, not wanting him to know just how close to defeat she was.

'Well, I said I thought I'd have to come back with a lesser offer for this place, and here I am. I've heard how badly your courses are going, and also how you've had to stop work on your latest hare-brained scheme to do up your barn, so I thought you might want to reconsider my offer. Even though my courses and my business are going very well indeed, my offer has gone down, I'm afraid.' He grinned maniacally.

'I'm not interested in any offer you might want to make,' she said. 'I wasn't then, and I'm not now.'

'Are you sure you don't need to speak to the owner before making such a rash decision? I don't think they'd turn their nose up at £500K. That is my final offer now. I won't be coming back again, so if you send me away but then change your mind on this, it will be too late. I'd get on to the owner if I were you.'

Cara sighed. 'I am the owner, and I'm still not interested in selling to you. And it doesn't matter what you do, I won't be changing my mind, so I'd like you to leave and never come back.'

She stood up then, and Lily came up alongside her from the kitchen. Everything fell silent for a minute until Joe appeared in the doorway.

'What are you doing here?' he said to Luke as soon as he saw him.

'He's just leaving,' said Cara firmly.

'You heard the lady,' Joe said, opening the door again and sweeping his arm towards the exit.

'You really are going to regret this. But that's up to you,' Luke shot at Cara before stepping through the doorway and making his way back across the garden.

'What a hateful man he is,' said Lily.

'And persistent too,' agreed Cara. 'I just don't know where he's getting all his information from. He even knew about the barn,' she said.

'Well, if he's behind the visit we had from the suits, then he would know. It makes sense, doesn't it?' Joe's jaw was clenched, and Cara appreciated his anger on her behalf.

'I guess so. But why is he going to all this trouble to get the guesthouse? Why can't he be happy with what he's already got?' Her shoulders slumped in near defeat.

'People like that always want more. They're never satisfied,' Lily said.

At that point, Joe's phone rang. 'It's the council calling me back,' he said.

He went outside to answer the phone, and Cara followed him out to see if she could pick up any news from his side of the conversation. He was doing all the listening, though, so she had to wait patiently instead. She wandered round the garden looking at all the work he'd been doing that morning and taking comfort from being in nature.

She turned when Joe called out to her, now off the phone. 'Well, that was a very interesting conversation. Firstly, I was right about the permitted development regulations. They do cover us for the work we want to do on the barn. That's the good news.'

'And the bad?' Cara clasped her hands together, almost in prayer.

'They've agreed to send you some paperwork documenting your right to convert the barn, but until it comes, we can't do any more work on it. And also...'

'What? Don't tell me there's more,' Cara groaned.

'I gave them the names of the men who came round, and the person I spoke to confirmed they don't actually work for the council.'

'Damn that man! I'm going to make a complaint about him if it's the last thing I do.' Cara stomped off across the gravel to work off her anger.

When she turned round to come back again, Joe was still watching her, understanding her need to vent her frustration.

'Well, we've got their names, so you could try, but whether they're their real names or not, you'll have to see. It might all be a waste of energy anyway. How would we prove that it was Luke who's behind all this?'

Even though she knew he was right, Cara was still furious.

Cara called the council herself first thing the next morning, but as Joe had said, even with the names of the men, she couldn't prove it was Luke who'd put them up to their deception. However, the woman she spoke to at the council did take her complaint seriously.

'I'm very sorry about this, Miss Rafaelli and I will pass your complaint on to the right people.'

'Thank you. I appreciate that. And can I ask you about my documentation as well? I really do need it sooner rather than later. Is there anything I can do to speed things along a bit?'

'Well, you could make an appointment and come in. I can check when the next free appointment is, if that would help.'

Cara waited while the woman checked on her computer, crossing her fingers that there'd be an appointment soon.

'I'm afraid there are no free appointments for the next month, so I think you'd be better off waiting for the paperwork to come through,' she said.

Cara rang off, frustrated yet again that she hadn't got anywhere with her phone call. She was worried about how long the paperwork was going to take, because in the meantime, she'd only be able to offer one course at a time, and right now, she didn't even have that. Money would soon start drying up, and then she'd be in real trouble all over again. She had very few tutors left who were loyal to her, and soon, the villagers would lose interest too if she couldn't get the barn finished. She had no idea what she was going to do.

Lily was sympathetic as Cara recounted her conversation a little while later, after she'd finished the cleaning.

'I don't know if this will make you feel any better, but I've been hearing on the grapevine that a lot of the tutors are feeling disgruntled with Luke for not paying them as promptly as he should be, and in some cases, he hasn't paid them at all.'

'If I were a lesser person, I'd say that serves them right, but instead, that makes me feel terrible on their behalf. Still, no-one's contacted me wanting to come back here and work with me, so what can I do?'

'I know. Would you be prepared to take them back though if any of them did want to get in touch?' Lily asked.

'Of course. Beggars can't be choosers. But genuinely, I'd be happy to have them working for me. I'm not the sort of person to bear grudges.'

'Okay, well, that's good to know if the subject comes up again.'

The rest of the morning passed slowly by, and then Lily went on her way, leaving Cara alone with nothing but her thoughts. She was surprised Joe hadn't called her to catch up on the news, but she knew he had to work with his mum, and that he couldn't spend all his time with her.

She did at least have a couple of new bookings for the following week, and these were nothing to do with courses, so something else must be working. Lily had been trying to put up a new post on the guesthouse's social media every day, including of the newly decorated family room, so maybe that was it.

Cara longed to go out for a walk, but right now, she felt like a pariah in her own village, so she didn't relish the prospect of seeing people who'd shunned her in preference for Luke's fancy hotel setting. She'd never felt so isolated in Watersmeet Bridge, in fact, and that made her incredibly sad.

By the time the paperwork did come through for the barn, it

might well be too late to turn the guesthouse's fortunes round. It was already limping along, and she had no idea how to put it right. Any self-confidence she'd built up was fading fast, and although she hated herself for having the thought, she wondered if she might come to regret not taking Luke up on his offer to buy the guesthouse. Except, in her heart, that would only make her loathe herself more, and as for Penny – well, she'd probably never speak to her granddaughter again.

Anyway, Luke's offer was ancient history, and she knew she could never really bring herself to sell the guesthouse to him.

After making herself yet another cup of tea, she reviewed the positives. Finn was holding his event at the guesthouse in a week's time, and that would bring in some more money for her. Work would be able to start again on the barn at some point in the near future, and she still had guests booking in to come and stay, so it wasn't all hopeless. She pulled herself up straight and tried to concentrate on the good things. When the phone rang, she jumped after being so deep in thought about everything.

'Watersmeet View. How can I help you?'

'Hello, Cara. This is Eileen Evans. We spoke before about me running a beginners' crochet course for you. Then I cancelled and went to work with Luke at the big hotel.'

'Ah yes, I remember. How are things?' Cara didn't have it in her to be rude, nor to gloat if things hadn't worked out for her.

'Terrible, if I'm honest. I should never have changed my mind. I've run two courses for Luke, and as yet, there's no sign of any money coming my way. So I know it's really cheeky of me, but I wondered if you'd still be interested in me running a course for you.'

'I'm sorry to hear that about Luke not paying you, Eileen. That's terrible. I'd be happy for you to run a course here. If that would work for you, why don't you come in and see me so we can chat it over?'

Eileen rang off, and Cara had to admit, she felt a small sense of triumph at luring one of her tutors back from Luke, even though it was really Eileen who'd lost out. Still, she'd welcome her back with open arms, and she would pay her properly as well.

CHAPTER FIFTEEN

Joe had stayed away from the guesthouse for a couple of days, full of remorse for what had happened with the council over the barn. The mess Cara now found herself in was all his fault, and although he'd tried to make good, she'd have to wait ages to get permission. He wished he'd never suggested converting the barn at all. He'd told his mum all about it, and of course, she'd leapt to his defence, but it was no use. He needed to stop meddling and get back to his original plan. Although, right now, he was no longer sure of what that plan was.

He'd gone out for a walk early this morning to try to clear his mind and to make sure that he was doing the right thing. The coastal path was usually quite empty at this time of day, with the exception of a couple of dog walkers he didn't know anyway. But just as he reached the brow of the first hill, when it was too late to turn round without being seen, he saw Hamish out for a walk alone.

'Morning, lad. How are you these days? I haven't seen you in a while.'

'I know. I'm sorry. Things have been a bit hectic.'

'Why don't we walk together, and you can tell me more about it?'

Joe studied his granddad's craggy face and saw only kindness there despite his sometimes gruff manner. 'That would be great.'

'So, what's been happening?' Hamish stared ahead, and that gave Joe the confidence to say what was on his mind. It wasn't long before he was telling Hamish the whole story.

'I've made such a mess of everything here that I think it's for the best if I just push off now before I make things even worse.'

'Have you spoken to Cara about this? Is this what she wants?'

'I haven't, no, but I can't imagine her wanting me to stay now.'

'And what about your mum? How will she manage without your help with the gardening business?'

Joe grimaced. 'I don't know about that one. It's the only thing I can't sort out. I can send her money, but I can't find anyone who can work with her apart from me.'

'If you don't mind me saying, I think you're being a bit hasty with all these decisions. It's not your fault about the barn. It was a good suggestion, and it will come good in time for Cara. I shouldn't think she holds that against you for one minute. And maybe she does want you to stay. I'm sure your mum does too.'

Joe pondered what Hamish had said. The way he painted the picture, there was still a lot going for him if he stayed in Watersmeet Bridge, so why did he see it so differently? The more he tried to think it all through, the more unclear it became.

'I honestly don't know what to do for the best, Granddad.'

They stopped at the top of the cliff and looked out at the bay. 'The thing is, Joe, I believe you do know, but perhaps you're frightened to commit yourself to staying here from what you've told me before. It sounds like there's nothing for you in London now. I know there's a big world to explore out there, but there's also a world of opportunity for you here. You just have to be brave and take that chance.'

'But it's such a risk, isn't it? I don't know if things would work out if I stayed.'

'But what if they did? Then your mum would have your help,

you'd have a share in your own gardening business as well, and you might be in a proper relationship with Cara too.'

Once again, Joe's head snapped to his right to look at Hamish. 'What do you mean about Cara?'

'It's as clear as anything to the rest of us that you two like each other. So why won't you both do something about it?'

Joe threw up his hands. 'She won't want to have anything to do with me now.'

'You don't know that. Why don't you just talk to her? You're making an awful lot of assumptions otherwise.'

They turned and started walking back down the hill, the bracing wind behind them now.

'So do you really think I could manage to run the gardening business alongside building up my digital business? It's taking so long to get things off the ground since I came back, and I'm worried it's never going to happen.'

'It's going to take some time to get yourself established, so you will have to be patient. But I believe it will happen for you in time, and when it does, you'll be in charge of your own diary, so you can fit the gardening in around your other work or vice versa. If you like living here and you do want to stay, I think you can easily make a go of it with these businesses. I think you just have to trust yourself and the people around you.'

They were both quiet for a few minutes as they descended the hill. Soon, they were standing outside Hamish's cottage.

'How's Penny?' Joe asked. 'I can't believe I've taken all your time and not even asked you how the two of you are.'

'She's fine, and much better now Cara's taken over the guest-house. I think we should go and see Cara though. It sounds like she needs some support right now. Anyway, give what I've said some thought, and let me know how you feel in a few days.'

'I will, and thanks for listening.' He turned to give his granddad a hug.

'You're always welcome.'

Hamish walked away up his garden path, and Joe turned to continue towards the High Street. He glanced at the guesthouse as he went by, but he didn't go in. He needed some time to process what Hamish had said, but he was relieved to have talked things over with him. Now all he needed to do was to make a final decision, once and for all.

Penny stopped just outside the garden gate. It had been a while since she'd been to her beloved guesthouse, and suddenly, she was overwhelmed with emotion. Why had she stayed away for so long? This had been her home all her adult life, and the sense of loss she experienced as she stood there staring at it was profound. She was almost afraid to go in.

'Are you all right, love?' Hamish asked, taking in how white her knuckles were as she held onto the gate so tightly.

'I don't know. I feel a bit emotional, that's all, and it's taken me by surprise.'

'Shall we sit down for a minute?'

Penny nodded, and he led her away from the guesthouse for the time being, over to their favourite bench that looked out across the bay.

'I feel silly now,' Penny said after she'd taken a few minutes to calm herself.

'It's not silly to be overwhelmed sometimes,' Hamish said. 'It's been a while since you were last here, and you're not the owner any more either. Maybe we shouldn't have left it so long.'

'I'm ready now,' she said, and they both got to their feet.

Penny went through the gate with no problems and ambled slowly up the path, taking in the blossoming flower beds full of colour: petunias, primroses, tulips, all looking glorious in the summer sun.

'Sheila and Joe have done a great job in keeping the garden maintained here, haven't they?'

'They certainly have, but then they had the best teacher, didn't they?' Hamish laughed, and Penny slapped his arm playfully, knowing he was trying to distract her.

He pushed the front door to the guesthouse open a minute later, and she went inside.

'Grandma, Hamish! Oh, it's so lovely to see you both,' Cara cried as soon as she saw them. 'How are you?'

'All the better for seeing you,' Penny replied, folding her arms around her granddaughter and basking in the joy of her embrace.

'Oh, me too. I really needed a hug from you today. Shall we go and get a drink?'

She led the way to the kitchen, and Penny and Hamish followed. Penny settled herself at the table while Cara bustled around making tea and digging out some biscuits. Penny cast her eye around the kitchen, noting with fondness that everything was much the same.

'So, how is everything, Cara?' Penny asked once Cara had put the cups and biscuits on the table and taken a seat too.

'Things have been hard, I can't lie. That damn man, Luke has been interfering every step of the way, and I just can't seem to have any success without him ruining it. But the tutors who went with him are now having problems with getting paid, and one of them has already asked if she can come back to me. So maybe he'll get his comeuppance as far as that goes. And then there's the issue with the barn conversion.'

She explained what had happened and what she'd done to try to sort it out.

'Well, it sounds like it's only a matter of time then before that gets dealt with,' said Hamish.

'It is, but it's time I can't afford to keep wasting. I want to get on and get the rest of the guesthouse redecorated, but I can't do that if I haven't got any money coming in. It's a vicious cycle.'

'Could you go into the council and see if you can get the paperwork you need?'

'They've told me they don't have any appointments for a month. There are lots of good things going on here, but I'm also having to deal with lots of obstacles, and it's all just so frustrating.'

'Business can be like that, but it does sound like you have a lot of potential to make a go of turning the guesthouse round. You mustn't give up, Cara. I know you can do this.' Penny picked up her cup and took a sip of tea.

'Anyway, how are you two?' Cara changed the subject, obviously desperate to talk about something else.

'We're fine and enjoying our quieter lives,' said Hamish.

'You both look so much better, even since I last saw you,' Cara said. 'You must be so relieved Sheila and Joe agreed to take over your gardening business.'

'Definitely, and I can see what a good job they're both doing around the village,' said Hamish. 'It was the right decision for me, and for them.'

'And how are things with you and Joe? He wants to help you too,' Penny asked over the rim of her cup, a mischievous look in her eye.

'Well, I thought that, but I just don't know,' Cara replied with a shrug.

'Has he taken you up on the idea of running a course? He'd be really good at that, I'm sure,' said Penny.

'Not yet, no. And I can't force him, can I? I've got a business to run, and I need to prioritise people who want to work with me.'

'How's Lily working out? Is she still here with you?' Hamish asked, picking up another biscuit, trying not to worry too much about Cara's dismissal of Joe.

'Oh, she's a godsend. She's picked up the job easily, but she has so much marketing experience as well, and she's run a course for me too. There's just a whole wealth of experience in this village, and I really want to tap into it for the benefit of the whole community.'

Penny smiled and relaxed her shoulders knowing that she'd made the right decision in handing things over to her granddaughter.

'Just try to bear with Joe a little, Cara, would be my advice,' Hamish said then. 'He does want to stay and help his mum, but he's worried about the future. I think he needs to talk to Sheila about how to run the courses alongside their gardening work, which is perfectly possible for them to do, and then they can really start to build their business empire.'

They all laughed then, but as much as Hamish hoped Cara would reflect on his words, he also prayed he was right about Joe's intentions.

Sheila had arrived early at her first gardening job today, and after talking through her client's requirements, she'd been left on her own to get on, so she had some time to think. She'd talked with Joe about his plans so many times now, and every time, she'd held back from asking him to stay, because she didn't want to pressure him. But now she was getting desperate, and she didn't know what to do for the best.

She tipped the salvia plant gently from its pot and teased out the roots before placing it in the middle of the hole she'd already dug out for it in the border. Then she filled the hole back in. The weather was beautiful now, and this particular customer liked to have colourful borders throughout the seasons.

Sheila sighed as she reflected on how hard it was to be a parent. She only wanted Joe to be happy, but the more she thought about it, the more convinced she was that he'd be happier if he stayed in Watersmeet Bridge rather than leaving all over again to look for more regular work elsewhere. But he had this idea – he'd always had it – that she needed protecting, and it was worse since the divorce, and now it was colouring his decisions about his future. No matter how hard she hinted, he didn't understand he'd actually be helping her more by staying and sharing the workload with her in the gardening business. She didn't want to have to find someone else to work with her when they worked so well together, and he was so good at the job.

Should she tell her son what she was thinking, or would he be upset at her for interfering? It was definitely a risk, and one she was worried about taking for fear of driving him away.

Sheila carried on working on the flower bed for the next hour, trying to work out what to do for the best, and when she next glanced up, Joe was approaching along the road.

'All right, love?' she said as he stopped at the gate and leaned over it towards her.

'Hi, Mum. Looks like you've been busy this morning. Do you fancy stopping for a cup of tea?' He waved his Thermos at her, and she smiled as she got to her feet.

'That sounds like a great idea.'

'Here you go,' he said as she joined him on the garden bench, passing her a cup from the flask.

This was one of the many reasons Sheila loved her son so much. He was just naturally so helpful and thoughtful, and people who were related to you weren't always like that. She'd been lucky with Joe, because she knew not all families got on so well. She didn't want to lose that, but she didn't want to hold him back either.

'So I wanted to talk to you about how to fit in running the courses Cara has offered us around the gardening work.'

Sheila raised her eyebrows, glad he was thinking about this. 'I definitely want to take her up on it, but even if we took turns, we'd lose quite a bit of gardening work for each week one of us was off.'

'What if we just asked the gardening clients if they'd be prepared to let us miss a week that week? Do you think they'd mind?'

'Well, we can only ask. I suppose it would be the same if we went on holiday. If there were any clients who desperately wanted a visit, the other one of us who was gardening that week could probably squeeze one or two extras in.'

'Exactly,' said Joe with a smile. 'So shall we give it a try? Do you want to offer your course to Cara first, or shall I?'

Sheila worried at one of her fingernails. 'I'm so nervous about doing it, Joe, but I can't keep putting it off, so maybe I should go first?'

Joe patted her hand. 'I think that's a good plan, and I can help you get ready. I do also want to see if I could run a course for the networking group at some point, but that can come later.'

'You seem much more enthusiastic about it all than before, if you don't mind me saying,' Sheila said, lifting her hand to shield her eyes from the sun.

'Yes. That's down to Granddad, who made me see sense.' Joe laughed and stood up. 'We won't know if we can make this work until we try, so all we can do is give it a proper go. I have to be at my next job shortly, so I'll get off now. Will you let Cara know you're ready to run a course?'

Sheila nodded. 'Yes. I'll pop in there when I leave here.'

By the time she'd finished working on the garden, it was lunchtime but instead of stopping to eat, Sheila decided to make her way to the guesthouse to speak to Cara. She wandered back through the residential streets until she reached the High Street, where she turned right to go to the guesthouse. She admired the garden as she passed through it, noting what a good job Joe was doing with it. That would be one customer they could easily cancel during the weeks they were running courses. Cara definitely wouldn't mind.

She pushed open the front door and stepped inside to the cool hallway, where she found Cara busy with paperwork at the front desk.

'Hello, Sheila,' she said as the door creaked open. 'How are you?'

'I'm fine, I think,' Sheila said with a laugh. 'I've come to tell you that I'm ready to run a dressmaking course if you'll still have me.'

Cara clapped her hands together and stood up. 'That's wonderful news, and yes, of course I still want you. Let me get the diary up, and we can see when the best date is for us both.'

Penny was up and out early the next morning and making her way towards Watersmeet Bridge before she'd even had breakfast. Today, she'd be having her breakfast at the big hotel so she could do a bit of spying on Luke. She called out greetings to the other villagers as she made her way along the cobbled street, feeling more excited than she had in ages. This man was making Cara's life a misery, and she'd do all she could to stop him. She'd never liked him, and she was sure she could find something he was doing that she could use against him to make him leave Cara alone.

Penny crossed the little bridge over the harbour to the hotel a few minutes later and used the automatic door to make her way inside. The entrance was plush, with marble floors and luxurious décor but it seemed impersonal to her. She went over to reception to ask about having breakfast.

'Good morning,' she said to the woman at the desk. 'I'd like to book in for breakfast this morning, please.'

'Are you staying at the hotel, Madam?' the woman asked with a frown.

'I'm not, but I've eaten breakfast here before as a non-resident.'

'Just a moment, please, while I check our availability.'

Penny tutted, unable to help herself. Surely a hotel this size would have a free table for just one person. She leaned on her stick, trying to keep calm.

'Ah, yes, here you go. I have a table for one. What name should I book it under please?' The young woman looked up at her.

Penny had to think quickly, because she didn't want to give her real name. 'Mrs. Ferguson,' she confirmed, liking the way Hamish's surname sounded.

'Thank you.' The woman put the details in and then picked up her phone to call for someone to come and take Penny to her table.

A minute later, a young man arrived to guide her to the restaurant, but when Penny arrived at her table, she wasn't pleased at all.

'Is this where you mean for me to sit for my breakfast?' she asked. 'In a cramped corner by the toilets, and with no view of the beautiful harbour this hotel is famous for?'

The young man didn't have an answer and looked flustered in the face of Penny's irritation.

'I'll sit here for a moment while you go and get your manager for me, please.'

Penny sat down and waited. Five minutes passed and no one had come to ask her what she wanted for breakfast, or to talk to her about her complaint. She was becoming steadily more agitated, and yet she knew that wasn't good for her. Finally, she stood up and made her way slowly back towards reception, where there was no sign of the member of staff who'd taken her to her table, nor of any other staff in the dining room. She slowed down and took in some of the disgruntled looks on the faces of the other diners. People were looking at their watches and tutting loudly about the delays.

Penny continued on her way, but instead of going up to the desk, she took a seat in a wingback chair in the foyer and settled back into it to listen to what was happening here. She was hungry, but that could wait for a while. She had work to do and didn't want to miss the chance.

As guests walked to and fro, all she heard were complaints.

'They clearly don't have enough staff.'

'A thirty-minute wait for breakfast. Shameful!'

'The staff they do have are obviously run off their feet. But it's no excuse in a hotel like this and charging these rates.'

'We won't be staying here again, that's for sure.'

'How have they got so many good reviews?'

After just half an hour, Penny had heard enough. It was miserable listening to so many unhappy customers, but it sounded like the hotel had only itself to blame for not keeping a closer eye on their manager. She wondered if the owners even knew how bad things were. She stood up slowly, slipped on a pair of sunglasses, and carefully made her way to the exit. As she was going out, Luke was coming in. She'd recognise his smug face anywhere. Well, she hoped he got what was coming to him. These days, everyone wanted to review everything down to the very last detail, and she was sure at least some of the guests she'd overheard this morning would say their piece somewhere.

She ambled back across the bridge and then along the High Street towards the café, where she knew she'd get a good breakfast, and in super quick time. Once she'd placed her order and taken a seat, she sent a message to Hamish asking him to join her and waited for him to arrive. She wasn't happy about what she'd seen at the hotel – far from it. She took no pleasure in seeing another hotel in the village performing so badly, and thankfully, it wouldn't be down to her to make it known to the wider public just how bad things had got there. Luke would get his comeuppance, as people like him always did eventually, and Cara wouldn't have to worry about him in the longer term.

'Hello, love,' Hamish said a little breathlessly when he turned up a few minutes later. 'Where have you been this morning? You should have told me you were going out, you know.'

'I'm sorry I didn't say, but I had a job to do, and I thought you might try to put me off.'

She filled him in on what she'd seen that morning, watching as his eyes widened in surprise at her news.

'Well, I honestly don't know what to say. I'm shocked to hear that about the hotel. It's always been held up as such a bastion of luxury hotels, and the best place to stay in Watersmeet Bridge. It's very sad this Luke fellow has let things get so bad.'

Helen came over with their breakfasts then. After thanking her, they concentrated on eating, but Penny's mind continued to whirl with the events of the morning and the wider implications for the village as a whole.

CHAPTER SIXTEEN

'Morning, Cara. Here's your post for today.' The postie handed her a pile of letters, gave her a quick wave, and turned to go on her way.

Cara sifted through the letters, handing enquiries over to Lily to deal with and keeping the ones that looked like invoices or other official documents for herself. There was a brown A4 envelope with a council stamp on the front. Cara held her breath as she tore it open, praying it contained the paperwork they needed to let them get on with the work on the barn. She pulled the contents out, studied the covering letter, and then shuffled the pages so she could find what she was looking for. And there it was. A temporary certificate giving them approval to carry on working.

'Yippee!' she cried out, to Lily's surprise. 'We've got permission at last.'

'To carry on converting the barn?'

'Yes, thank goodness. They've sent this while they get the formal documentation sorted. That's all thanks to Joe being persistent with them.' Cara held the paperwork lovingly to her chest.

'Oh, that's great news. We'll soon be able to use the barn for courses now then.'

'I must call Joe to ask him if he can come back and carry on with the work he was doing, and then I can try to book Ed in so that he can finish everything off. This is a great start to the day.'

She took her phone outside to the garden and sat down on the bench to call Joe.

'That's wonderful news,' Joe replied when she told him what had happened. 'I can come over this afternoon and carry on with the work, if you like.'

'Oh, would you? That's just what I was going to ask. I'm going to call Ed as well to see when he'll be able to come back and finish off when your work is done.'

'Great idea. I'm so glad it's all coming together. I should be with you just after lunch.'

She rang off, still giddy with delight. Things were going her way again, and she was back on track with her plans. She left a message for Ed and went inside to check how Eileen's crocheting course was going.

The day flew by, and the minute Eileen's course attendees had packed up and left, Cara got straight on to clearing up for Finn's team to come in and get ready for their event. There was no doubt this was a lifeline when she needed it most, but because space was so tight, it made it hard work to keep on top of everything.

She just about had time to check everything was tidy before there was a knock on the back door. Finn appeared, followed by two more chefs, who soon got to work preparing their ingredients for their event that evening. Cara left them to it, not wanting to get in their way, and escaped out into the garden to go and look for Joe. She found him in the barn, still hard at work.

'Hey, Joe. How's it going?' she asked.

He pushed his hair out of his eyes and wiped his brow before turning his gaze on her. 'Not too bad at all. I should only need another couple of days to be finished. Is Ed able to come back after that?'

'I don't know. I had to leave a message when I called him earlier, and he probably hasn't even had a chance to listen to it yet. Hopefully, he'll be able to come back soon though. Thanks for all you're doing. I really appreciate it. You will make sure to give me an invoice for your time and materials, won't you?'

'I will, I promise,' he said with a grin. 'Thanks for booking in my mum to do her course next week. She's excited and scared at the same time, but once she's done one, I think she'll be fine.'

'Yes, I agree. I'll be around to help her if she needs it as well. But the course is already fully booked, so that's a good sign.'

'That's great news. I'll make sure to tell her when I get back. I'd like to book a date with you as well to run a tech course like you suggested, if you're still up for that. And I emailed the networking business team to see if they'd like me to do something for them too.'

'I definitely still want you to run a course for me, please. We can look at the diary while you're here, if you like. And it's really good you contacted the networking team as well. They'd be mad not to take you up on that offer.'

'Talking of which, I don't suppose you're free to have that dinner you offered me tonight, are you? No worries if not.'

She smiled at his attempt to look nonchalant about it. 'I'd love that, Joe. Why don't you come in now and wash up? I'll go and look at the diary while you do that.'

Joe appeared in the reception a few minutes later. There was a definite buzz from the guesthouse kitchen now, as Finn and his team had got to work.

'What's going on?' Joe asked, cocking his head towards the dining room.

'Finn's holding an event here because he's had so many enquiries. It's a birthday dinner, I think. They're handling it all themselves and splitting the profits with me.'

'That sounds like a good deal,' Joe said.

'Yes, I think so, although it's a bit odd to just be renting out the space but not getting involved. Still, I need the money right now, so I can't complain. Come on through to the kitchen and I can see what there is for dinner.'

She took some chicken, leeks, and pancetta from the fridge and turned to Joe. 'How does chicken and pasta in a creamy sauce sound?'

'Fantastic. Can I do anything?'

'Not at all. Have a seat, and I'll find some wine as well. I'm really glad we've got the chance to spend some time together,' she said.

'Me too. This is like our first proper date, isn't it?' he said as he sat down at the table.

Cara smiled as she put a chilled bottle of white wine down on the table. 'Yes, I suppose it is.'

And with those words, they moved on from their recent doubts and into the next phase of their relationship.

Sheila had stayed up late night every night in the days before her course, finishing off her works in progress so she had plenty of examples to show the course attendees. She'd written pages and pages of notes to explain what she'd done, and she'd spent a long time rehearsing what she wanted to say, only to realise she didn't need the notes after all. She'd been dressmaking all her life, so she was confident there was little that would come up that she wouldn't know how to handle. The only worry she had was that she only had the one sewing machine, which might prove difficult in terms of making sure everyone went home with something they'd made during the week.

She'd put a call out via her crafting group and had also asked some of her customers whether they knew anyone who'd be prepared to lend her their sewing machines for a few days, but hadn't heard from anyone as yet. Now it was Saturday, and she was as ready as she ever would be for Monday. She got up early and made her way to her first gardening job of the day, trying to get everything up to date before taking her week away.

'Morning, Gladys. How are you?' she asked her customer when

she arrived an hour later. 'Everything's looking pretty good. Shall I just give it all a good tidy?'

Instead of answering, Gladys flapped her hands excitedly at her. 'I've found you two sewing machines!' she exclaimed.

Sheila's eyes lit up. 'Really? That's marvellous. Thank you so much, Gladys.'

'They're going to drop them in to the guesthouse for you as well. I told them about your offer to do some work for them free of charge in payment, and they were both very grateful.'

Sheila chatted with Gladys for a bit longer, but she was delighted by the good news. How kind everyone was when you needed a bit of help. She sent a message to Cara to let her know and then cracked on with the gardening job. By the time she'd finished and was able to check her phone, there was a reply.

'Three others have already been dropped off too, so it looks like you'll have six now. Such good news!'

Sheila could hardly believe her good fortune and finally began to relax a little in anticipation of running her first course.

Monday came around all too quickly, and the nerves returned with a vengeance.

'Morning, Mum. Are you okay? You're not letting your nerves get the better of you, are you?' Joe asked when he came down for breakfast.

'I woke up so early, and I've just been sitting here worrying,' she confessed.

'Have you done all you can to prepare?' he asked.

'You know I have,' she answered with a little shrug.

'I do know, and so do you, so try not to worry. Have you had something to eat?'

She pulled a face. 'I can't face anything.'

'Well, that's no good. You'll be so busy once you get there that it'll be hours before you can get something to eat, and we don't want you fainting.' He popped a slice of toast in the toaster and reboiled the kettle, emptying her cup and swilling it round.

'Would you be able to bring my sewing machine over for me this morning, please? It's heavy for me to lift on my own.'

'Of course, and I'll come in and check everything's working as you want it to as well.'

'Thanks, love. Once I get going, I know I'll be fine, but it's the not knowing that's worrying me at the moment.'

'I know. This will be me in a couple of weeks, and you'll be the old hand then,' he laughed, handing her a fresh cup of tea and a buttered slice of toast.

'Less of the "old", thank you.'

An hour later, they were on the way to the guesthouse in the van. Sheila had all her materials and notes carefully packed in one bag, and her equipment in the other. The sewing machine was wedged in between the lawnmower and the power washer they used for cleaning patios.

She went in with her bags, hoping she'd find Cara in the reception, but there was no sign of her. She must still be doing the breakfasts, Sheila guessed. Joe arrived carrying the sewing machine and set it down on the floor, out of the way.

'I'll go round the back way and see if Cara needs a hand in the kitchen.'

Sheila took a seat in the comfy armchair in the reception area and waited for Cara to let her know the way was clear for her to set up. She took the opportunity to have one last read-through of her notes.

'Morning, Sheila,' Cara said a few minutes later. She looked puffed out, and Sheila understood what a strain this all was for her.

'Morning, Cara. Is everything okay?'

'Yes, it will be. Joe's helping me to finish tidying the kitchen, but all the guests have finally gone now, so I can show you in and help you set up, if you like.'

Sheila followed Cara into the dining room, and Joe met them there from the kitchen. The sewing machines had all been stored in a corner.

'Show me where you want the tables, and I'll put the sewing machines on them,' Joe said.

For the next twenty minutes, Sheila directed, and Joe and Cara moved tables and chairs round to fit her vision. Joe put a sewing machine on each table, and Sheila put a pack of tools and materials down on each one as well.

'I think that's it,' she said finally, casting one last critical eye over the setup.

'Excellent,' said Cara. 'I'll just finish up in the kitchen, and then I'll be in reception if you need me for anything at all. Lily's also in today, so she'll be able to find me if I have to go elsewhere. It's going to be great, Sheila. I'm sure of that.'

'Thank you both so much for your help,' Sheila told them.

A moment later, the door opened, and one of the attendees came in. 'You must be Sheila,' she said with a smile. 'I'm so looking forward to this.'

Joe had heard back from the networking business team almost immediately, and now it was his turn to run a course in Barnstaple. His mum's course had gone so well the previous week, as he'd known it would, but now he had his own nerves to deal with. Despite all his mum's reassurances that morning, he was still on edge as he made his way over on the bus. The confidence he'd built up from running regular courses in his old job seemed to have temporarily deserted him.

Fortunately, he only needed his laptop and a few leads to run his course. He would send the PowerPoint slides to each attendee by email, together with some details of the services he offered, which saved him from having to carry loads of stuff around with him.

He arrived at the hotel nice and early and was met by the man who'd run the previous meeting, Tom.

'Great to see you again, Joe, and thanks so much for offering to do this. I've put the projector and screen in place for you, and hopefully, you'll have everything you need. I'm just going to make sure tea, coffee, and biscuits are on the way, but I'll be back in a minute.'

Joe got to work plugging in his laptop and charger and connecting it to the projector. Within a few minutes, his PowerPoint was showing perfectly on the screen, and he thanked goodness for his good fortune. Even when you were confident with technology, it didn't always do what you wanted it to.

He turned to cast his eye around the room. He counted twenty places and experienced another moment of nervousness as he considered all those faces staring at him with high expectations. This would be his first time running his own course and he wanted to make a good impression. He took a deep breath and went through his presentation one last time. It was a simple guide to setting up your own free website, and by the end of the session, that was what he aimed for everyone to have achieved. There would be some people who'd take it all in without any difficulty, but there would also be others who'd struggle. He smiled as he thought about Cara's initial aversion to technology. He had her permission to use her as an example to show just how far she'd come, and he was going to use the guesthouse's website and social media to demonstrate how both things had helped to improve their business.

The door creaked open, and he looked up, expecting to see Tom. Instead, he found the first attendees arriving, and he switched straight into course-leader mode.

'Morning. Find yourselves a seat. Tea and coffee are on the way.'

Tom returned shortly afterwards, and the drinks arrived just after that. Joe circulated among the attendees, chatting easily to them and trying to put them at ease. In no time at all, Tom was guiding everyone to sit down, so he could do the introductions, and then Joe was looking out at all those expectant faces. But instead of feeling nervous, he was excited about what he'd teach them that day, and having already spoken to most people, he was comfortable about teaching them what he knew.

By the time they started the first break, he'd gone through the basics of setting up a website on WordPress, and it was time for everyone to set up their laptops ready to get started on their own sites after the break. The rest of the morning flew by, and by lunchtime, there were only a couple of people who were struggling.

'How are you getting on?' he asked one man as they were getting their lunch.

'A bit better after asking you some questions before, but I'd be grateful if you could have a look at what I've done so far.'

Joe went and sat with him to eat his lunch and soon got to the bottom of the problems.

'I think the theme you've chosen is complicating what you need to have on the site for your business. A simpler one, like the one I used as the example, might be easier for you starting out.'

He changed the theme back to an easier one and then showed the man how to change the header and add things to the sidebar.

'That looks a lot better,' he said with relief. 'I was trying to run before I could walk, I think.'

'Just take your time and get to know it for a bit first, and then, when you're more confident, you can start experimenting with other themes.'

It was time for the second half of the day, and Joe returned to the front of the room to encourage everyone else to focus. His task for the afternoon was to introduce everyone to the basics of social media. He used Cara's Facebook page to show them all how straightforward it was to set up, and how they could keep it simple at first.

Soon, the attendees were setting up their own pages and firing questions at him once again.

'Do I really need to have social media pages?' was a constant refrain, so Joe tackled it before the whole group.

'I know a lot of you hate social media, but if you're a small business, you need at least one way of letting people see what you're up to. You can do this with just a website, but you can see how the guesthouse has been able to enhance their static website page with daily updates on their Facebook page as well. Putting up photos of events – or shots of the garden, in this case – are all ways of drawing customers into your business. You don't need to be on every social media platform. I'd advise against that myself. Just choose one and do it well.

Soon, it was time to bring the session to a close. Joe couldn't believe how well things had gone and how positive the attendees had been.

'Thanks very much for coming, and please do make sure you've left me your email address, so I can send you the slides from the session, as well as details of the services I offer, in case any of you want a bit more help after today.'

With a final word from Tom, the event was closed. Tom made his way round picking up feedback forms while Joe answered a few more questions before everyone went on their way.

'These feedback forms are all really positive, Joe, and I wanted to say well done too. It was a great day, and I learnt a lot myself. I think we'll definitely want to do another session in due course.'

Ed had finally been able to free up some time to finish off the plastering work in the barn, estimating it would only take a couple of days to do the whole thing. As always, he'd arrived early, and Cara and Lily had kept him going with cups of tea throughout the first day. He'd also offered to move on to some more decorating on the second floor of the guesthouse while he was there, and although it would be a bit of an inconvenience, Cara had accepted his offer, as the room was free.

For the first time since taking over the guesthouse, Cara's finances were looking healthy. She was gradually reducing the outstanding debt, and she was running weekly courses again, as well as working with Finn to let out the kitchen on a regular basis. The guesthouse was full most weeks, and the courses were helping with that.

She still couldn't quite believe the turnaround in her fortunes as far as the courses were concerned. Almost all the tutors had come back to her after having a bad experience with Luke, and it seemed his attempt to run courses had faltered before it had even had a chance to get going. She really hoped she'd seen the last of him now.

'I heard the hotel's been having problems with really poor service,' Lily had told her just the week before. 'Customers have left some awful reviews online, apparently.'

'That's a surprise, isn't it? Everyone has always said it's *the* best hotel to stay in here, but suddenly, everything's changed. I just can't work out why. But the one good thing in this sorry tale is that Luke has disappeared and is leaving me alone, which, I must admit, I'm relieved about.'

'I wonder if he's been told to lie low for a while, so maybe he's been sent off to one of the other hotels while they sort things out.' Lily looked like she'd given it a lot of thought.

'Let's hope he stays there for the long term, wherever that is.'

So now Cara had only her own business to think about. And the next item on her list was planning how to start using the barn. The proper certificate was through now as well, so there was nothing to stop her, but she needed Joe's help to get the technical setup in place before she could start taking bookings.

She went back outside to see if he was in the garden today. Things had been going well between them since they'd shared dinner together, and her attraction to him was steadily growing. She was ready to move things on to the next level now, by inviting him to spend the night with her, but she didn't know if he felt the same way. With all these thoughts buzzing in her mind, she circled the gardens, but there was no sign of him.

She turned back towards the guesthouse, disappointed not to be able to talk to him, but as she approached the front door, she heard voices.

'Hey, Cara. How are you today?' Joe asked as she pushed open the door.

'I've just been looking for you in the garden. I couldn't remember if you were due to come today or not.' She gave him a warm smile. 'I wanted to talk to you about the barn, if you've got a minute.'

'I do, and I wanted to talk to you about my tech course.'

'Oh goodness, that's in a couple of weeks already, isn't it? Do you need lots of stuff?'

They went back out to the garden and walked round to the small shed where the tools were now being stored since work had started on the barn. Joe told her about his minimal requirements to run the course.

'I'm really looking forward to it after running the one for the networking business team. It went so well they've already asked me to run another one – for the council this time.'

'That's fantastic news,' she said. 'I always knew you could do it though.'

He took her hand and pulled her round the side of the shed, out of sight of anyone who might see them. And then they kissed. Cara held onto him tightly for fear of losing her balance while in the throes of passion. When he pulled back, his eyes were shining bright with his own feelings.

'I can't even remember what it was I wanted to talk to you about now,' she said with a weak laugh.

'The barn, I think, but I'd much rather be kissing you.'

It was in that moment she felt something shift inside her as her heart opened to the idea of having a proper relationship with him. She couldn't bear the thought of not being with him now, and she hoped he felt the same.

'Ah yes, the barn,' she said, suddenly regaining her ability to think as she stepped back. 'I want to add something about it to the website, and to start promoting it on social media. I'll ask Lily to create a flyer for me, but I wondered if you'd help me set things up again initially.'

'Of course. That should be easy enough. When do you think the barn will be ready then?' he asked, pulling on his gardening gloves.

'By the end of this week, I hope. I've already got a couple of book-ings for evening parties. I need to speak to Helen at the café about catering for those. And I want to spread the word in the village about it being a community hub for everyone to use at a reasonable price.'

'Well, I could come round one evening this week, and we could have a go at sorting it out together. What do you think?'

'That sounds great. I can make dinner again as well, if you'd like,' she suggested.

'How about tomorrow then?' he asked, and she smiled at his enthusiasm.

'It's a date,' she agreed.

She left him to his work, already looking forward to the date, but also to getting the website and social media updated with details of the community barn. She was excited by the idea of it and hoped that the community would get on board to make best use of it.

CHAPTER SEVENTEEN

Even though Cara was looking forward to seeing Joe this evening, she was nervous. She'd made a lasagne for dinner so she could just pop it in the oven while they were working and not have to worry about it, and she'd prepared a salad, which was ready and waiting in the fridge. A bottle of Italian red wine was on the table, which had already been laid.

This all left her with just the one remaining problem: what to wear. She'd tried on her whole meagre wardrobe and still couldn't decide what to choose. They'd be working for a bit, and she wanted to be comfortable for that, and not to look too eager for what she hoped might follow, but she also wanted to look good. She sat down on the bed, holding her one and only dress to her chest so she could assess it in the mirror one last time. A quick glance at her watch told her she didn't have much time left, so it was time to make her decision.

Once the dress was on and she was looking at herself in the mirror, things didn't seem so bad. She gave her hair a final brush, berating herself for still not having had her fringe cut, checked her makeup even though it was only ever minimal, and went to slip her shoes on before making her way back to the kitchen.

She'd told Joe to come through when he arrived, which had seemed like a good idea at the time, but now she kept glancing anxiously at the hallway to see if he was there. After checking on the lasagne, she made her way to reception so she could see when he came through the gate. And a few minutes later, there he was. He was wearing a jacket and a smart pair of chinos, which reassured her she'd made the right decision to dress up a bit.

Cara went to the door to wait for him, and he beamed as soon as he saw her. Her heartbeat skipped a little, and goosebumps came up on her skin at the thought of how she felt about him.

'You look gorgeous,' he told her when he reached her.

'Thank you,' she replied, trying not to blush. 'You look very smart as well. Come on in.'

She turned to go inside, but he caught her hand and pulled her into an embrace – only a quick one, as he was holding a beautiful bunch of flowers and a bottle of wine, and his laptop bag was on his shoulder as well.

'Sorry,' he said. 'These are for you.'

She took the flowers, delighted he'd thought to give her some. She led the way down the hallway to the kitchen, where Joe placed the bottle of wine on the table and his laptop bag on the floor.

'Dinner smells amazing,' he said with a smile. 'Thanks for going to all this trouble.'

'No trouble at all. It was really nice to have a reason to cook for a change, and to be able to make the time to do it. Why don't you pour out some wine, and I'll serve?'

They sat down a few minutes later, and silence fell as they tucked into their delicious meal. Cara sensed a bit of awkwardness between them, but on her part, it was only because she had a sense of expectation about the rest of the evening, and she didn't know if Joe felt the same.

'This is really wonderful, Cara.'

'Thank you. It's my mum's old recipe, and it never fails.' She smiled as she said it, happy to have someone to make it for.

After Joe cleared the plates, he got out his laptop so they could do some work. They added a page to the website about the community barn and how to make bookings, and then they moved on to writing some social media posts to let the village know the latest news. Cara sent Joe some recent pictures she'd taken of the barn.

'It's already looking so good, Joe. Thank you. I just hope we can keep this momentum going now.'

'Judging from the interest the other day, I don't think you'll have any problems. Your only stress might come from being too busy.'

'I'm going to ask Lily to work full-time from now on, and perhaps she'll manage the barn as part of her work as well. What do you think?'

They both looked at each other, and suddenly, the moment to stop work and think only about themselves arrived. Joe closed down his laptop and put it away, while Cara poured them out another glass of wine each. She took Joe through to her grandma's old sitting room, wincing a little at how old-fashioned it looked. She made a mental note to ask Ed to redecorate the living quarters as soon as she could afford it.

Joe sat down next to her on the old sofa, and the next thing she knew, she was in his arms, and they were kissing once again as though it was their first time. Everything else was forgotten except their feelings for each other.

'Can I stay with you tonight, Cara?' Joe asked when they finally paused for breath.

'I'd love that,' she told him softly, and they moved to her bedroom. Thankfully, she'd put her clothes away after trying them all on earlier, and they were able to continue what they'd started in the sitting room while lying on her bed.

Joe paused to remove his shirt, and when Cara went to take off her dress, he helped. In no time at all, they were skin to skin, and for Cara, it had never felt so good. Joe was considerate and loving, nothing like her ex at all, and he made her feel special. It was a long time before they finally fell asleep in each other's arms. Cara's final thought as she drifted off to sleep was that she only wished she didn't have to get up so early the next morning.

———

Cara had decided to celebrate the opening of the barn by holding an open day over a Saturday lunchtime for villagers to come along and have a look at what was on offer. Helen at the café had supplied canapés, and she'd bought some sparkling wine and soft drinks from the wine shop in the village as well.

Joe had tidied up the gardens the day before, and they'd set up a gazebo on the lawn next to the barn for the drinks and food. She'd asked Lily to work the whole day to help her get ready for the big event, and to be on hand to help with anything else that might crop up.

A Pilates instructor had contacted Cara about booking a weekly early-evening session, and today, she was going to be doing a taster session for anyone who wanted to have a go. She arrived just before 11 am armed with mats and balls and rollers of various shapes and sizes.

'Hello, Cara. Lovely to see you again,' she said, looking the picture of health and fitness in a crop top and leggings.

'You too, Katie. Do you need a hand to set up at all?'

'No, no. I should be fine. I've invited a couple of my regulars to help me get the session started, and then anyone else can join in if they want to as they arrive.'

Cara wasn't sure anyone would come, but soon they did, and they all seemed to know what to do, so she just pointed them in the right direction. The class was full in no time, much to Cara's delight, and she was confident about getting a regular booking from Katie for the future.

'Cara, sweetheart, this is amazing,' Penny told her a few minutes later.

'It is, isn't it?' she agreed, handing her grandma a glass of wine and a canapé.

'You must be so pleased at the way everything's come together,' Hamish said.

'I am, but it has definitely been hard work getting here, and I couldn't have done it without all of you.'

Joe and Sheila arrived shortly afterwards, and Cara was delighted when he kissed her cheek in front of everyone. They were an official item now, and she couldn't be more delighted. Gradually, all the course tutors arrived as well to take a look at the barn in all its glory.

'This is wonderful, Cara,' Eileen told her. 'What a lovely venue for us to hold our courses in. I can't wait.'

Cara introduced Eileen to Sheila then, knowing they'd have a lot in common. The Pilates session finished, and the attendees all came out to have a drink and join the festivities.

'Hello, Cara. I'm Jacqui, the line-dancing lady. We spoke the other day on the phone.'

Cara put out her hand. 'Lovely to meet you. Have you had a chance to look at the barn to see if it would work?'

She led Jacqui across the lawn, and they looked at the barn together.

'This looks great,' Jacqui confirmed. 'I have to hold classes at the church hall in Lynford at the moment, which is fine, but it's a bit of a way to go, so it would be lovely to offer something nearer to home.'

'That's great news. Well, let me get you a drink, and I hope you'll stay and chat to people while you're here.'

Zoe and Ed turned up next, and she shared a hug with them both. 'It's so good to see you guys. Thanks so much, Ed. You and Joe have done such a brilliant job.' She waved at Joe, and he came over so she could introduce him.

'Joe, this is my best friend, Zoe, and Ed you know already.'

Joe shook hands with them both. 'I hear congratulations are in order,' he said. 'You'll be able to have a great party in the barn now.'

'We definitely will,' Zoe confirmed. 'I can't wait to start planning everything.'

Ed pulled nervously at the collar of his shirt as if the very thought of party-planning made him ill.

'I've had a couple of party bookings, actually. It's amazing how many ideas people have for using the barn that I'd never have come up with on my own.'

Cara glanced round the garden to check everyone was okay and was thrilled to see so many villagers had come out to support her.

'You've done such a brilliant job,' Joe told her as she turned back to look at him. 'I always knew you'd save the guesthouse.'

'Did you really?' she asked. 'I'm still waiting for something to go wrong at any minute. I wish I had more confidence in myself.'

'You definitely should. I don't think you could have done much better than this.'

Cara knew she was falling in love with Joe in that moment, but she didn't want to voice her feelings right then, in front of everyone. She just hoped everything continued to run smoothly for her, and between them both.

She said goodbye to Zoe, who had to get off to The Bistro to let Olivia and Finn come along and see the barn.

'I'll see you soon for a catch-up,' Zoe said as she kissed her good-bye. 'And Joe is wonderful,' she whispered with a wicked grin.

Cara watched her friend go with a huge smile on her face and wondered how she'd got so lucky to find herself here, with everything working out for her. She'd never imagined such good fortune in all her wildest dreams. Today was the culmination of months of hard work, and she knew all too well how fragile her success was. But she was determined to keep working hard, and with Penny and Hamish, and Zoe and Joe beside her, she was more confident now than she'd ever been that she could make it work.

Monday morning rolled round quickly, and with Harriet finally running her ceramics course, it was shaping up to be another very busy day at the guesthouse. Cara had asked Lily to work the whole day, and she was going to be covering reception and Harriet's course while Cara focused on managing the barn.

Once breakfast was over, she took her laptop outside to sit in the barn and think about how she wanted to promote it from here onwards. Joe was off running a course for the council over in Barnstaple, so he'd shown her how to add photos to the website, and some other tasks, so she could start doing it all herself.

She brought up the website and had another look at all the pages, pleased with the decluttering Joe had already put in place, as well as the updating work Lily had started doing. When she spotted the placeholder page for the breakfasts, she remembered some photos she had on her phone of their breakfast range and began by adding those in. Then she added some photos of the open day they'd just had for the barn together with details of how to book the venue. She had a booking for a course for the coming week, when Joe would be running his website course in the dining room, but after that, there were still quite a few gaps in the barn's diary. She wanted to get some more bookings during the day, and to encourage more in the evenings as well. It was going to be a lot of hard work, but with Lily's help, she thought she could pull it off.

After a couple of hours of staring at her computer, Cara stood up and went outside to look at the garden, desperate for a bit of fresh air and some time to relax. She wandered round the pristine flower beds, enjoying the sight of all the summer flowers coming up. She spotted some vibrant purple geraniums coming up now in the borders, alongside the irises and crocosmias, and the riot of colour and fragrance was just heavenly – exactly what she needed to take her mind off everything.

As she stood there soaking in the joys of the garden, a man came up to the gate and stepped inside. He was wearing a suit, and her heart sank at what his arrival could mean. He was smiling, though, so she was hoping he had good intentions.

'Hello,' he said when he reached her.

'Hello. What can I do for you? I'm Cara Rafaelli, the owner.' It was the first time she'd used the phrase, and she was surprised at how easily it tripped off her tongue.

'Hello, Cara. Good to meet you. I'm Stephen Nelson. I own the hotel at the other end of the village. I believe you've met Luke Johnson, who was the manager of our hotel until recently.'

Cara's face fell. 'Please don't tell me you've come to harass me into selling. I really thought I'd heard the last of all this.'

'Actually, I'm here to apologise for all his harassment, and to reassure you that you've seen and heard the last of him. We had to let him go recently, because we'd had so many complaints about the hotel and his behaviour.'

Cara's face paled. 'Oh my goodness, I'm so sorry. I appreciate you coming to tell me, but I really am so sorry to hear that.'

'Thank you. It's going to take us a while to get our reputation back, but we're going to do so by concentrating on our core business, which means we won't be running any more courses. I've made sure all the tutors have been paid what they're owed, and I've advised them to contact you in the future. I saw you were opening this barn as well, so I figure you'll be looking for as much business as you can get.' He gave her a kind smile, and she returned it.

'Thank you for that. I really hope you can get things back on track and if there's ever anything I can do to help, you only have to ask.'

He put out his hand, which she shook firmly. Cara watched him go, amazed at what he'd said about Luke but relieved she wouldn't have to worry about it all any more. She was glad all the tutors had been paid as well, and she hoped she'd hear from them all in due course.

She made her way back into the guesthouse to see how Lily was getting on, and to tell her the news.

'How's it been going this morning?' she asked as she put her laptop bag down next to the desk.

'It's been crazy-busy, Cara, I can't lie. I feel like I've only just about managed to keep on top of everything.'

'You should have messaged me. I would have come straight back to give you a hand.'

'I know, but you were busy, and I didn't want to bother you on my first day working full-time. I'm sorry. I think I've got things under control now, but there have been so many messages from tutors, and Harriet has needed quite a bit of hand-holding.'

'Is she okay now? Shall I go in and check on her?'

'I think she'd appreciate that.'

'I have news about the tutors, but I'll tell you when I come out again. Don't worry about dealing with those messages for now. I'll handle them. Give me a few minutes, and then you should go and get some lunch. Thanks for all you've done this morning.'

Cara slipped into the back of the dining room, where everything seemed to be going well. All heads were down, and the attendees were obviously focused on what they were doing. Harriet was going round the group giving advice and encouragement as they worked on shaping their clay by hand into small pots.

Cara coughed discreetly, and Harriet looked up.

'Is everything going okay?' Cara asked quietly when the older woman came over.

'Yes, all good now. It was a bit chaotic at first, but everything's going okay now. I'll have to take everything home with me each day to fire things in the kiln, but that's fine. It's going to be a matter of learning as I go.'

Cara nodded, knowing exactly how that felt. She left Harriet and her students to it and went back out to reception to fill Lily in on the latest news about Luke.

Joe had led another successful course for staff from the district council this time, and as the day drew to a close, he was starting to think that he might enjoy doing more of these sessions. Tom from the networking business team had been really helpful in spreading the word about his courses, and he already had another one booked in the south of the county the following month. He'd have to stay overnight for that one because it really was a bit too far for him to travel in one day, but he was excited at the prospect of it.

The last person left, and it was just him and Tom clearing up again.

'Another great session, Joe, with lots of great feedback. How did you think it went?' Tom asked.

'Yes, I really enjoyed it, and I felt a bit more confident this time. I've got another session lined up already, thanks to you spreading the word. I really appreciate it, Tom.'

'No worries at all. Have you thought about doing this as a full-time job? You've got really good presentation skills, and there are plenty of jobs crying out for someone with your digital knowledge. There's even one at the district council.'

Joe stopped and considered his reply. 'A few months ago, I would have jumped at the chance, but I'm pretty settled in Watersmeet Bridge now, and I have enough work of my own to keep me busy.' He was intrigued by the thought of it though.

'Well, there's no harm in taking a look at the job. If you change your mind, it's up on their website.'

They finished packing up, and Joe made his way back to the bus stop to return home. He'd already been thinking about getting a car if he was going to be doing this much travelling, but it would be a big investment when his income was so inconsistent at the moment.

Once he was on the bus, he reflected on what Tom had said about taking a full-time job as well. He quickly found the district council's website and took a look at the job he'd mentioned. It sounded right up his street, but it was based in Barnstaple, and it involved travelling all around North Devon. He could definitely do the job, but would he want to? Joe closed the website, put his phone in his pocket and stared out the window for some distraction. He didn't need this right now, just when everything was going so well with Cara, and his own business was taking off. He was happy as he was... wasn't he?

The only good thing about taking a permanent position was that he'd know he had some regular income coming in, and he'd also know exactly how much it was going to be. But then he wouldn't be able to help his mum with the gardening business, and his own business would fail immediately. That was all the practical stuff, but what about his heart? Cara was steadily taking more and more of it, and what was more, he was very willing to give it to her. He didn't think he could stand to be away from her now.

The bus trundled down the hill towards Lynford, and he smiled at the thought of being home soon. He'd come to love Watersmeet Bridge in no time at all, and he enjoyed being part of the new community. He wouldn't want to have to start all over again somewhere new.

He jumped off the bus and started the walk through the village back home, forgetting all about the job for the time being. It was a fine summer's evening, and he was looking forward to seeing Cara and telling her all about his day, as well as finding out how everything was going for her.

As he approached his favourite viewing spot, he saw she was already there, sitting on the bench looking out across the bay. He stopped to study her for a moment – her long, wavy hair, her calm, beautiful face, and just the way she held herself with so much inner strength. He loved her, he realised, and that certainty made him both excited and nervous about laying his own heart so openly on the line. They had a power over each other now, if she felt the same way he did, and that could be both good and bad.

Sensing him there, perhaps, she turned to look at him and gave him a smile that was full of love, leaving him in no doubt as to her feelings for him.

She waved, and he went over, dropping down onto the bench

next to her. He leaned towards her for a kiss and put everything he was feeling into it.

'Hey,' she said finally. 'Is everything okay?'

'Yes. I missed you today, that's all.'

She blushed then, and his love for her deepened even further. 'I missed you too.'

'How's your day been, anyway?' he asked, tucking a wild piece of her hair behind her ear.

'A bit better than yesterday for Harriet's course. It's hard, running a ceramics course without any pottery wheels or a kiln on site, but she's managing okay. I don't know if she'll want to run another one from the guesthouse dining room. We'll just have to see. I'm going to have to employ Lily full-time, I think, now that the barn's up and running – and of course, that depends on us continuing to do well.' She sighed.

'Try not to let it overwhelm you. You're doing okay so far, and you've only just opened the barn.'

She leaned against him, and he put his arm around her. 'It really helps having you to talk things over with, and to reassure me.'

'Have you got anything on in the barn this evening?'

'Yes. It's the first Pilates class, so I want to be around to make sure that everything's okay for them. I shouldn't need to do it in the future, but as this is the first one ...' She glanced at her watch. 'I'd better get back, actually. What are you getting up to tonight?'

'I need to catch up with Mum to see how the gardening's gone today and what she needs me to do tomorrow, but I can come over later, if you'd like?'

'I'd like that very much,' she said and gave him a soft kiss goodbye.

CHAPTER EIGHTEEN

Cara had planned for Joe to run his course in the barn so the photography tutor could have the dining room for the beginners' photography course. She was looking forward to having him around all week even though he was going to be busy. Their relationship was developing quickly, and she missed him whenever they were apart. She wanted to tell him she loved him, but she was still afraid to bare her soul. There was no denying it any more now on her part, and she was desperate to know whether he felt the same.

Now they'd completed their first full week with courses in both the barn and the dining room, she and Lily had a better handle on how their routine needed to change. She was keen to ask Lily to work full-time permanently, but she worried in case the finances wouldn't stretch to that long-term. She'd been thinking of offering her a full-time contract just until the end of the summer for now, with a promise to review things then, when she'd have a better view of the situation.

Lily was on bedroom-cleaning duty this morning, and Ed was decorating the last bedroom on the second floor. Cara was in reception and managing both courses. Luckily, the photographer hadn't needed any help, and she didn't think Joe would either, but she was on hand just in case. She'd brought her paperwork up to date over the weekend, and she dealt with bookings as and when they came in now, so there was very little else for her to worry about.

She heard the sound of footsteps on the stairs and prepared to direct guests to the right course, and to answer any questions. Some of the guests weren't attending courses, so they might have other questions to deal with too.

'Good morning,' she called as they appeared one by one in the reception area. She was glad she'd put up a sign pointing to the photography course, as half the guests disappeared off that way. Most of the others were looking for Joe's course, so she pointed them in the direction of the barn.

'Can you recommend a good walk for us this morning, please? Nothing too strenuous though.'

Cara turned her attention to the remaining guest and told them about the coastal path leading out of the village.

Soon, she was alone again. Now would be a good time to go out and get supplies while everything was quiet. She grabbed her phone and her bag, let Lily know she was going out, and set off for the village. Just as she was approaching the gate, she saw Tom from the networking business team coming the other way.

'Hi, Tom. How are you?'

'I'm fine, Cara, and really glad to see your business doing so well.'

'Thanks. Yes, we seem to have turned things round – at least for now. What can I do for you, anyway?'

'I'm here to see Joe, actually. I told him about a job with the council the other day, and I want to find out if he's going to apply for it like I suggested. He's so good at these courses, and he really knows his stuff, so this job is just right for him.'

Cara was so stunned to hear those words she couldn't think of anything to say. She just stood there nodding as if it were the most normal thing in the world to hear that Joe had been considering taking a job but hadn't told her about it.

'Right,' she said, finally finding her voice. 'He's in the barn this week.' She pointed it out to Tom before saying goodbye.

Cara made it to the bench across the road and sank onto it as she tried to make sense of what Tom had just told her. Joe hadn't mentioned anything about this job opportunity, but that didn't mean he had applied for it. Or maybe he really hadn't, and she was just thinking the worst. What was she going to do with this information? She'd just have to ask him and see what he said, she supposed, but in her heart, she was afraid to do that, because she wasn't sure she'd like his answer.

She stared out to sea, paralysed by her thoughts and her own inaction. This had always been her greatest fear – that she'd fall in love with him and give him her heart, only for him to up and leave her, and for her heart to be broken all over again. She took in a deep breath. She could let that happen again, or, this time, now that she was stronger in herself and had more self-confidence, she could confront this head-on. She loved him, and she didn't want him to go. All she had to do was to find the confidence to tell him that.

She stood up and turned to make her way into the village, conscious of time passing and the need to get back soon. She completed all the jobs on her checklist in robotic fashion, all the while trying to deal with the jumbled thoughts milling around her brain. What if she told Joe how she felt but he didn't feel the same way? What if his work was more important to him than the life he'd been building here? What if his mum could now manage without him and Sheila encouraged him to go? What if, what if, what if, on a constant repeat, until she thought she was losing her sanity.

She found herself back at the gate to her own guesthouse, afraid to go in and deal with everything. But eventually, she pushed the gate open anyway, straightened her shoulders, and lifted her head high. She could deal with this. She would have to, one way or another. But should she bring it up to Joe or wait for him to tell her?

She glanced at the barn as she went by. The door was open, and she could see Joe at the front of the class teaching his students something in his friendly, confident, open way. She only hoped he'd be the same way with her when they had the conversation about their future – a conversation that would now come round much sooner than she'd ever expected.

Joe was pleased with how the first day of his course had gone, but he was worried about Cara's reaction to him when he went to see her afterwards. She'd been distinctly cool, and he couldn't work out why. In the end, he'd just left without making any plans to see her that evening, thinking she might just need some time on her own.

He'd been surprised to see Tom as well, since he hadn't said he'd be coming. Not only that, but Tom had come specifically to put pressure on him to apply for the job with the council, and he still hadn't really decided whether that was something he wanted to do now he had so much at stake.

He made his way home and was glad to see his mum already there.

'Hello, love. How did the course go today?'

'Really well, thanks.'

'You don't look very pleased. Is everything okay?'

'Not really, no. I need your advice about something.'

Joe told his mum all about the job and the pressure from Tom for him to apply for it.

'Hmm. Well, it does sound like a good opportunity, but, as you've said, there's a lot more at stake for you now. What would you stand to lose if you did go for it?'

'Well, I'd be leaving you in the lurch, for one thing. I don't know if you could manage the gardening business on your own.'

'You know, though, that I would never stand in your way if this was something you really wanted, so that one doesn't count. What else?' she pressed.

'Well, I'm just getting my tech business off the ground and

settling into life here. I don't really want to have to move somewhere else and start all over again where I don't know anyone.'

This time, his mum rolled her eyes. 'Anything else?'

'Cara,' he said quietly.

'At last. Could you stand to lose her at this point? Because she can't go anywhere else. Her future is here.'

'I couldn't stand to lose her, no. But I am intrigued by this job.'

'Why? What would you gain from leaving here to go and do that job?'

Joe gave that one some real thought and realised he didn't know. The main reason he'd wanted to get a permanent job originally was so he'd have a regular income coming in to help his mum out if she needed it, but what with the gardening business and her fledgling dressmaking company doing so well, none of that seemed to apply any more.

'Things have changed since I was first looking, and to be honest, you don't need my help any more. You're doing perfectly well on your own.'

His mum smiled. 'Joe, I love how protective you are of me, but you're right. I am managing on my own, so when you make this decision, it won't be about you needing to help me any more. It should be about what's best for you.'

'You're right, Mum. Thanks. What's for tea? I'm starving.' He'd have to give it all some more thought when he was on his own, but for now, he needed to think about something else.

Back in his room later, he wondered why Cara had been so cool with him earlier. What might have upset her? He sent her a quick text.

Hey, how did your day go today? You didn't seem very happy earlier. Is everything okay?

He saw she'd read his message, and he waited a few minutes expecting her to reply, but when she didn't, that was when he knew something was up. He wanted to go and see her and have things out, but part of him was afraid to know what he'd done wrong.

Except he didn't think he'd done anything wrong, so maybe it was something else that was worrying her, and nothing to do with him at all.

He pulled on a hoodie and went back out to the kitchen.

'I'm just going round to see Cara,' he said. 'I won't be long.'

'Okay, love. Have a good evening.'

He made his way through the village towards the guesthouse, noticing how busy the High Street was in the evenings. The Bistro was full, and it looked like everyone was having a great time in there. He still wanted to go, and he'd love to take Cara on a proper date there sometime.

There were a couple of other places doing good business too – a newly opened wine bar, and a desserts-only venue. He wasn't sure whether they'd have the staying power to be there next season, but it was good to see them all having a try.

He arrived at the guesthouse and turned in at the gate, crossing the garden and pushing open the main front door. He didn't know whether he should have let Cara know he was coming in case he surprised her by just turning up.

I'm in reception. Is it okay if I come through?

He heard a door open along the corridor, and suddenly, Cara was standing in front of him in her pyjamas, not looking best pleased to see him.

'What are you doing here, Joe? It's late.'

'I'm sorry I didn't let you know. I was worried about you and thought I'd just come over and see you. I'll go if you'd rather be on your own.' He turned back towards the front door, unable to hide his disappointment at her rejection.

'No. Look, you'd better come in as you're here now.'

She'd already started walking back along the corridor by the time he'd turned round, leaving him in no doubt as to her mood. She went into the old sitting room and sat down in the armchair.

'I've obviously done something to upset you,' he began, 'and I'd rather know what it is so we can move forward, hopefully.'

Cara didn't know where to begin with what she needed to say. She still couldn't believe what Tom had told her, and the longer she'd stewed on it, the angrier and more upset she'd become. Now she'd have to be honest and tell Joe what was on her mind.

'You'd better sit down.' She waved him towards the sofa. 'I saw Tom today before he came in to see you,' she said once he'd taken a seat.

Joe swallowed but didn't say anything, so she waited. 'What did you two talk about?' he asked finally, when it was clear she wasn't going to enlighten him otherwise.

'He told me he was there partly to persuade you to take the job he'd told you about.' She struggled to finish the sentence without starting to cry.

Joe's face fell. 'You have every reason to be cross with me for not telling you about it, but it's not a done deal. I haven't applied for the job, because although it sounds like a good position, I'm not sure I want it. I didn't want to tell you about it, because I knew it would upset you if you thought I was looking for a permanent job elsewhere. Which I wasn't.'

It was Cara's turn to feel bad now. 'So you haven't applied yet ... but are you going to then?'

'I don't know. I talked it over with my mum earlier and realised she isn't dependent on me any more. But I'm settled here, and I think you and I have something good going. So I wasn't looking for something like this, but now I know about it, I feel curious about the opportunity. I suppose it would be great to have my cake and eat it.'

Cara was pleased he felt they had something good going, but she still didn't feel that reassured by what he'd said. 'So even though you think that you and I "have something good going", it's not good enough for you to want to stay here and not go elsewhere when a job comes up.' She'd done air quotes around his words and felt petty, but at the same time, she was hurt.

'What I'm trying to say is, I don't want to leave here. I want to be with you, to commit to what we've started. That's important to me. But at the same time, I'm interested in this job. If I were going to apply, it would be on the basis of doing it differently to the way they imagine it, because I want to stay here.'

Her anger disappeared in an instant. 'I want to commit to our relationship too, because I've fallen in love with you, Joe. I tried hard not to, but in the end, I couldn't help it.' She released a sob, and then the tears flowed.

And Joe was by her side then, hauling her into his arms while she cried her heart out.

'I'm sorry, Cara, for giving you the impression I was planning to leave. Well, that was Tom's fault, actually, but still, I'm sorry. You need to talk to me when you're worried about something you think I've done, not just hold it all inside.'

'I know, but I've been let down so many times, it's just my natural instinct to expect that to happen again and again.'

'It's been hard for me to let my guard down as well, but you've still found a way into my heart. I love you too, you know.'

She looked up at him in surprise. 'I didn't expect you to say it back to me.'

'What kind of idiot would that make me?' he said with a laugh.

They kissed softly then, and he wiped away her tears.

'I'm sorry for jumping to conclusions,' Cara said after a minute. 'I do think you need to be more open with me though. I can only understand what you're thinking if you tell me.'

'I know, and I'm sorry I didn't. I guess I've just got out of the habit of sharing my news with anyone other than my mum.' He rolled his eyes. 'Sorry, that sounds pretty lame, but I hope you know what I mean. I guess I was flattered when Tom told me about the job, but I didn't expect him to put pressure on me to apply for it. It's full-time and based in Barnstaple, with travel all round North Devon, so I definitely don't want to take the job with that level of responsibility.'

'But you've obviously looked at it and given it some thought,' Cara replied.

'Well, yes, I looked at it out of interest, but when I saw all the details, I knew that wasn't what I wanted.'

'But you want something more than what you're already doing?' She was struggling to understand exactly what it was he was looking for.

'Yes, I think so ... Oh, I don't know. I'm just not sure.'

'It sounds like you need to do a lot more thinking about it. Maybe you should give them a call and have an informal chat?'

'That sounds like a good idea. I should probably get off, as I've got the second day of the course to run tomorrow. Are we okay now? I hate to leave after such an upset evening.'

'No, it's okay. It'll do you good to have an early night. I'll see you tomorrow, but thanks for coming over to see me tonight.'

They kissed goodbye, and Cara went straight to bed, but she lay awake for ages trying to make sense of all Joe had told her. She ought to be most delighted about the fact he'd told her he loved her and wanted to be with her, but there was an underlying restlessness to him she didn't understand. And she knew that it wasn't going to be easy for him to feel fulfilled by his work and at the same time, ready to make a commitment to staying in Watersmeet Bridge. She had no influence over his decision either. This was something he was going to have to sort out on his own.

Joe took Cara's suggestion on board and decided to give the council a call about the job the next day. He had to focus on the course first, though, and avoid getting distracted by anything else. He waited until his lunch break, and while his course attendees were busy eating and chatting, he made the call.

'Hi. My name's Joe Harris, and I'm calling for more information about the Digital Trainer job you've advertised on your website, please.'

'Joe Harris? Have you done some work for Tom Stewart from the networking business team?'

'Yes, that's right. He told me about the job, actually.'

Joe chatted with the man on the phone for about fifteen minutes, and by the end of the conversation, it was clear they really wanted someone who could work full-time, was based in Barnstaple, and had their own car to get around in. When Joe returned for the afternoon session of his course, he had a lot to think about but no time to do so right then.

Fortunately, the afternoon flew by, and with no sign of Cara, he made his way out along the coastal path to think about what to do. He'd already weighed up the pros and cons so much when he was lying awake last night, but it still didn't make the decision any easier for him. If he applied for the job and got it, he'd have to leave Cara behind, and even if she agreed to continue their relationship, it would be difficult to maintain it when he was no longer in the village. He'd also be abandoning his mum, and that thought ate at his conscience. So, bearing all that in mind, why couldn't he shake his interest in this job?

A permanent job would give him the same financial security he'd had before, doing a job he was good at, and one he'd enjoy. But if he carried on as he was, he could build on his relationship with Cara, support his mum, and continue building his own businesses in a place he'd come to love. And wasn't that why he'd left his previous job and his life in London anyway?

He spotted a bench and sat down to take in the view and some sea air. He'd miss being here and being able to take walks like this, he thought. In fact, the whole idea of having to move somewhere new again filled him with dread. He knew what he needed to do in his heart, but his head was telling him to apply for the job anyway, and he didn't know how to get past that.

He was so deep in thought that he jumped when his phone rang.

'Hi, Joe. It's Richard from the council. I've been thinking about our conversation this morning, and I really would like you to apply for the job, but I sensed some difficulties on your part with some of our requirements. So I'd like to ask you to apply anyway, but to explain in your covering letter what you'd be looking for in an ideal world. It might not come to anything – I can't promise we can meet your needs – but I'd hate to have discouraged you from applying when you come so highly recommended. And I enjoyed talking with you this morning as well.'

'It's really good of you to come back to me with that suggestion, Richard. Thanks. I'll get something off to you tonight.'

Joe rang off with a smile and stood up to make his way back home. Maybe luck was on his side after all.

After a quick hello to his mum, he settled himself down in his room and opened his laptop. His CV was pretty much up to date anyway, so he was able to review it quickly and save it before turning his attention to his covering letter. Once he got started, he found he was able to compose it easily, explaining that what he'd really like would be a contract for a regular amount of part-time work per month, and that although he'd be happy to travel around the county, he wanted to maintain his base in Watersmeet Bridge. So not full-time and not based in Barnstaple. He couldn't really see them ever agreeing to his demands, but he had nothing to lose, so he went ahead with it anyway, not giving any more thought as to why he even wanted this job so much when it would completely upend the new life he'd been working so hard to build.

He then had to copy and paste his whole CV into the council's application form – a long and tedious process – but once that was done, he was finished. He copied everything into an email, and before he could change his mind, he sent it off to Richard at the council.

He stared at his computer for a good few minutes wondering if he'd done the right thing. But in the end, he decided they could only say no, and if they said yes, then he might well be able to have his cake and eat it after all. The job would give him some security while he and his mum navigated the choppy waters of running their own businesses, and it would allow him to stay in Watersmeet Bridge. If it all worked out, he really would have the best of all possible worlds. He just had to hope Cara would forgive him for not telling her about the job originally, and that she'd be pleased if she found out that he was staying here for good.

As he packed his computer away to go back out to the kitchen and help his mum with dinner, he marvelled at the way his life had changed so much for the better in such a short space of time. If this job worked out for him, he'd have everything he could have ever wanted.

CHAPTER NINETEEN

Cara had been ruminating on the situation between her and Joe ever since he'd come round to see her that night. She ought to have been thrilled to find out he loved her, but instead, she was just worried about where things would go between them. In essence, he seemed to be saying that although he loved her, he still wasn't happy with his life in Watersmeet Bridge, and that if the right job came along, he'd be off like a shot. Obviously, that thought didn't make her happy at all. She needed a solid commitment from him.

So she'd stayed out of his way as much as she could, sending Lily to check on the course instead and keeping to the guesthouse, where she wouldn't have to talk to him. She was being a coward, and she knew it, but she needed to get things clear in her head. That was proving easier said than done though. How could he love her and want to be with her but still be considering applying for a full-time job based in Barnstaple and travelling all over the county?

She muttered to herself as she went through the paperwork, but when she heard the front door open, she pulled herself together and focused on her work.

'Hey, Cara. How are you? I thought I'd come and see you to stop you avoiding me as you've been doing all week.' Joe smiled at her to soften his words, but she knew he'd seen right through her.

'Well, I can't lie. I have been avoiding you, but I've had a lot on my mind, and I was hoping it would be easier to deal with if I didn't have to speak to you as well.' She looked at him defiantly, willing him to argue with her, because she was in the mood to argue back if he pushed her.

'And have you managed to deal with it?' he asked.

She stood up then, so that they were face-to-face. 'No, I haven't, for your information. I'm still just as confused as I was the other day.'

'Do you fancy a quick walk, then, to get some air?'

She hesitated, knowing they should try to sort things out, but not really feeling up to the conversation. 'Okay, let's go,' she said, finally making up her mind. She grabbed her bag and followed him out the front door, looking for Lily on the way. When she saw her, she gave her a quick wave, and Lily came over.

'I'm just popping out for a few minutes. I won't be long. Will you be okay?'

'Of course. See you soon.'

They were soon on the coastal path again and walking away from the village.

'So do you want to talk about how you're feeling now?' Joe asked as they headed up the hill, towards the cliffs overlooking the bay.

'I'm cross with you, Joe. That's the bottom line. You say you love me, but at the same time, you're talking about applying for jobs that will take you away. That's not fair, and you weren't honest with me about it either. I hate not knowing where I stand with you.'

'I accept all that, and I have apologised for not telling you about the job. But I hadn't applied for it at that point, I'd only heard about it. Being interested in it and applying for it are two different things. And as I said – and meant – I do love you, and you're a large part of why I felt unsure about applying, because I don't want to leave you. As it happens, I took your advice and gave them a call about the job to find out more.'

She turned her head to look at him directly then for the first time since they'd left the village. 'And what did they say?'

Joe filled her in on both conversations. 'So last night, I sent off my application, clearly stating I was only looking for a contract for part-time work, and that I'd want to be based here.'

'And if they say no?'

'That will be the end of it. And to be honest, that's what I'm expecting them to say. I'm asking a lot of them, really, but this is what I want.'

'And what if another job comes up? Are you really committed to staying here for the long term, Joe, or will you always have it in the back of your mind to leave?'

Joe swiped his hand through his curly hair, and she realised this was really the crux of the matter for her. 'It's not about leaving, Cara. I've told you that. But I guess I'll always be interested in jobs that give me more security financially than I have now.'

'Okay. I understand that vulnerable feeling, of course I do. But my answer to that has been to throw everything I have into making things work here so I can keep the guesthouse going. I know it won't ever be easy, but I have no choice but to try. And that's what your mum has done as well. Both of us have made Watersmeet Bridge our home, so we're invested in making our lives here work for us. You have the same chance to do that as well, and your businesses seem to be going from strength to strength now, so wouldn't it make more sense to pour all your energy into your life here, rather than spreading yourself so thinly by trying to find work outside the area?'

They reached the bench, and Joe took a seat, looking like he really needed it after all Cara had said.

'What you've said does make sense, and maybe you're right. I don't know why I'm so drawn to this other work when I have every-thing I need right here. It's something I've asked myself again and again. It's not a question of commitment. I think it's just that I'm always worried about turning down work in case one day I don't have any. But now I have a roof over my head and regular work coming in, I should be able to let that feeling go. But it's a hard one to shake.'

Cara took his hand, finally understanding his vulnerability but not knowing how to reassure him further that everything would be okay.

Cara was up early the next day to make sure everything was running like clockwork in the barn before the day's courses got underway. There was less than a week left until Zoe and Ed's engagement party, and there was still so much to do. She threw her dressing gown round her shoulders and shivered as she made her way to the bathroom. It felt unusually cold for the time of year, and she brushed her hand across the nearest radiator, expecting the heating to have come on. The radiator was stone-cold, which stopped her in her tracks. By contrast to the cold, a bead of sweat broke out on her forehead at the thought of what this could mean. She stepped outside her bedroom, looked up and down the corridor to make sure no guests were lurking, and rushed to the next nearest radiator. When she found this one was also off, she tried to suppress a rising feeling of panic.

She rushed back to her en suite to check the hot water, and once again, there wasn't any. Now the panic overwhelmed her. She threw on some clothes and went downstairs to check the boiler. There was a red light flashing on it when she pulled the panel on the front of it down, and no light in the little window. That didn't seem right. She'd have to call Penny – there was nothing else for it – even though it was really early. She simply didn't have time to try to find the instructions for the boiler when she had breakfasts to make and courses about to start.

'Gran, I'm sorry to ring so early, but I've got a bit of a problem,' she said when Penny answered.

'Okay, try not to panic. I'll send Hamish round to have a look, but try pressing the little button above the red light to see if that will reset it.'

Cara went back to the airing cupboard while her gran was on the phone and tried pressing the button, but the red light remained stubbornly lit up. Hamish arrived just as she was emerging from the cupboard, so she said goodbye to her gran to talk to him.

'Don't worry, lass. We'll get it sorted. I think we just need to reset the pilot light.'

Cara took some reassurance from Hamish's confident air and crossed her fingers while he fiddled with a dial on the front of the boiler, turning and holding it to see if the pilot light would come back on. She held her breath as he let go of the dial and the light flickered back into life.

'Oh, thank goodness. Hamish, you're a lifesaver,' she cried, wrapping her arms around him in gratitude.

'It's okay for now, but you should probably get someone in to look at it sooner rather than later in case it's a sign of a bigger problem.'

Her heart sank. That would be the last thing she needed right now. Hamish left, and she ran through to the kitchen to get started on the breakfasts, now running half an hour late. Guests were already coming in, and most of them looked grumpy.

'Why's there no hot water, Cara? And it's so cold.' They all had the same complaint, and now their breakfast was going to be late as well.

'All I can do is apologise,' she said, 'but it should warm up soon and I'm making a start on breakfasts now.'

'Is there anything we can do to help?' one lady asked, and Cara could have cried. The next thing she knew, all the guests were carrying things through from the kitchen to the dining room – cereals, juices, pastries, and bread for toast were relayed along a chain and delivered to the main table.

Cara cracked on with the hot breakfasts, and soon, everything was calm once again as guests took their seats and enjoyed their food.

Cara made sure to visit each table to check they all had everything they needed, including hot drinks.

'Thank you all so much for your help this morning,' she announced with glistening eyes. 'You've all been marvellous.' And she really meant it.

For the first time ever, she cleared the tables but left all the washing up in the kitchen to be dealt with later. She messaged Lily, asking if she could come in earlier to give her a breather so she could at least have a shower, and Lily was soon on her way.

'Oh, Lily, thank you so much.' She gave Lily the rundown of her morning and explained she hadn't even had time to check that everything was in place for the courses.

'Look, I can do that while you go and get yourself ready.'

So Cara dashed off and left Lily in charge, and by the time she was back, about twenty minutes later, the courses were already in progress. Cara breathed a huge sigh of relief. Lily had really come into her own today.

'Thanks so much, Lily, really. I'm going to go and sort out the kitchen, if you wouldn't mind holding the fort here while I do that.'

'Of course. No worries at all.'

'You could also give the plumbing and heating guy a call to see if he could come and check the boiler over for me as soon as he can, to make sure everything's okay.'

'Will do.'

Despite the stressful start to the day, Cara was heartened by the way the guests had come to her aid, and also by the support she'd had from Lily. She hoped she could repay them all in some way, and soon. At least it wasn't the depths of winter, so it hadn't been too cold for the guests, but she hoped the heating engineer wouldn't find anything worse wrong with the system.

She was due to meet with Zoe shortly to go over the final details before the party and make sure everything was organised and in place. After all that had happened that morning, she worried there was something she might have forgotten, and she needed Zoe to reassure her it was all going to be fine. When she glanced up and saw Zoe coming across the garden, she'd never been so glad to see her friend.

It had been a few days since Joe sent off his job application, and he still hadn't heard back from the council. He kept thinking about giving Richard a call to see if there was any news, but then he shied away from pestering him, preferring to wait and see.

In the meantime, he'd decided a proper date between him and Cara was long overdue, so he'd spoken to Finn and asked if they could squeeze the two of them in for an early dinner. Luckily, The Bistro had had a cancellation, and Finn offered the table to Joe and Cara instead. When Joe invited her, she didn't sound as excited as he expected, but she'd said yes, so he'd put her muted reaction down to tiredness. He persuaded himself all she really needed was a night away from the guesthouse.

He was looking forward to spending the evening with her, and to talking about their future together. It would do them both good to get out in the evening, and he'd put in more effort than usual in his appearance. He set off to collect Cara about ten minutes before their booking time, and it only took him a few minutes to get to the guesthouse.

When he opened the front door, Cara was already waiting for him, and he beamed at her.

'You look amazing,' he told her. 'Ready to go?'

'Yes, of course.' She smiled at him, but she looked a bit unsure, making him worry she was still annoyed at him about the job.

'You okay?' he asked.

'Yes. I'm fine.'

Joe took her hand, but she didn't say any more, and his anxious feeling only deepened, convincing him that perhaps there was more on her mind than eating at The Bistro.

They arrived a few minutes later, right on time for their reservation, and Joe opened the door to let Cara go in first.

'Hey, you two. Lovely to see you at last,' Zoe said. 'Let me take you to your table, and then someone will be over to take your drinks order shortly. Have a lovely evening.' She gave them both a final smile and went back to the front desk.

'I guess that means Olivia's on maternity leave now,' Joe said.

'Yes, she must be by now.' Cara turned her attention to the menu, and Joe's spirits dipped a little further at the lack of conversation.

'Is everything okay, Cara?' he asked again. 'You just don't seem yourself tonight.'

'Let's order our drinks and our food, and then maybe you can bring me up to date with your job situation,' Cara said.

So that was it. She'd obviously been worrying and wondering what he was going to say about it. At least he could reassure her on that front.

'Okay. Good idea.'

They both ordered a glass of white wine and pondered the menu.

'What do you fancy eating tonight?' he asked, trying to kickstart the conversation.

'I'll have the sea bass, I think.'

'Sounds good. No starter?'

'No. I'll get too full.' Cara took a sip of her wine but didn't question him about what he was going to have.

Their server came over then, and Joe ordered the calamari, followed by the hake in a white wine sauce.

'I hope you'll share the calamari with me,' Joe offered as their server took their menus away.

Cara shrugged but didn't say anything. She looked like she was barely holding her emotions together.

'Look, you're obviously on edge, but I can tell you I haven't heard anything about the job with the council, so it's probably going to be a no from them, and that's what I've been expecting anyway. I don't want to move away, Cara. I've told you that, and I've been keeping you up to date whenever I can. I don't want it to spoil our evening tonight, not when we've been looking forward to coming here for so long.'

'Well, neither do I, but I just don't know what to think any more. If you don't tell me what's going on, what am I supposed to think? You don't volunteer any information despite me telling you several times I hate being kept out of the loop.' Tears sprang to her eyes, and he was devastated at the turn the evening was taking.

'Oh, Cara, please believe me about this. I've told you everything that's happening and if I haven't mentioned it, it's because there was nothing to say.' He reached out to take her hand, but she pulled it away and searched in her bag for a tissue. Joe didn't say anything else, trying to let her regain her composure. He didn't want to upset her further.

Cara finally looked up at him after wiping her eyes and blowing her nose. 'Okay, if that's all the update there is for now, I accept that, but it is difficult not knowing what your plans are. It feels like at any minute you might be offered the job and you'll decide to leave, and that makes me nervous about our future.'

'I really never intended to make you feel like that. I'm sorry. I do want to stay here and settle down. I want to get to know you better, if that's still what you want. As far as the job's concerned, I'll only accept it if it's on my terms, which I've been very honest and upfront with them about. There's nothing more to it than that.'

'So no matter what happens, you're going to stay? Can you promise me that, Joe?'

'I can and do promise you that, Cara.'

The starter arrived then, and they both fell silent while it was served.

'That looks and smells amazing,' Cara said with a small smile.

'Try one,' Joe said, desperate to move things on, and he was delighted when she did.

Joe tried one himself then, after dipping it in the salsa verde on the side and it truly was delicious.

'It seems like everything I've heard about the food here is true,' Cara said then. 'I can't wait to taste my main course.'

Joe smiled and hoped Cara was feeling reassured now about what he'd said. The evening seemed to be back on track, and he just hoped it continued that way.

Cara had been feeling down since her date with Joe at The Bistro – down on herself, as well as down on him. She'd been longing to taste the food at The Bistro for so long, and when she'd had the chance at last, she'd been too upset with him to really enjoy it. She'd believed him when he'd told her there was no news about the job, but she wished that she hadn't been forced to ask for that information. No matter what she told him about how fragile she felt about getting involved with someone else again, he didn't seem to volunteer any information about his plans any more readily.

But it was time to let it go now. She was hosting Zoe and Ed's engagement party this evening, and it was important to her for it to go well for her friends, and for the guesthouse. Joe had been invited with his mum, so they'd see each other tonight, and maybe they could put things behind them and move forward. She really wanted to, and she hoped he did too.

Lily was coming in today and working the whole day to help Cara out, which she really appreciated, especially as it was a Saturday. She had breakfasts to do as always, and then Lily would be there after that to help her make sure everything went according to plan.

She made her way along the corridor towards the kitchen, eager to get the show on the road. In five short months, she'd begun the transformation of the guesthouse from a dilapidated business on the verge of closure to a modern hospitality venue offering accommodation, courses, and a place to hire for both businesses and individuals from her community. She was pleased with all she'd achieved. The only thing missing was someone to share that success with. She wanted that person to be Joe, but for that, he needed to commit to her fully, and to prove he wanted to stay in Watersmeet Bridge for good.

Soon, the guests started coming in, and her mind had to focus on making breakfasts for them all, and she was relieved to be able to think about something other than Joe for a while. By ten o'clock, the dining room was all cleared and tidy, and the kitchen was back to normal as well. She made her way out to reception to find Lily already installed behind the desk.

'Morning, Cara. Breakfasts all done?'

'Morning, Lily. Yes. Like clockwork today, thank goodness. And thanks to you too for coming in today. I really appreciate it.'

'No worries at all. I've got the checklist at the ready. Shall I make a start cleaning the top floor, and you do the first? That way we can get it done quicker.'

'That sounds like a plan. Hopefully, we'll meet somewhere in the middle. We both need to keep an ear out for any deliveries that might come, that's the only thing.'

Lily nodded and then disappeared upstairs. Cara wasn't far behind her. An hour later, Lily joined her on the first floor, and they finished the last room together. All the rooms had been decorated now, and there was only the downstairs left for Ed to do. Cara was looking forward to upgrading her own living space at long last.

They were just putting the cleaning supplies and equipment away when the florist arrived with her delivery for the barn.

'Morning ladies,' she trilled, as she came in.

'Hello, Rachel. How are you this morning?' Cara asked as she came out from behind the desk.

'I'm smashing, thank you. The sun's out, and I'm raring to go.'

Rachel's enthusiasm was always infectious, and today was no exception.

'Let me show you to the barn then, and you can make a start. Would you like a drink?'

'No, no. I'm fine, thank you.'

Cara walked Rachel round to the barn and unlocked the door.

The sun was already streaming in through the windows, so it was warm inside.

'Lily and I will start setting out the tables as well shortly, but we can put your arrangements on them later if you need to get off,' Cara said.

'I don't need to be anywhere else for a while, so it would be nice to stay and put them out myself. I'd also like to get some pictures to use on my website, if that's okay,' Rachel replied.

'Of course. I'll be back in a minute, and we can make a start.'

With Lily and Rachel's help, they'd set the tables up around the edge of the barn in no time, designating one table at the end of the barn for the engaged couple. Rachel put out all her small displays on the tables, as well as two larger ones on stands in the far corners of the room. At the same time, Lily started hanging up the bunting Zoe had supplied.

'Goodness, it looks beautiful already,' Cara said when they were finished.

'It really does,' said Rachel with a smile. 'Well, I hope you have a lovely evening. See you soon.'

By lunchtime, the drinks deliveries had been made to the kitchen, and Cara put the white and sparkling wines together with the beers and soft drinks in the smaller kitchen fridge. Around mid-afternoon, Sophie arrived with several trays of food from the café. It was all light finger food and designed to be easy to store in the larger fridge in the guesthouse's kitchen. It was a tight squeeze, though, and it left Cara thinking they might need to invest in more fridges in the future.

Finally, the band arrived and started their sound check in the barn, and not long after that, Zoe and Ed turned up. Cara had just finished changing into her evening outfit and was making her way to the barn when she saw them coming towards her across the garden.

'Congratulations, you two!' she called as they approached.

She led them to the barn, and after a huge gasp of delight, Zoe threw her arms around her.

'Cara, it looks amazing. Thank you so much.' Zoe looked like she might cry for a minute, but then she blew out a long breath and smiled.

'You're so welcome. I hope you both have the best night celebrating. I'm just going to get the food, and I'll set it up with Lily. The drinks are all out for you. Lily's pouring out the sparkling wine right now, so off you go and get started.'

Cara studied the scene in the barn for a moment before dashing off to get the food platters.

An hour later, and the party was in full swing. Cara breathed out a sigh of relief from her vantage point outside the barn, where the air was a bit cooler. Lily had decided to stay and enjoy the party as well, and Cara was glad that she was getting some time to relax.

Cara's only concern was that there was no sign of Joe. His mum had come, and so had Penny and Hamish. They were all sitting together at a table inside and seemed to be having a good time, not in the least worried about Joe, so her mind had gone into overdrive. She'd concluded that it must be her fault he hadn't come after their horrible date at The Bistro the other night. Maybe she'd pushed him too far and he'd made the decision to take the job and leave. That would prove her right about his lack of commitment, but it would also leave her with a broken heart.

CHAPTER TWENTY

The next morning, Joe woke early, still feeling guilty about his decision not to attend the party and the worry his absence would undoubtedly have caused Cara. But after their date, he'd been unable to shake the feeling that she wouldn't believe his commitment to her and Watersmeet Bridge whatever he said so he'd decided not to go to the party.

His decision had also been impacted by an email he'd received on Friday from Richard at the council, telling him they'd like to offer him a job but that they could only offer him the original full-time one based in Barnstaple. And now he had a dilemma: should he stay despite the tension between him and Cara and show her he meant what he said about wanting to settle there, or should he take the job if their relationship was effectively over anyway and just leave? His mum would be okay without him helping with the gardening now her dressmaking work was going so well, and she was offering courses, so he had no one to answer to but himself. He just had to work out what he wanted from his life.

If he took the job in Barnstaple, he'd have to move again, find somewhere to live, and spend most of his time travelling to deliver courses. Most importantly, he'd be on his own, without his family and without Cara. But if he stayed, would she even want a relationship with him?

He finally hauled himself out of bed, still no closer to making a decision about his future. He found his mum in the kitchen making breakfast.

'Morning, Mum. How did the party go?'

Sheila's eyes lit up. 'Oh, Joe, I wish you'd come. It was such a lovely evening, and everything went off really well.'

'Did Cara ask where I was?'

'No, she didn't, and I deliberately didn't say anything to her about why you weren't there. That's up to the two of you to sort out on your own.'

'Well, as I said, I don't think she would have wanted me there anyway. To be honest, I think she's lost interest in a relationship with me after what she said to me on our date. I'm beginning to wonder if I made a huge mistake in coming back here.'

Sheila winced. 'I hope that's not what you really think. I've loved having you here, and so has your granddad. I think you and Cara need to talk again, and properly this time. She certainly looked a bit lost without you there last night.'

'We've done so much talking though, Mum, and nothing I say seems to get through to her. Now I've missed the party as well, she'll probably hate me even more.'

'She doesn't hate you at all, Joe. Far from it, I think. The only thing I can say is that if talking hasn't worked, maybe you need to do something to show her you want to stay. Have you sent a reply about the job yet?'

'No, not yet. I just don't know what to do.'

'Maybe you should get out for some fresh air today and give yourself some time to think it all through,' Sheila said.

'Yes, maybe. What are you getting up to today?' he asked.

His mum gave him a cryptic smile. 'Oh, this and that, you know.' She wandered off back to her room, leaving Joe bemused by her manner and her statement. He set about making himself some toast and thought about what his mum had said about showing Cara that he wanted to stay.

An hour later, he was high up on the coastal path with the wind blowing in his hair, and thinking again about how much he'd come to enjoy living in Watersmeet Bridge. He loved the walks and the views, and that was a real positive to living here. He'd also really enjoyed being able to spend time with his family after so long away. As he walked further along the path, he started ticking more positives off in his mind – his fledgling business, the courses he was running for Cara, the community – and he realised, even without Cara, there was so much more to his life here than he'd appreciated. But Cara more than anything was the reason he wanted to stay, and that understanding helped him to make his decision at last.

He whirled around suddenly and started making his way back home. He had to see Cara and tell her how he really felt before it was too late. He was almost running down the hill on the way back, such was his need to get home. He had an important job to do first before going to see Cara, and once that was done, he could get on with saving their relationship. He only hoped she'd believe what he had to say to her when the time came.

Joe arrived back to an empty house with no sign of his mum, but that was fine. It wouldn't take him long to do what he had to do, and then he'd be gone again. He shut the door of his room behind him and took out his laptop. It was strangely freeing to say no to the job offer from Richard at the council. He'd been so flattered by the invitation to work for them, and this had led him to consider doing a job he really didn't want to do. All his life, he'd found it hard to say no to things and he'd become a bit of a people-pleaser in the process, but now it really was time for him to please himself by doing what he knew would make him happiest. He typed out a quick email, and after reading it through, he sent it before he could change his mind again.

He took in a deep breath and released it, feeling happier than he had in weeks. After closing his laptop, he stood up and made his way back outside again. Now it was time to see whether Cara could forgive his indecision and accept what he had to tell her.

Cara had been awake since dawn worrying about why Joe hadn't come to the party yesterday. She was sure it was her fault for having pushed him away so determinedly on their date at The Bistro, and she was full of regret. Even Sheila had kept her distance from her last night, so Joe must have told her what had happened.

He'd been trying to be more open with her since she'd mentioned it to him, but instead of appreciating his efforts on that front, she'd been even more critical.

She finally realised she wouldn't be able to bear it if he decided to leave because she hadn't told him how she really felt. So, as soon as she thought it was a suitable time to visit people on a Sunday morning, she left the guesthouse and set out for Sheila's cottage, hoping to catch Joe and talk to him honestly about her feelings for the first time in a while.

She'd hardly lost sight of the guesthouse before she saw Joe coming towards her on the path. They both stopped in their tracks when they spotted each other and smiled tentatively before carrying on, until they were standing face-to-face.

'Joe, I... I thought you might already have left when you didn't come to the party yesterday,' she said, her voice catching at the very idea.

He lifted his hand towards her cheek and caressed it gently. 'I would never leave without telling you, and anyway, I'm not going anywhere,' he said before kissing her softly.

'Oh, Joe, I'm so sorry for everything. I've got so much I want to say to you.'

'Me too,' he said with a smile.

They wandered over hand in hand to the bench overlooking their favourite view and sat down before it, enjoying the silence of the morning and just being with each other.

'I've been unfair to you, Joe, and I'm sorry,' she began. 'I know you've been doing your best to be open with me, and I haven't appreciated it enough. I just wanted you to know my worries have come from a good place. Because I want you to stay here in Watersmeet Bridge. I don't want you to go.' She swallowed, knowing she was opening herself up to his rejection, but also knowing it was time for her to ask for what she wanted and to stop getting in the way of her own life and what she wanted from it.

'That's what I want too, Cara. I want to be with you, not doing a job that takes me away from you and our life here. I'm sorry it took me so long to realise it.' He took both her hands in his. 'I love you, Cara.'

Her eyes filled with tears. 'And I love you, Joe.'

He pulled her into a hug, and then they sat side by side for a moment, enjoying their closeness and their shared love for each other.

'So you really have decided to stay?' she asked finally, hardly daring to believe it.

'Yes. I promise,' he said with a chuckle. 'Richard did offer me a job, but only the full-time one, and I realised I didn't want it, because my life is here now, and being with you makes it even better.'

'So you turned it down?'

'Yes. It was an easy decision in the end. I'd be happy doing occasional courses for the networking group, but mainly, I want to be based here, running courses for you, gardening with Mum. That's enough for me.'

'I really think there could be a lot more scope for you to run different courses for me. I'm so glad you've chosen to stay, Joe.' She couldn't believe how well things had turned out for them both.

'I honestly feel such a sense of relief having finally made the decision. I don't have to worry about any of it any more. I am sorry I missed the party though. I just thought you might not want me to come after our disastrous date.'

She turned to look at him. "I don't blame you for not coming, but you did miss a good night.' She smiled at him. 'But there will be lots of others in the future, I hope. And we'll have to go back to The Bistro another time.'

'I'd like that. Have you got time to go for a walk this morning?'

'Yes. It's all quiet back at the guesthouse. I'd love a walk on the path up to the sea.'

They set off hand in hand, enjoying the fresh air and the quiet of the day. There was no one else around either, and it felt special to have the path and its wonderful views all to themselves.

'I feel so lucky to have these walks and views on the doorstep. I wouldn't swap them for the city now. It's funny how things change, isn't it?' Joe said, turning to look at her.

'Yes. I think you and I have been on similar paths, searching for something we thought life in the city would bring, but in the end, we found it here at home instead. I did love Exeter in the beginning, but after a while, I craved something else. It was good to get the experience, and to get it out of my system, though.'

'So no regrets about taking over the guesthouse then?' Joe asked.

'None at all. It's been hard getting it all off the ground but so worth it in the end. I've learnt a lot in the past six months, and that will probably never end.' She laughed and he joined in with her.

'What's next for you then?' he asked.

'I've got so many ideas for expanding the business, but I need to take it slowly. I can employ Lily full-time now, so that will give me some breathing space to think about what I want to do first, and also to get away from the guesthouse like this more often. I hope you and I will be spending more time together too. How about you?'

'More of the same, really – building up my digital business, running more courses, doing a bit of gardening, spending time with you. That's all I need to make me happy. I feel settled here.'

It was almost the end of Cara's first season at Watersmeet View, and she was looking forward to a slightly slower pace of life as she moved into autumn. She still had a good number of courses scheduled on the calendar, though, and they were going to keep her and Lily busy all the way through to Christmas. She couldn't complain about that, of course – she was lucky to have that business to rely on when so many others didn't – but she was glad things wouldn't be quite as hectic as they'd been for the past few months.

All the redecorating was now done, and she'd been able to replace some of the older furniture, giving the guesthouse a slightly more modern feel. Soon, she'd be turning her attention to the outside of the building, getting a fresh coat of paint done, as well as some repairs to the guttering and fascia boards. It wasn't very exciting, but it was necessary work, and she was glad it would be done before the winter winds and rain came. There would always be work to do, but once all this was done, the main problems would have been dealt with.

She was off for lunch with her grandma and Hamish today, leaving Lily to hold the fort. She had complete confidence in Lily's ability to deal with anything that might come up, but she wasn't far away if there were any curveballs.

The garden was looking beautiful as she stepped outside, and she allowed herself a little tour before leaving. Roses were still blooming in the main circular flower bed, and the scents were heavenly as she passed by. Joe and his mum had also planted some dahlia tubers earlier in the year, and they were flourishing now, all around the garden. The colours were delightful, and Cara's heart lifted as she took in the results of all their hard work and dedication. She was able to pay them to come a couple of times a week now, and she knew her business was important to them.

Cara turned right out of the garden, glancing briefly across at the sea, before continuing on her way to Hamish's cottage. The view was always enticing, but she didn't want to be late for lunch, and she was looking forward to seeing them both.

A few minutes later, Hamish greeted her at the door with a kiss and a hug before ushering her down the hallway and through to the courtyard back garden. The sun was shining brightly, but there was a table with a parasol over it, and Cara was thankful for the chance to sit and eat outside.

'Hello, Cara, darling,' said her grandma. 'How are you?' Penny gave her a quick kiss and a long hug before gesturing for her to take a seat at the table.

'I'm really well, thank you. You're looking good too,' she said. 'Retirement obviously agrees with you.'

Penny laughed. 'I can definitely recommend it.'

Hamish returned with a chilled bottle of rosé and three glasses.

'Ooh, wine at lunchtime. Are we celebrating?' She glanced between the two of them as a mischievous grin broke out on their faces. 'Well?' she asked when they didn't say anything.

Penny leaned over and showed Cara her left hand, which was now boasting an elegant diamond ring. 'We got engaged,' Penny said softly.

Cara's eyes filled with tears. 'Oh, that really is the best news. I'm so pleased for you both.'

'Well, we have a favour to ask of you now,' said Hamish. 'So hang on until you hear what that is.'

'Whatever it is, you know I'll do it in a heartbeat,' Cara replied, wiping her eyes.

Hamish poured out small glasses of wine and went back to the kitchen, leaving Penny the job of telling Cara what the favour was.

'We want to get married as soon as possible given our ages,' she said. 'And I wondered if you would give me away.'

Now the tears fell, and for a long moment, Cara was speechless. Hamish returned with three bowls of salad and a box of tissues on a large tray. She grabbed the tissues and wiped her eyes.

'I'd be honoured to give you away, Grandma,' she said. 'I hope you know that.'

'And there's something else, please. We'd like to have our lunch and reception in your lovely new barn if you can fit us in.'

Cara clapped her hands together in delight. 'What a wonderful idea! That will be my wedding present to you both,' she said.

'Cheers then,' said Hamish, raising his glass.

'Cheers and congratulations to you both. I can't wait. So, tell me everything you've been planning for it,' Cara said.

They all tucked into their salads while Penny and Hamish explained the wedding was set for a fortnight's time at the Watersmeet Bridge church, right at the other end of the village.

'We'd like to invite our close friends and family to the wedding and then walk back through the village so all our other friends can see us,' said Penny.

'Then we can assemble in the barn for lunch and our reception,' finished Hamish.

'That all sounds wonderful. I'd be happy to organise the florist and a local band, if you'd like, as well.'

'That would be lovely. Thank you,' said Penny with a smile.

'What a wonderful occasion to end the summer with,' said Cara.

'Indeed. Everything's worked out well in the end, hasn't it?' said Hamish. 'Even that grandson of mine finally came to his senses,' he said with a laugh.

'We both did, and I'm very glad Joe has decided to stay.'

'How is he? We haven't seen him for a few days,' said Penny.

'Well, I saw him yesterday, and he was fine. I think this past month, he's really relaxed more, and he feels more comfortable with his life here. His digital work is picking up all the time, and we've planned another course for him to run too.'

'I'm so glad,' said Penny. 'He's definitely made the right decision to stay here, I think.'

The day of the wedding dawned sunny and bright, and Cara breathed a sigh of relief as the sunlight streamed in through her bedroom window. She rolled over to stare at Joe, knowing these were a few precious moments she could steal before he woke up. She could still hardly believe they'd managed to get together, and that everything was going so well for them. Joe had stayed with her most nights for the past week and had made his mark on the bedroom they now shared. She wanted to ask him to move in but was afraid of scaring him off. She was ready for them to take that step though. She just needed to summon up the courage to ask him.

'What's going on in that head of yours?' he asked suddenly, his voice groggy with sleep.

She gasped at being caught out. 'I was taking my chance to ogle you without you knowing what I was up to,' she laughed before lying down again and resting her head on his shoulder.

His arm slipped round her, and he drew her gently against him. 'Oh, I *know* you were doing that,' he said, 'but you were deep in thought about something as well, and I'm wondering what that is.' His eyes were fully open now and focused on her.

She bit her lip, wondering whether to tell him or not, and then she remembered they'd promised each other not to keep any more secrets. She circled the hair on his chest with her finger until he grabbed her hand and stopped her by leaning over for a kiss.

'You're making me worried now,' he said, staring down at her afterwards.

She closed her eyes briefly. 'I was wondering if you'd like to move in with me,' she blurted once she'd reopened her eyes.

'I would love that,' he said before kissing her again, more soundly this time.

'Really?' she asked when they came up for breath. 'It's not too soon for me to ask you that?'

'If you're ready to take that step, then I am too,' he replied. 'But now that's sorted, we have to get up and get ready. We've got a wedding to attend.'

Cara smiled at how easy a conversation it had been after all her worries. She was so glad she'd asked, and now they were going to have a wonderful day.

An hour later, they were dressed in their best clothes and making their way to pick up the bride and groom for the walk to the church. Lily had arrived at the guesthouse and would make sure everything was sorted in the barn for when they came back later.

'You look beautiful,' Joe said softly to Cara as they wandered along the path towards Hamish's cottage.

Cara had finally had her hair cut in the village and had left it flowing down her back over the floral dress she'd bought to wear for this special occasion. She felt wonderful in the dress, and she was so happy she was fit to burst.

'You look pretty good too,' she told Joe. 'I had no idea you'd look so good in a kilt.'

They both laughed. Hamish had asked Joe if he'd be prepared to join him in wearing a kilt on his wedding day, and Joe had agreed, if only to please him.

'I was worried about how I'd look, I must admit, but I'm pleasantly surprised about it now. And Granddad will be happy anyway.'

They arrived at the cottage to find Sheila already there, on door-opening duty.

'Morning, you two. You look fabulous,' she said, kissing them both as they passed by into the cottage.

'You look lovely too, Sheila,' said Cara as she came in. 'Your dress is wonderful. Is it one of your own?'

'It is. And thank you. I'm really pleased with it. Now, Penny and Hamish are almost ready. They're in different rooms, so you can go in and see them separately. I'll wait here for you.'

Cara went in to see her grandma, hoping she wasn't feeling too nervous. 'Morning, Gran. How are you?' she asked after knocking gently on the door.

'I am absolutely fine and almost ready to get this show on the road,' Penny said as Cara went in.

'You look amazing,' Cara told her as she took in her sage-green dress and bolero. 'Well, if you're ready, shall we go and join Sheila? Joe has just gone in to see Hamish.'

As they walked out into the corridor, they met Hamish and Joe coming the other way. Cara took Joe's hand to lead him back to Sheila so Hamish and Penny could have a quiet word.

'I've got your corsage here, Cara, and your buttonhole, Joe,' Sheila said, passing them their flowers.

'Oh, these are beautiful. Rachel's done us all proud. Penny's bouquet is gorgeous.'

Penny and Hamish appeared then, and they gathered together outside the front door to make their way. Sheila and Cara walked either side of Penny, and Hamish and Joe walked together behind them in their matching kilts. There were already well-wishers lining the High Street, and it was a joyful experience waving at everyone along the way.

In no time at all, they were at the church for the very short ceremony – by request of the bride and groom, who'd both been married before – and soon, they were married and back out in the churchyard once again.

The journey back to the guesthouse took a bit longer, as there were so many more people, but it was a heartening experience for them all.

'That was a simple service but so poignant, wasn't it?' Joe said to Cara as they meandered along the street.

'It was beautiful, and I think it meant so much to them to formalise their relationship that way.'

Joe took her hand and gave her a meaningful smile. She wondered what he was going to say, but he didn't say anything. He just kept smiling.

They were soon back at the guesthouse, where friends had gathered for the reception. It was such a wonderful day that they were able to have drinks outside. Cara and Joe joined Lily to serve to the guests.

Cara had never seen Penny look so happy, and she was delighted they'd been able to have such a glorious day. Finn had provided an extra special buffet for them all, and after setting it all out with his team, he announced it to the guests before joining them inside.

Cara sat down next to Joe after putting her plate down on the table before her.

'This is amazing,' said Joe after his first mouthful.

Cara groaned as she took hers as well, savouring the delicious taste of hot smoked salmon. 'It really is,' she agreed.

'We'll have to ask Finn to cater for us as well when it's our turn,' Joe said then, with a wink at Cara, and as she looked into his eyes and saw the love she felt for him reflected back at her, she knew it wouldn't be long before that magical day took place in their future too. She raised her glass to Joe, her heart full of love and happiness.

The End.

READ AN EXCERPT FROM THE BISTRO BY WATERSMEET BRIDGE

BOOK 1, WATERSMEET BRIDGE SERIES

Olivia went over what she was going to say to her father one last time as the train rattled its way towards Bristol. Years of habit kept her back straight, her knees pressed together, her ankles crossed and her hands folded lightly in her lap, but her mind was racing with what she was about to do. There would be no coming back from the ultimatum she was going to give, and she was still unsure whether she was doing the right thing. But the job offer from Café Express had come at just the right moment and it was time to put herself first. Her mind returned to her speech and she was soon lost in her thoughts again.

The train finally squealed to a halt and people all around her stood up, impatient to get off the train and on their way to work. Olivia picked up her bag, left the carriage and set off on foot for the short journey to the company offices, leaving the grand old station behind her. She pulled her woollen coat tighter around her and made her way towards the river Avon, resisting all the coffee shops with their glorious early morning smell of roasted beans. The bright March sunshine calmed her and took her mind off the impending showdown with her father. As she approached the white metal bridge across the river, her long ponytail swinging behind her, she wished things hadn't come to this between them.

In no time at all, she found herself on the pavement outside the gleaming windows of the high-rise offices of La Riviera, the restaurant chain her father had spent his life building up. She was soon swept up by all the other employees making their way inside. The automatic doors swooshed open, and a second later she was crossing the sand-coloured marble foyer. Using her ID badge, she passed through the barrier and walked towards the bank of lifts. Several other employees were already waiting there, but even though she recognised some of them, she didn't speak to anyone, and no-one spoke to her. She studiously avoided eye contact, after several years' practice, refusing to let her guard down long enough to let anyone else in.

The lift arrived and she followed everyone else inside, squeezing herself into the back corner. The lift stopped at every floor as people made their way to work, but eventually, she was alone, speeding up to the executive suite of offices. This was where her father dominated the rest of the company, and where she was planning to do battle with him. She drew in a deep breath, trying not to let fear overwhelm her. She had put up with his behaviour for long enough. Now it was time to break free.

'Ah, the lovely Miss Fuller. I trust you had a jolly weekend?' Ryan started badgering her before she'd even taken off her coat.

'I'm sure you've got far more important things to do than annoying me, Ryan.' Olivia busied herself hanging up her coat on the stand in the corner of the office they shared with two other members of the Sales and Acquisitions team, and steadfastly ignored him. His eyes never left her the whole time she was booting up her computer and she willed him, for once, to leave her alone. As Marcus and Jake arrived, Ryan became distracted enough to give up bothering her, and she released a slow breath.

It wasn't long until the start of the Monday morning briefing, so she quickly scanned her emails to see if there was anything important she needed to know beforehand. She planned to speak to her father straight afterwards. He was a stickler for punctuality and if she upset him by being late, she would already have lost her advantage.

'C'mon, gorgeous. Time to go and listen to your old man's pearls of wisdom.' Marcus gave her a salacious wink before turning towards the door.

Olivia worked hard not to roll her eyes at him. She was used to the jibes of her colleagues. She didn't appreciate their taunts, of course, but she'd found it was best to simply ignore them. That way, they usually lost interest fairly quickly. She picked up her notebook and pen and joined the others on the walk to the boardroom. She stayed a few paces behind the rest of the team, who had joined them from adjacent offices. They were all men, hand-picked by her father or his lackeys for their ruthless business approach, and rejected by her, almost every one of them, for their cheesy come-ons. She'd made the mistake of letting one of them in once, but never again. She was still recovering from that experience and the effect it had had on her. Her trust in men had been severely damaged when she'd found out he only saw her as a way of gaining favour with her father. Somehow, though, she still held out some hope. Surely there was a man out there for her somewhere who would respect her for who she was and what she wanted to do with her life, rather than because she was the daughter of their wealthy boss?

She came to a stop, as everyone else had done. They were still in the corridor and clearly unable to enter the boardroom. She stood on her tiptoes and strained to see what was going on. Other people were doing the same, so raising herself up made no difference to her view. Marcus pushed his way to the front and bent his head to study something on the glossy wooden door. Next thing, he walked back to rejoin Ryan and Jake before the three of them turned around and made to go past her.

'That's a first. Who'd have thought old man Fuller had it in him to break with tradition like that?' grumbled Jake.

'What's happening?' Olivia was startled out of her usual silence by the sudden change of plan.

'The meeting's been postponed to this afternoon.'

ALSO BY JULIE STOCK

From Here to You series

From Here to Nashville - Book 1 - From Here to You

Over You - Book 2 - From Here to You

Finding You - Book 3 - From Here to You

From Here to You series

Domaine des Montagnes series

The Vineyard in Alsace - Book 1 - Domaine des Montagnes

Starting Over at the Vineyard in Alsace - Book 2 - Domaine des Montagnes

A Leap of Faith at the Vineyard in Alsace - Book 3 - Domaine des Montagnes

The Watersmeet Bridge series

The Bistro by Watersmeet Bridge

Standalone

Bittersweet - 12 Short Stories for Modern Life

ABOUT THE AUTHOR

Julie Stock writes contemporary feel-good romance from around the world: novels, novellas and short stories.

When not writing, she can be found reading, her favourite past-time; running, a new hobby; or cooking up a storm in the kitchen, glass of wine in hand.

Julie is married and lives with her family in Cambridgeshire in the UK.

For more information:
julie-stock.co.uk

ACKNOWLEDGMENTS

This book has been a long time coming, it has to be said! I finished the first draft in 2021 but then life got in the way, and try as I might, I couldn't seem to work out where I wanted the story to go. With each new, not-quite-finished draft I lost more and more confidence. But then this year, knowing I was about tot turn 60, and also feeling that my life was once again on a more even keel, I finally found the determination to get to the end. It has taken a long time but I think the story is better for it. I hope you agree!

Thanks as always to my family and friends for their support and advice during the most difficult times.